Sisters

of the Silver Moon

Book One, The *Gypsy Moon* Trilogy
Sisters of the Silver Moon

© Veronika Sophia Robinson
© Cover illustration by Sara Simon
© Under The Same Sky, lyrics by Mandy Bingham
Author photograph by Dave Hollins

ISBN: 978-0-9931586-1-2
Published by Starflower Press
www.starflowerpress.com
June 2015
New Moon in Gemini: *The Scribe's Moon*

British Library Cataloguing in Publication Data.
A catalogue record for this book is available from
the British Library.

Other novels by the same author:

Mosaic
Bluey's Café

For the full list of the author's non-fiction titles,
visit: www.veronikarobinson.com

Sisters

of the Silver Moon

by Veronika Sophia Robinson

Starflower Press

Azaria Chantel Loren Chamberlain (11th June 1980–17th August 1980) was an Australian baby girl who was killed by a dingo on the night of 17th August 1980 on a family camping trip to Uluru (at that date known as Ayers Rock), in the Northern Territory. Her body was never found. Her parents, Lindy and Michael Chamberlain, reported that she had been taken from their tent by a dingo. Lindy Chamberlain was, however, tried for murder and spent more than three years in prison. She was released when a piece of Azaria's clothing was found near a dingo lair, and new inquests were opened. In 2012, some 32 years after Azaria's death, the Chamberlains' version of events was officially confirmed by a coroner. - Wikipedia

Author's note:
I was twelve years old when Azaria Chamberlain's death made the headlines all around my country. It was the year I started secondary school. From the moment I heard the news, I knew that Lindy did not kill her child. I knew it with every cell of my being. Her baby's name has stayed with me over the years, and the story still breaks my heart. Nothing can ever undo the pain that family went through, and the untold damage the media caused, but I hope the naming of my main character, Azaria, is a small token of me saying "I remember".

Azaria is pronounced A *zar* ee ah

For my Paul.
Then, now, and always.

*"What cannot be said,
will be wept."*

The Springtime

The Gathering Moon

"How much longer do you think they'll be?" Caroline Lafferty asked her daughter.

The subtle scent of freshly brewed lavender tea, entwined in the slowly rising steam from two earthenware mugs, was part of their mid-morning ritual on the old veranda. Wildflower honey melted effortlessly in the hot brew.

Car breathed in the morning air, then eyed her daughter up and down while waiting for an answer.

It had been several years since Azaria Linden had seen her twin sister, Astrid. Eight years of estrangement had weathered Azaria's heart, wounding her a little more with each passing year. It wasn't Azaria's choice for them to not be on speaking terms. In fact, she'd tried many times to heal the rift: a lesion that continued to fester for Astrid. It all came about simply because Azaria had loved her sister so much that she couldn't bite her tongue any longer.

Azaria smiled, and said: "Eliza-May thought they'd arrive at 11am." Raking her slender fingers through her lustrous, long, silver hair, she smiled hopefully. "And Astrid? When is she expected?" she asked her mother.

"About the same time." Car sipped her tea, Astrid's life story playing through her mind. It was the hardest thing in the world for a mother to watch her child suffer, but if there was one thing Car Lafferty knew, it was that Astrid was a ticking time bomb. However, she was family, and it simply wouldn't be a family reunion if her own daughter — Azaria's twin sister — wasn't there.

Mother and daughter sat on the porch swing in comfortable silence for several minutes, not looking at anything in particular, but not missing a moment of the view before them, either. Life here in the Rocky Mountains suited both of them. It always had. The open-plan mountain home had been in the maternal family for generations, built from local wood and stone. The site was blessed by being in a suntrap, as well as for its outstanding views. A priceless legacy: the property featured over seven-hundred acres of pristine mountainside, thick forests, flower meadows, caves, waterfalls, a sacred spring, and clean mountain air. In the distance, groves of Colorado blue spruce, some one-hundred feet high, marked out the lakes near their local town in the valley below: a vibrant, artisan community; a haven for artists, writers and musicians.

A small bear cub had taken to playing near the veranda steps each morning. They laughed as he tumbled out of an old oak drum which had caught last night's rain. It tipped over, and he bounded away, pride wounded, calling for his mother.

Azaria smiled as she thought of her grandchildren. It had been well over a year since they last visited. Sighing, she had to admit that a year was like a lifetime in the lives of children. They were even more precious, somehow, because her other three daughters showed no sign of blessing her with grandchildren. Bella, sixteen, and Ruby, fourteen, were the light of her life even though she rarely saw them these days. She even took to learning how to Skype so she could keep track of them. How would they fare in the countryside now? Laughing out loud, Azaria couldn't help but think of their mother, Eliza-May, who was constantly frustrated at their world of texting, tweeting, and Facebook. She, of all people, wanted them back out in the fresh air, away from the distractions of modern life and pernicious technology, but felt trapped in the culture and could find no escape.

"Why are you laughing?" Car asked, setting her mug on the wooden table beside the porch swing.

"Teenagers and fresh mountain air. Things are a bit different these days, aren't they, Mom?"

"Ah, those girls will be fine. Just fine. It's your sister who concerns me. I hope this new man is good for her. I really do. I hate to even say it, but I wish she was coming on her own. Bringing this new chap with her is a hindrance to any sort of healing between you both. She's starting to turn her life around. I know you think differently, Azaria, but she really is trying. Astrid just doesn't have your sense of self-worth. She never did have. Everything is a lot harder for her, you know?"

"Mom, I agree about the self-worth, but most of her troubles are self-inflicted. They always have been. She didn't have to run away when she was fifteen. She didn't have to get pregnant. She didn't have to adopt her baby out and then spend the rest of her life regretting it."

"You will try and bite your tongue this weekend, won't you, my love? After all, it's not every day that I have my whole extended family here to celebrate my eightieth birthday," she winked, hoping to appeal to Azaria's kind nature.

"Of course I will, Mom. I won't do or say anything that will wind her up. I promise. I know it probably wasn't easy for you to convince her to be here. I still can't believe you persuaded her to come back to the mountains. It doesn't seem real. I suppose that's why I've been so quiet this morning. I haven't really been able to process it. But, you know, I am glad she's coming. Maybe we can find a way to heal this rift, even with the new beau in tow."

"Rift? Is that what you call it?" Car laughed. "Rift? The gulf between you girls is wider than the Grand Canyon. It's not right. Twins are meant to be close, like your two daughters are. Luna and Starr are inseparable. They even share an apartment. God help any man who comes between them!"

"Well, Astrid and I probably would have been close if she was born on the same day."

Car smiled wistfully, her wrinkled hand gently resting

on her daughter's leg. "It might have been nearly 57 years ago, but I remember your births as if they were yesterday. Mirrors of your personalities. You, easy and calm; gently slipping into the midwife's hands as the Sun rose over this valley. Astrid," she laughed, shaking her head, "dear Astrid. We had no idea I was carrying twins. Even after I birthed you, we had no idea. And then when I started contracting again, and Sally, the midwife, realised what was happening, I thought the baby would just slip out like you did. Knowing her the way I do now, I should have guessed Astrid would get stuck on the way out and end up needing the midwife to pull her out. I should have known that girl would try to kill me. Stubborn little thing!"

They both laughed at the truth of it.

"Some things never change," Azaria mused, and gently squeezed her mother's hand. Their relationship had always been easy and comfortable: more like best friends, than mother and daughter. Azaria often felt guilty that her sister didn't share the same mother-and-daughter ease, and that Astrid had been so desperate to estrange herself from family.

"Look, there's Eliza-May!" Azaria stood up, ruffling her hair a little, then walked off the wooden veranda, down the five wide steps, and into the rambling garden: an eclectic mix of native wildflowers, many already in bloom.

Azaria, a natural gardener, planted her first seeds as a barefoot toddler: determining her career path as a herbalist. The blue flax leant at an angle, as it did every year, and was now about 20-inches high.

Leaving a trail of dust in its wake, it would be another two minutes before the red station wagon finished its long drive up the mountainside. The morning rays of late-Spring sunshine warmed Azaria's skin. It was good to be alive! Breathing in the fragrance of the minty leaves of wild bergamot made her smile. It always did. The pink flowers, like ragged pompoms, cheered her on. In a week, she'd harvest the leaves to make mint tea, and use the oil from them to treat any respiratory ailments next Winter. Teas, tinctures, balms, oils and essences. They were her speciality, and had made her renowned around the mountains. Azaria turned around. "Are you coming, Mom?" she asked excitedly.

"I am indeed." Car's steps were slower these days, deliberate and measured. It had been a long life, and mostly a good one. A year ago, her beloved husband died quietly in his sleep. She gave thanks for the 58 years they'd had together, but the loss of his companionship chipped away at her, despite the constant and abiding love of her daughter and strong community support.

Azaria was at her mother's side, day and night, nurturing her heart, ensuring she ate regularly, and cosseting her as she walked through the obscurity of grief. The pain of losing a lifelong lover hung around like pewter clouds on a dreary Winter's morning. Oppressive and tormenting. But still, each day Car gave herself a constant 'to-do' list: hang out the washing, bake scones, knit booties for the premature babies at the local maternity hospital, help Azaria gather herbs, stroll to the beehives, write to her great grandchildren, organise meetings of the local knitting group; and there was also her weekly meet-up with local musicians to play her drums and guitar. Twice a week she gave music lessons to teenagers. Car lived a full life, and even though it felt different now she was a widow, her days had purpose and meaning. Determined to make every day count, she forced herself out of bed even when she would rather have stayed there with the covers over her head.

They stood, that sunny morning, Car and Azaria, their arms linked, tears of anticipation sliding down their cheeks. Ah yes, it would be a grand weekend: a celebration to remember. Even the heart-shaped alpine arnica flowers seemed to agree: their sunshine-yellow faces beaming up from near Azaria's feet.

Azaria's other three daughters would arrive later on that day: Kara, the eldest, at almost 40 years old, and married to a well-known and respected Boston doctor; and 24-year-old twins, Starr, a journalist; and Luna, a school teacher.

James Megane pulled into the driveway, bringing the rental car to a standstill, his wife Eliza-May crying gently at the sight before her. "Oh, James, look at Mom. She looks like a goddess. I'm sure she gets more beautiful and radiant with each passing year. Bella? What do you think? Ruby?"

"Yeah, she looks pretty cool. Doesn't really look like a grandmother, though," Bella glanced briefly at her silver-headed foremothers before returning her view to the cellphone in her hands. "There's no signal. Oh my God! There's no bloody signal!"

"Language, Bella," James said sternly. "None of that this weekend, thank you very much."

"I can't believe it! You don't understand! You never understand. What am I going to do? I can't be away from Smudge for four whole days. I can't not be in contact! This is a disaster. A disaster, I tell you! I want to go home! Dad, I want to go home."

This was not how Eliza-May and James wanted to start the long weekend, but they were both resigned to the inevitability of bringing a rebellious, love-struck teenager to the heart of the mountainside.

"They're quite pretty, aren't they?" Ruby said, her lyrical voice barely a whisper, as she took in the sight of her grandmother and great grandmother. Reflecting on her friends' grandmothers, it struck her how different her own grandmother looked. Nope, no tight perms or elasticised waistbands in *her* maternal line. "Beautiful, I think."

13

"Yes, honey, they are." Eliza-May, at thirty seven years old, saw her mother with new eyes.

"Do you think I'll look like grandma when I'm old?" Ruby asked, eager to follow the line of maternal beauty on display before her.

Eliza-May felt her shoulders relax a little. She loved her mother dearly, but often felt light years away from Azaria's life views. Still, she was deeply proud of this woman who engendered respect wherever she went: her mother, known locally as The Herb Lady. On other days she was known as The Bee Whisperer. Both descriptions were accurate, but words failed to denote the esoteric wisdom for which Azaria was renowned.

"Bella, I know this is going to be tough, but this weekend isn't about you. This is about your Great-Granny Car. This is her weekend, and all of us, including the *bad bad* Aunty Astrid, are making this about her. I expect you to be on your best behaviour. Anything less, and I'll be deeply disappointed."

Bella dropped her head, partly in fury, but mostly in shame that she'd made such a fuss. She was secretly looking forward to seeing her Aunty Astrid. She'd heard stories, but doubted they could all be true. But oh how she was missing Smudge already. Mentally counting down the hours until their reunion, Bella held the secret inside: this was meant to be the weekend that they finally did it. She'd promised him. So far, for the past five weekends, she'd made excuses: headache, homework, friend visiting, on her period, her dad grounding her for coming home late. It was true that she wanted to have sex with him, but she was scared, too. She was the only virgin left amongst her friends, and desperate to be rid of that wearisome title, but horrified at the thought of doing something so life changing. Whenever she wanted to talk to her mother about it, her father walked into the room. She'd felt so alone in her fears. This weekend gave her some breathing space,

14

but being away from Smudge amplified her fears that he'd dump her for a new girlfriend: someone more willing to put out. She flicked her mop of chestnut-coloured curls and reluctantly stepped out of the rental car. The drive from Denver airport had taken far too long.

Ruby scrambled out first, however, desperate for a cuddle with her grandmother. Azaria breathed in the scent of Ruby's silky, flaxen-blonde hair–so different from Bella's hair–grateful to hold her grandchild. She'd been there on the night of her birth, and always felt bonded to Ruby despite living so far apart. Unlike any other child she'd ever met, it was as if Ruby wasn't quite of this Earth. Like a poet, somehow caught in Dreamtime. That she still retained an innocence and purity, despite being 14 years of age, was nothing short of a miracle to Azaria. She squeezed her even tighter. "I love you so much, my child."

"I love you too, Granny." Ruby squeezed in closer to Azaria, loving the feel of her gentle curves against her own body. "I'm so glad we've come for the weekend. I wish we lived here. I could sit on the hill and draw flowers every day. I could wear flowers in my hair all the time!"

"Maybe we can talk to your parents about you coming to spend the Summer here. What do you think?" she whispered softly into the strands of blonde hair.

"Do you think so? Do you really think I could?" Ruby sighed, nudging her head against her grandmother's soft bosom, a familiar place of comfort and safety indelibly printed into her heart from an early age. Ruby imagined a Summer here, full of flowers, and clouds, and walks by the river. She felt happy already. It was a way of life distinctly removed from the one she lived in New York.

Eliza-May knew she didn't have a chance of hugging her mother until Ruby was well and truly loved up. Instead, she embraced her own grandmother.

"Granny Car, it's so good to see you. I'm so thrilled we're all gathering to celebrate your birthday. Is there

15

anything we can do to help get ready?"

"You should know better than to ask that. Your mother has everything under control. You know what Azaria's like! Every last dot covered." Car smiled, and said "Your family is looking good, Eliza-May. Real good."

They shared a gentle laugh, but Eliza-May maintained her poker face. The last word she'd use to describe herself was good. "Oh the air, Grandmother, it's just so fresh up here. Sometimes I forget what it's like. I can't believe I ever moved away. I must have been crazy. I am crazy. Why on Earth do we live in a city when we could have this every day?"

Ten years of depression, breathing in New York pollution, had taken its toll. Her ears constantly rang to the jarring resonance of fire-engine sirens and the distressing bell sounds of ambulance vehicles. It was as if her own life was always in a state of high alert, and Eliza-May could feel her adrenal glands fully stretched as they accommodated her aversion to all the ways of city life. Her feet had forgotten what it felt like to walk on grass, and her eyes couldn't remember the last time they'd looked at an unpolluted night sky to see the stars.

Prozac was a way of life to Eliza-May, despite Azaria's constant attempts to treat her naturally through herbs. Counselling had failed to get to the root of her emptiness and silent desperation. The love and vigilance of her family kept her dog-paddling at the surface—just—but she lived with a constant fear that any day now—*any* day now— she'd go under. She'd drown, and no one would see it happening. Life felt overwhelmingly bleak to her.

James overheard her, and pecked Car on each cheek. "We live in the city so we can pay the mortgage." He chuckled, "We can't all be farmers and herb growers."

Twelve years as a partner in a top New York legal firm conditioned him to a life of work before family. The thought of anything different always tugged at his

16

conscience. It had meant the world to his wife that he was taking this weekend off so they could all come to spend time with her family. He did it for one reason: he loved Eliza-May with all his heart, and lived daily with the knowledge of just how much she'd given up by leaving the mountains to follow her heart and be with the man of her dreams. Not a day passed by when he didn't pinch himself that she had made such a sacrifice. Not that Eliza-May considered it a sacrifice. Of course not. She believed that when you loved someone, you turned your life inside out and upside down to be with them. It was simple: you didn't do anything less than that for love.

Neither of them, however, dared acknowledge the connection with her murky depression and the compromised life she lived. Not once. If they had, their whole life would have to be turned upside down.

"Bella, come here!" Azaria called out, as she watched the older girl leaning against the bonnet of the car attempting to get signal for her phone.

"Hey Gran," she smiled sheepishly. "I can't get any signal." She shook her phone, horrified at its sudden impotence. The reality of four days without contact with the outside world filled her with fear.

"You can use the landline. Who is it that you need to call so desperately?" Azaria asked, swinging the girl up off the ground like she did each time they met. It was getting harder to do with each passing year, but she had a tradition to maintain: the Granny Swing!

"Smudge. He's my new boyfriend. He's so hot! He's nineteen, and works at the gym as a fitness instructor."

"And remind me again how old you are?" Azaria asked, knowing full well that Bella's 16th birthday had been just a few weeks ago.

Azaria said "Come onto the veranda while we wait for Astrid."

"The bad bad Aunty Astrid?" Bella laughed, mimicking

17

her mother.

"Does your mother still call her that? She's not bad, just, well, you know, a little misguided at times."

"Oh Gran, you make it sound like she's a teenager. She's your age!"

"Trust me, my darling, you can be misguided even when you're nearly fifty seven!"

As they headed towards the steps of the veranda, Azaria casually held out her other hand, knowing that at any second Eliza-May would catch hold of it.

"I've missed you, Mom," she sniffed. "I never thought this day would arrive."

Azaria felt a pang in her heart. Despite Eliza-May being beautifully dressed, and wearing a gorgeous smile, she knew that her second-born child was not happy. Not happy at all. It made Azaria ache every time she thought about it, but she also knew that there were only so many times you could reach out to someone. At some point, you had to step away and let them find their own way.

"Let's just make sure that you and I get some time alone together this weekend. It'll do us both the world of good. Everything is prepped for the party, so we can just sit back and relax for now."

Eliza-May helped her mother to fetch the glass pitchers of home-made lemonade with blueberry-filled ice cubes. The scent of tangy citrus penetrated the old kitchen, bringing back a childhood of delicious summertime memories. She looked up at her mother, desperate to say something, longing to reach out and share the pain that filled every pointless waking day. A word, a sound, some sort of SOS to reach through the molasses of numbness that kept her imprisoned in a lonely world. But as she watched Azaria Linden, flitting from one side of the kitchen to the other, sorting drinks and cookies on trays, she didn't have the strength to say a single word. Her mother looked so happy, so thrilled to have her family right here where they belonged: home.

Eliza-May wondered how it was possible that she was born from a woman who loved life so passionately whilst, for her, every day it was a struggle to even breathe. The effort it took to simply exist was exhausting.

Azaria looked over, as if she sensed something was amiss, but when Eliza-May plastered a smile across her face, a ritual she was well rehearsed in, they both stepped out to the veranda.

"Whose car is that?" Bella asked, cosying up next to her great grandmother.

"Could be your aunties. I'm sure Luna has a Volkswagen now."

The electric-blue bug drove steadily up the steep mountainside, slowing down for each pothole and bump.

"Will Aunty Starr be with her?"

"They're never apart, those two. They spend every waking minute together, when they're not working. So, Bella, tell me about this boyfriend. I want to know everything."

As Car reached for her hand, Bella's first thought was: Oh no you don't!

Three minutes later, the doors of the blue VW opened at the same time, and identical twins jumped out and ran up towards the veranda, their long chocolate-brown hair swishing behind their shoulders. They might have been twenty-four years old, but they ran like young kids, filled with excitement about the weekend ahead. At every family gathering, they were the light and life of the party.

Ruby was the first to greet them, taking them hostage in a group hug. "I have the best aunties in the whole world!" she said, grabbing their hands and leading them up to the house. "The best!"

"Kara isn't bad, you know," Luna laughed.

"Yeah, but you two are my favourites!" she whispered, as if it were a trade secret.

19

o giggled, and then parted so Azaria could
ler twins. "Look at you two. I still can't tell
" She bent the top of Luna's ear over to reveal
rthmark. That had been the way she'd always
.........ed them. Everything about them was the same:
the way they laughed, cried, and day-to-day mannerisms.
Even their vocal tone was identical. Over the phone,
Azaria didn't have the option of doing a birthmark check.
The small patch of dark-brown skin had made the world
of difference in her parenting style.

"We thought we'd make it easy for everyone this
weekend. I'm wearing blue clothes, and Starr is wearing
green."

"And you won't swap them around and trick us like
you did last time?" Azaria asked, not entirely convinced.
"Because, I always feel like a bad mother when I can't tell
you apart."

"You're the best mother in the world. That's why we
trick you...so we can prove to the world that the great
Azaria Linden is actually human." Luna kissed her mother
on the forehead. "Love you Ma, it's so good to be here."
They squeezed each other tight, and then Azaria caught
the green fabric of Starr's dress in the corner of her tear-
soaked eye.

"My darling, Starr. Thanks so much for coming. I know
you've got deadlines looming."

"We're thrilled to be here. Is the bad bad Aunty Astrid
here yet?" Starr asked.

"Why does everyone call her that?" Azaria asked,
hands on hips.

"I love how you get just that little bit protective of her,
despite what she's done to you," Starr laughed.

"Let's get something clear before she turns up:
Astrid hasn't done anything to me. We simply had a
misunderstanding."

"Well, then, Ma...this is the perfect weekend to clear

it up." She linked arms with her mother, so delighted to be on home soil again. "Hey, do me and Luna get our old bedroom this weekend or are we relegated to the barn?"

"All my girls get their own rooms. I've made up the loft in the barn for Astrid and her boyfriend."

"Boyfriend? Do tell?" Luna asked. "Please tell me he's better than that last idiot she was married to."

"I don't know anything about him. Car says that Astrid met him through work. So we're all going to be kind and give him the benefit of the doubt. Aren't we, girls?"

Everyone got the message, but Azaria couldn't stop their secretive giggles.

Kara arrived twenty minutes later. Without her husband.

"William has to work this weekend," she said, not making eye contact with anyone as she said it. She was fed up with making excuses for him. William had never attended any of her family gatherings. Aside from his own wedding, twenty years ago, that was the only time he mingled with the Linden family. He considered himself to be of a higher socio-economic echelon, and didn't deign to spend time with people 'from the land' as he referred to them.

Azaria knew the truth, but kept it to herself. If there was anything she learnt early on, it was that you couldn't choose your daughters' husbands for them. A part of her was thankful that Luna and Starr had each other, and hadn't yet walked down the aisle. It made their lives infinitely less complicated, though she dreaded the day when one of them met the man who would sever their tight relationship.

Bella eyed up her aunt Kara. "Bit overdressed, aren't you? We're in the middle of nowhere. Why are you wearing that suit?" She didn't mean to sound so harsh, but as the words tripped over her sassy tongue she saw

21

Eliza-May glaring at her and tried to backtrack. "I mean, you look pretty. Really pretty, Aunty K. It's just that we're hanging out on a veranda and eating food all weekend. You don't need to wear doctor's-wife clothes out here."

Kara kept her chin up. She'd discovered years ago the importance of appearing strong, and how to hold her emotions inside. The wall came down, like the door to a vault, and she laughed out loud to disguise the pain, overexaggerating her response. "Yes, silly me. I'll get changed shortly." She kicked herself for not packing casual clothes, and hoped that once the partying was underway no one would notice her rigid formal attire, which, ironically, was a perfect metaphor for her life.

Kara seated herself beside Granny Car, thankful for her grandmother's emotional solidity. The elder of the family, she could always be relied on for tenderness. Car had a way of seeing right into the heart of a person, and leaving them feeling that bit better without ever having to say too much. Sometimes it was the simple wink of an eye, or the unobtrusive touching of someone's shoulder. At times, it was nothing more than the affirmative 'mmm' as she let them keep talking. Car's time in an Indian ashram, many years ago, had given her a strong spiritual foundation. It was the silent witness to many people's stories.

Azaria felt her tummy start to rumble. Where the hell was Astrid? Couldn't she have the courtesy to at least arrive in good time for her own mother's eightieth birthday party? Azaria took a walk around the garden, breathing in the sweet, medicinal scent of lavender after she plucked a few leaves. The last thing she wanted to feel was aggravation. Surely Astrid could just have said 'no' if the party was too much of a hardship?

Closing her eyes and offering a silent prayer up to the heavens, she asked: "Please let this weekend be memorable. Help us all to find a way to open our hearts and receive what we need. Especially Astrid."

Welling up with emotion, she acknowledged that although forgiveness hadn't been easy, she had managed it. She just couldn't understand why Astrid didn't return the sentiment. It wasn't as if Azaria had been the one who was out of line. It was Astrid. Way out of line! The rest of the guests would be here in a few hours, and she really wanted to have family time before the party started. It was important to establish a sense of family after all this time.

The distant hum of a vehicle reverberating across the valley brought Azaria's thoughts back to the garden, and as she spied the trail of dust winding its way up towards her mountain home, she wondered if this was Astrid. Of course it was: Astrid, straddled on the back of a motorbike! In three weeks, they'd both be fifty-seven years of age. Azaria laughed at herself, standing there, barefoot by the herbs, her long, white, muslin skirt gently blowing in the breeze, the sunlight shining through to reveal the taut muscles of her long legs: supple and strong from years of daily yoga asanas.

Azaria's striking silver hair made her immediately identifiable whenever she went down into the town. With full-bodied waves, it came midway down her back, and framed her friendly face.

Azaria adored the feel of the earth beneath her bare feet, and the sweet, unmistakeable perfume of mountain air. This was her home. This was her life. She had no desire to travel and see the world. For Azaria, the whole world was here on this mountain. It had everything she could possibly need.

Astrid, on the other hand, kissed bitumen, and breathed New York pollution as if it were life-saving oxygen. She hated country living. At least that had been her story since she left home more than forty years ago. Not once did she let anyone interrupt her script.

How was it even possible that her and Astrid were twins, Azaria wondered.

23

The motorbike's engine continued to be revved for at least a minute after the rider brought it to a stop. Azaria's heart sank. She wondered if he was making a point. Perhaps it wasn't Astrid she needed to worry about, but her bonehead boyfriend. Why did she have to bring him?

Azaria breathed in deeply, and made her way to the front of the house, then stood back for a minute and watched curiously as Astrid took off her motorcycle helmet and began introductions. She looked relaxed, and so pleased to be finally establishing a relationship between her beau and her family.

Astrid had the same high, defined cheekbones as her sister, but that was about where the similarities ended. Azaria smiled at how those cheeks were accentuated even more by the short, razor-cut hairstyle. For years, Astrid had dyed her hair burnt-orange, with tar-black roots, as homage to her first husband, Rory, a firefighter who was killed on duty. Azaria wondered if this was something she ever shared with her boyfriends, and if she planned on dyeing it another colour as symbolic of moving on at long last.

In the Autumn of her life, Astrid stood tall, a stunning-looking woman. Her slender body was clad, skintight, in biker's leathers, highlighting her toned figure. Though, to Azaria's mind, she could do with putting on a stone or two. *Too skinny*, she said to herself several times.

Whatever reservations Astrid had about this family reunion certainly didn't show on her face now. It was as if she'd never been away, and, disconcertingly, seemed like a different person. There was no hint of her telltale temper. How odd, Azaria thought to herself. Something about the picture in front of her didn't seem quite right. She tried to dismiss the thought. Perhaps she was just feeling her own discomfort about all the wasted years between them. If only they'd had a relationship like Luna and Starr had. If only.

Once Azaria was confident that everyone had hugged her sister, and that the bonehead boyfriend had a clear idea of who was who, she moved away from the flourishing, bronze fennel leaves, and offered her arms wide to her sister. She half expected Astrid to fob her off with something like "don't be stupid", and was most surprised when her sister fell into her arms easily, as if it were the most natural thing in the world. "Thanks for inviting us," Astrid said softly. "It's good to be home."

If she didn't know better, Azaria would almost have thought she meant it. Perhaps the boyfriend had put her on a 'strictly good behaviour' warning, too?

"This is my partner, Bob," she said, introducing him with her hand now tucked firmly into his. "We met through work."

Azaria reached out her hand. "Nice to meet you, Bob." She was surprised that, despite the image she'd built up in her head about him, he appeared to be a very gentle man. His eyes were the colour of a baby-blue sky, and she understood why her twin was so smitten with him. He was a bear of a man: tall, solid, imposing. Protective, even. He didn't reach out for Azaria's hand, but scooped her up off the ground and gave her a huge hug. "I've heard so much about you!"

She was struck by how genuinely happy he was to meet her. He placed her securely back on the ground. Azaria felt a little dizzy. By his response towards her, he clearly hadn't heard everything. Especially the part about herself and Astrid not having spoken for eight years! Her thoughts were racing. What exactly had her sister told him? she wondered.

Drinks continued to be poured, and, a few hours later, Azaria invited everyone over to where the party was to be held, and waited for the other guests to arrive.

Under the Old Apple Trees

Beneath a floating canopy of muslin and silk georgette, a makeshift gazebo was erected between four old, gnarled apple trees. Azaria had spent days preparing the location for her mother's party. Trestle tables, made from wide tranches of ancient oak panels, stood firm. Along the tops, small clay pots with jasmine-scented beeswax candles flickered.

Cushions, gathered from all around the house, were scattered on the benches and on the grass. Fairy lights, marking out the party area, twinkled in the early evening light.

A lingering smile fell upon Azaria's face as she dreamily dragged her fingers along the trunk of an apple tree. Just last week, on the New Moon, she'd scratched her name—*Azaria Linden*—into a branch of apple wood, then tossed it into the lake, honouring an ancient ritual for drawing a soulmate into your life. It had been too long. The years with Jake Linden had been wonderful, but she'd been reluctant to enter into a new relationship after his death. After all, no man was going to be as comfortable as him. But lately, she'd wondered if perhaps it were true that we all had dozens of potential soulmates, or twin flames. If that were so, then maybe—just maybe—her heart would be open to the possibility of new love. She still had plenty of years left, so why not share them with someone? Car wouldn't be around forever, and Azaria's children were spread far and wide, and it made sense to have someone else to enjoy the bounty of this mountain life with her. *Apple-wood wishes*, she whispered. *I'm ready. I really am.*

Several students from Car's music group were hired to play throughout the evening, and catering students were brought in as waiting staff. As the band set up their instruments, and began tuning them, Azaria turned to see everyone taking their seats. There were forty guests, as well as family, who had travelled for the party. Eliza-May and her daughters helped to bring out the last trays of food. Before the musicians began to play, Azaria stood up to raise a toast.

She met her mother's watery eyes, and tried to hold back her own emotion. "This is to Car, the best mother in the world. I'm sure I can safely say she's also the best Granny, and Great Granny. Happy eightieth birthday, Mom. You're the best."

Glasses chinked around both tables. "To Granny Car," they each called out. After some music, there was a pause for speeches. Several guests spoke at length about the impact Car had had on their lives, and how she'd changed them in so many ways, not by what she said, but by how she lived.

The evening played out much like musical chairs, with people swapping seats, or getting up to dance. When Astrid stood up to slow waltz with her mother, Bob found himself walking over to Azaria and sitting by her side.

"This is such a great evening. I can't believe Astrid kept you all hidden away from me for so long. I know she's busy with work, but we really should have come over here before now."

His gaze held the woman he loved, as she swirled around on the makeshift dance floor. "She's so beautiful, isn't she?" He laughed as he said the words, realising that Astrid looked rather like her twin, despite their vastly different hairstyles and dress sense.

"How much has Astrid told you about our family?" Azaria kept her tone light, but she sensed Bob had no idea at all of what he'd just walked into.

"Everything. She loves you guys so much."

"How did you meet? Through work, you said? You're a counsellor, right?"

27

"Er, no. I was a client."

Azaria's head spun. A client? Astrid hadn't changed at all! Damn it! When would she *ever* learn? Azaria could feel the puncture marks growing deeper into her tongue. She'd promised Car that she'd not cause any trouble this weekend. But this? Someone had to say something!

She bit her tongue, again, and kept the conversation light. "So how long have you known each other?"

"Two years. We moved in together virtually overnight. I just knew she was the one."

The thought of Astrid being anyone's happily-ever-after seemed a strange concept to grasp. Astrid, the one-woman time bomb, always ready to detonate when she didn't get her own way. And this gentle giant thought she was 'the one'?

"I'm glad you're happy." The words slipped out before she had a chance to censor them, but as they tripped off her tongue so readily it occurred to Azaria that she was happy: for both of them. Everyone deserved love, even Astrid. Especially Astrid.

Azaria introduced Bob to friends, and even had a dance with him before the end of the evening. It was hard to imagine that he would ever hurt Astrid. He just didn't have a mean bone in his body. That he ended up in Astrid's life through contracting genital warts seemed ironic, to say the least. Talk about clouds having silver linings! What really engendered her to feel so warmly about him was his complete transparency about his past. No guilt or regret, or worse, blame; just the wisdom of another life experience.

Eavesdropping

After a lifetime of a 9pm bedtime, Car Lafferty begged permission to retire just a little after midnight. A standing ovation was one of her last memories of the evening, as she carefully climbed each of the steps on the veranda. This was the culmination of eighty years: beautiful friends and family, and a life well lived. The band played *September Song*. Car walked away with tears in her eyes. It was true: the days were getting shorter, and every single one was precious. To have all her family here, in one place, was the greatest gift of all.

The celebrations dimmed, and guests said their goodbyes. After the last visitors left, at one in the morning, Azaria stood in the kitchen sipping valerian tea. Bob seemed nice enough. The truth was, she really did like him. But a client? Everything about the situation was wrong. It reeked of overstepping boundaries and taking advantage of someone's vulnerability. But the truth loomed large before her: there was no way she could say anything to Astrid about it. Azaria had learnt her lesson eight years ago, the last time Astrid hooked up with a client. There are some things that are just better left unsaid. And this was one of them. She hoped the valerian would soon kick in so she could sleep peacefully.

The waxing Moon beckoned her outside. A slight breeze murmured through the mountains—its movements like the slow and graceful steps of her aging mother—causing Azaria's hair to wisp about her shoulders. Barefoot, she walked beyond the vast herb gardens, and for some inexplicable reason was drawn towards the barn. The window to the loft was open, and the lamplight hinted that Astrid and Bob were still awake.

It was wrong to eavesdrop, she knew that, but her

29

curiosity led her to sit right beneath the window in the shadow of some bushes. Their voices were softly carried on the breeze.

"They're real nice, your family. It's a shame we didn't come here before now. Life's too short to... Sorry, oh honey. I didn't mean it that way. Oh love, I'm so sorry. Come here, sweetheart."

Azaria's ears pricked up at the sound of her twin sister's muffled sobs. What had he said to upset her? She tried replaying his words over in her mind to find a clue.

"You have to tell them. They'd want to know. I'd want to know if I were in their position. That's what families are for. It is their right to witness your journey, just as it's your right to regret certain parts of your life. But they really love you, I can tell that. No one holds any grudges, least of all Azaria. Surely you can see that?"

Azaria stood up, careful not to step on any twigs. Have to tell them what? she wondered, her bare feet upon the dewy grass.

"Come on honey. Let's get to bed. Tomorrow's a new day. You might feel differently when you've spent a bit more time here."

As the lamplight went out, darkness fell across the grassy area below the barn. Her first instinct was to wake Car. But what could she tell her? She was a little too old to be spying on her sister, and even older to be telling tales. Throughout their childhood, it was always Astrid who was the tittletat. Azaria decided, at the age of three, that she'd never be like that.

She lay in her huge bed, flipping the blankets this way and that. She tossed and turned for the longest time. One thing was clear: Astrid didn't just come home for her mother's eightieth birthday. Something was weighing on her conscience, heavy as a boulder.

Barely an hour into sleep, and Azaria was woken by the first rays of sunlight. Bob's last words came rushing back

30

to her: *Tomorrow's a new day. You might feel differently when you've spent a bit more time here.*

Despite her aching muscles, and the weariness enveloping her body, Azaria showered and headed to the kitchen to prepare brunch for her family. Car was already there, sipping her morning cup of chai tea.

Greeted by the intoxicating zingy spices of cinnamon, ginger and cardamom, Azaria started to feel more awake.

"You don't look like you slept very well," Car said, as Azaria sat down beside her.

"I didn't. I barely slept at all." She filled her cup, unsure of how much to share with her mother. "Something's up with Astrid. I don't know what, but I…" she suddenly felt awkward about the idea of confessing to snooping on them last night. "Never mind."

"You can't stop now. What is it?"

Before Azaria had a chance to answer, Ruby came bounding into the kitchen, and nestled herself in her grandmother's lap.

"I could get used to this," Azaria laughed, kissing the flaxen hair on Ruby's head a dozen times, staccato style. "I so love having my grandbabies around."

"I want to live here. I don't ever want to go home." Ruby nuzzled into her grandmother. "Can't I just stay with you and Car?"

"Your mother would miss you far too much," Car winked at her.

"She wouldn't notice," Ruby said matter of factly. "She's too sad to notice how anyone else is feeling. Dad says she was born that way, and that we just have to get on with our lives."

"She was not born that way!" Azaria snapped. When Ruby flinched, Azaria pulled her back into her arms. "I'm not cross with you, honey. Your father is wrong. Eliza-May was one of the happiest girls you could ever meet. She was like you, in many ways. Always happiest

31

amongst the flowers and watching butterflies and making daisy chains. She wasn't born to look out of a high-rise apartment building."

"So why does she?"

Azaria sighed. "We can't help who we fall in love with. Your mother was born under the apple trees, but she grew up and fell in love with a man who was born on the top floor of a hospital, and rarely has his feet on grass."

"But if she's not happy, then…"

"Shhh," Car whispered, as James walked into the kitchen, still in his pyjamas.

"Morning ladies. Any coffee?"

"What? You don't want our famous lavender tea?" Azaria laughed, trying to dissipate her frustration that he didn't know his wife nearly as well as he should have after seventeen years of marriage. "Of course we have coffee."

She removed the kettle from the Aga, and filled the cafetiere. Freshly ground Nicaraguan coffee sent a robust aroma shooting around the kitchen, quickly overshadowing the chai tea spices.

"That should wake you up, James. Been busy at work?" Azaria wasn't sure why she asked him that. He was always busy. There was rarely a week when he didn't work at least six days.

"Quite," he said, grabbing a scone from the rack.

"Careful," Car said, "They've only just come out of the oven. Don't burn your mouth!"

It was too late. "Bloody hell!"

"DAD!" Ruby yelled. "You told Bella she wasn't allowed to swear this weekend."

Everyone laughed.

"Best behaviour never lasts very long," Azaria said, kissing Ruby on the head once again. "Right young lady, what would you like for breakfast? Car has baked cheese and chive scones, or I can whip you up some maple pancakes. Or there's muesli or my famous poached eggs on English muffins."

"All of them, Granny. I want all of them."

"And where are you going to fit all of them? Hmmm?"

"Dad will eat whatever I leave behind."

"I sure will," James laughed, patting his pot belly. Azaria liked James, she always had, but she could never reconcile how he could be so at a loss to his own wife's needs: her total disdain of city life, for starters.

"Everything it is then," Azaria said, lifting Ruby off her lap.

From out of the walk-in pantry, Azaria brought glass jars of marmalade and blueberry jam, and bottled peaches. Placing them on the table, she set about making quinoa pancakes. Ruby watched carefully, memorising the measurements. She poured the batter into a pan, and watched as bubbles grew in each pancake. Azaria set some English muffins to toast, and made poached eggs. The kitchen was alive with activity, and James continued to chat about his work and a high-profile case he was involved in with a celebrity.

Car listened, and also listened between the words. Home life for the Megane family seemed non-existent. Ruby's afternoons were filled with extra-curricular activities, and Bella had intensive tutoring six days a week. James was determined his daughters would get into the best universities. It occurred to Car, that Eliza-May was barely mentioned. Was their marriage doomed to failure?

Ruby ate a pancake straight from the pan, licking her fingers and dipping it into some maple syrup.

"Eliza-May and Bella still asleep?" Azaria asked when setting the table.

"Eliza-May is snoring, and Bell is up the back garden looking for phone signal."

"I told her she could use my phone," Azaria laughed.

"I think privacy is the keyword here." James laughed, raising his eyebrows.

"Of course. But if she changes her mind…"

"Gran, what are we doing today?" Ruby asked, sipping her grandmother's tea.

"Since your Mom's being a sleepyhead this morning, how about you and I take a dip down at the hot spring? We can be back by mid morning and then you can help me prepare for a late lunch. What do you think?"

"Wonderful. Just me and you? No one else?" she asked hopefully.

"Just me and you!" Azaria smiled, grateful that a teenage girl would think that hanging out with her grandmother was actually fun.

Ruby scoffed her pecan and cranberry muesli, shoved two scones into her pocket, and announced she was full.

"Mom, are you okay to keep an eye on things here? Make sure James doesn't eat us out of house and home," Azaria laughed, pinching his arm as she walked by.

"Come on, Rubes. Let's go."

The Hot Spring

Taking nothing with them but a bottle of spring water with lime slices, and two towels, Azaria and Ruby made their way down the hill. Colorado was stunning at this time of year. The mountainside setting was pristine all-year round, but today there was something in the air. Something hopeful.

Despite Ruby's constant and lively chatter, Azaria's mind kept returning to the conversation between Bob and Astrid.

And then, as if picking up her grandmother's thoughts, Ruby changed the subject.

"Why does everyone say *bad bad* Aunty Astrid?" the young teenager asked, squeezing her grandmother's hand a little tighter as they navigated a steep rocky outcrop on the path.

"I don't call her that."

"That's because she's your sister! Is she bad?"

"No, not at all. Astrid has a good heart. It's just that…"

"What?"

"Well, she's an impulsive person. Sometimes she acts before she thinks, and this ends up causing her, and others, a lot of pain. But no, honey, she's not bad. She never has been. Misunderstood, perhaps."

"Do you love her, Gran?"

"With all my heart. More than she could ever know."

"Why don't you tell her then?" Ruby asked, as if it were the most obvious thing in the world. "Is it true she ran away from home when she was fifteen years old?"

"Yes, she did. Here we are," Azaria proclaimed five minutes after they'd left the house. They stepped out of the forest of Douglas firs into the granite clearing, the steam from the pool rising up to meet them. Such a perfect

35

Spring morning: a powder-blue sky, and the air subtly scented with pine.

They discarded their dresses on the rocks, and carefully stepped into the warm water. It had been a whole year since they'd enjoyed sharing the pool together. This annual ritual was something they'd both come to cherish.

Azaria marvelled at the changes to Ruby's body in that time. Her flat chest and straight bony hips had softened somewhat and given way to breasts, soft as marshmallows, and shy curves. Azaria's heart clenched a little. Her baby grandchild was growing up. She was rapidly becoming a woman. Time waited for no girl. Truth be told, it didn't seem like that long ago that Azaria was a pubescent teenager herself.

Azaria sighed as her muscles instinctively relaxed in the warm water of the wild mountain spring. She started most mornings with a trip to the hot pool, the medicinal mineral waters a balm for daily life, followed by an hour of yoga asanas there in the sunshine with the warmed granite beneath her feet.

As lovely as it was having a house full of visitors, it disrupted her daily rhythm somewhat.

"Was Great-Granny Car mean to Astrid?" Ruby asked thoughtfully.

"No, not at all." She wondered how Ruby came to that conclusion. Caroline Lafferty was as kind and gentle as it was humanly possible to be, and had modelled how to be a good mother in a million different ways.

They sat in golden, companionable silence for a while, when the sound of a snapping twig caught their attention. A moose, browsing foliage of the quaking aspen, caught their eye. Ruby studied the majestic animal, and also noticed the claw marks of a bear engraved in the smooth bark of the tree. Everything about this secluded haven was a lifetime away from the world she knew in Manhattan.

The moose called out, his throaty, airy moo echoing

across the woods. Intrigued by his velvet antlers, Ruby was lost in a world so different from her daily life. Enrolled in an all girls' school, attending as a day student, she hated it, but somehow never lost her sense of wonder. Despite the bleakness of home life: a sister focused on boys, a workaholic father, an emotionally absent mother, and constant bullying at school, Ruby Megane remained a free spirit with dreams no one could erase. Her sole vision in life was to become a herbalist, just like Grandmother Azaria. And one day, she would. She was sure of it. Yes, one day she'd be living here on the mountains, spending her days infusing leaves and blossoms into tinctures, drying plants for tea, and blending oils to make healing balms. Like Azaria, she'd start each day with a dip in the sacred spring. One day, the taunts of spoilt, rich schoolgirls would be a thing of the past. Her father was adamant: university first, and then after she had a degree she could "play with herbs". Ruby, however, had other ideas. Plans were already in place. It was just a matter of time.

"What's the yellow flower?" she whispered, spying a blossom atop a strong stem, always keen to add to her knowledge of native flowers.

"Mule's ear."

"Gran, do you know all the flowers?"

"I try to. Remember, I've lived here all my life. I've had plenty of time to get to know them."

The lone moose, startled by a noise nearby, trampled through the woods, his large, cloven hooves thudding heavily on the forest floor, the vibration causing a gentle ripple across the water.

"If Great Gran wasn't mean, then why did Aunty Astrid run away?"

Azaria sighed, then thought it was best to start from the beginning. Ruby was a bright child. She could make up her own mind about who was right and who was wrong, if at all.

"Well, about a month or so before she ran away, I had my first period. I was so excited about it. Astrid, on the other hand, thought it was disgusting, and she hoped that she'd never have to bleed."

"I had my first period two weeks ago!" Ruby announced, excited to share in something her own grandmother had experienced. Her eyes were wide and wild, momentarily thrilled at the common connection they now shared.

"You did? Your mother never told me that." Azaria felt a tear emerge in the corner of her eye.

"Mom doesn't know," Ruby said, shaking her head. "She was in bed that day, so I never told her. Don't tell Bell, but I borrowed some pads from her bedroom. I didn't mean to steal them. It wasn't really stealing, was it? I just didn't want to make a fuss. She has tampons, too, but I didn't want to use them. It seemed icky to put them inside me."

"Your Mom doesn't know? Oh honey!" Azaria reached for her hand. "Thank you for telling me." A gnawing pain filled the pit of her belly. It was such a huge life change for Ruby to undergo on her own. She should have had someone to share it with at the time.

"Then what happened? With Astrid?" Ruby begged for more information.

"Well, she got her first period two weeks after me. Car asked us if we'd like a ceremony to celebrate our initiation into womanhood. I was so excited, and helped her plan it. We invited Car's eight sisters and our best friends to come and join us. You should have seen the beautiful white dress that Mom and I sewed. It was so pretty. I felt like a fairy princess!"

A tear slipped from her eye, not of sadness, but happiness. It had been the highlight of her teenage years, but also bittersweet. It was a turning point in more ways than one.

"Did Astrid wear a white dress too?" Ruby asked, her

eyes wide with curiosity. "I'd love to have a ceremony like that." That familiar dreamy look came into her eyes.

"Astrid wasn't there. She didn't turn up." It was just over forty one years ago, that fateful day, but it was stamped on Azaria's heart in a way that meant it was always there.

The Raging Moon

Where was Astrid?

At breakfast the next morning, there was still no sign of her sister.

Car Lafferty refused to be drawn into the child's drama. Astrid was already the queen of causing mayhem, her temper ready to flare at a moment's notice. She shouldn't have been surprised at this latest outburst. It was just like Astrid to try and ruin everything.

"It's washing day. Can you help me, Azaria? I'd like to get it out early while the weather is fine."

Together they brought wicker baskets to the laundry room, and began sorting clothes into piles.

"Can you strip the beds?" Car asked, her hands shaking.

"Mom? Are you alright?"

"Yes dear, just do the beds."

Azaria began in her parents' bedroom, stripping the blankets back, and removing the sheets and pillow cases. Popping them into a hamper, she carried it on her hip and headed to her bedroom, the one she shared with Astrid. She smiled to herself. A year ago, her hip hadn't been round enough to rest the basket on. Now she could, just like her mother, and

39

probably her mother before her. Her fingers ran along the woven edge of the basket, and she allowed herself a few moments of pride, before continuing with the task at hand.

It was so odd not to have Astrid here. There was so much she wanted to tell her about the New to the Moon ceremony, and how she really felt like a woman now. And that periods weren't a yicky thing. It would have to wait, though.

She lifted the pillow off Astrid's bed, and a small piece of paper fluttered to the floor.

I'm not coming back! Not ever. I'm not interested in all your hocus-pocus, and herbs and rituals. I want to be normal!

Azaria fell to her knees, unable to comprehend the enormity that small piece of paper held. Not coming back? It was impossible. Astrid was fifteen years old. She had no way of looking after herself.

Azaria dragged herself into standing position. It was time to tell Car.

"Gran, were you scared?" Ruby asked.

"I was terrified for her. Really, she was so young. Feisty, angry, and inexperienced at life. We'd spent our whole lives up here on the mountain. I knew she was desperate to leave, and travel to cities and explore the world, but I never imagined that she'd just run away."

"Did the police find her?"

"No, they didn't. From time to time she'd send a postcard saying she was okay, and not to worry."

"Did you worry? Did Granny Car and Grandpa worry?"

"Non-stop!"

"What none of us knew was that she'd been dating a local boy. They'd run away together. A year later, she sent

40

a photo of her new baby."

"She'd had *sex*?" Ruby asked incredulously.

"Yes, indeed."

"Did she bring the baby home?"

"No. No she didn't. We didn't get to see the baby."

"Why not? I didn't even know she had a child."

The Fire

Astrid, eight months pregnant, watched the flames in horror. Thirty-five firemen were on duty, the flashing red lights of their engines, and their unwieldy turbo hoses, warning every living creature to stand back. The city nightline was both simultaneously lit up and darkened by a fatal orange hue. The colour of death. Astrid screamed out for her lover, the father of her unborn child. "Rory, Rory!" Her voice, desperate, hoarse and raw, punctured the poisonous fumes. Falling onto her knees, overcome with smoke, the chief fireman ordered two of his men to take her away from the scene. Rory hadn't been seen for five minutes. He should have been out by now. He'd risked his life to save a baby who'd been trapped in a room. Time was running out.

Two hours later, as the huge inferno began to die down, Chief Harrison came and sat by Astrid's side. "It can't be possible. It's just not possible! He's too young to die! What about *his* baby?" It was the longest night of Ed Harrison's life. He'd mentored Rory through his fire training, and had never lost a fireman so young. He felt the loss personally.

Ed took the next few days off work, ensuring that Astrid had counselling, and was the

41

recipient of a payout from the fire department. He couldn't bring Rory back from the dead, but he could ensure that his child was looked after.

Astrid fought her way through labour pains, resisting all the way. She was meant to birth in four weeks from now, not three days after her lover had died. Screaming, she ordered the doctor to give her drugs. "Hurry up!"

"Astrid," he said softly, "this baby needs you to calm down. I can give you something for the pain, but I need you to try and relax."

"I don't want to relax. And I don't want this baby!"

The doctor shook his head gently, and moved away.

"I'll come back in a few minutes. In the meantime, the midwife is going to monitor you. I'm serious, Astrid, you have to calm down. You're not doing yourself or the baby any favours."

Within two minutes, the doctor was back in the room, having been alerted by a worried midwife.

"The baby's in distress," she whispered to him.

"Of course it is. Poor thing is trapped in an angry prison."

The baby was born by emergency caesarean just ten minutes later. When her fragile, bloodied body was placed in Astrid's arms, the only thing she had to say was: *I can't be this baby's mother.*

The midwives ignored her, and fussed around the baby saying what beautiful ruby lips she had. "And look at those eyes," they said. "She looks just like her mother."

Another midwife took photos. "You'll want these."

But Astrid didn't want the photos, and she didn't want the vile creature who was now screaming in her arms. Not when she still had her own screaming to do. Despite her protests, the midwives tried to help the baby latch on. "I am not feeding this child! Get her a bottle."

After several hours, and frantic, desperate crying from the baby, the midwives contacted social services asking for an adoption placement. Bottles of formula were brought to the baby throughout the night, and the unloved infant was taken to a nursery. One thing they did insist on was that Astrid name her baby. She did: Victoria.

The next morning, a kindly midwife, named Sarah, asked Astrid if she'd like to see her baby girl one last time. Maybe she'd like to say goodbye?

"I have lost the love of my life. He died because of a baby! And now he isn't here. He isn't here for his own child. Don't you understand that?" Astrid screamed. "I haven't even buried his body. Do you really think I want to be reminded of what has happened to me every time I see that child? No, I don't! There are a million other people who will be better mothers than I could ever be. Don't bother me again."

Sarah sighed, her heart aching for mother and child, and tried another tack. "Do you have family? Do you want me to contact your mother? Maybe I could see if any of them would help you raise the baby?"

Astrid fumed. She took the Polaroid photos from the side cabinet and said "Here, post them a picture of the baby. It'll just highlight what a failure I am to them. Again."

Sarah wrote down the address, and quietly left the room.

"Oh Gran!" Ruby cried. "That's so sad. This is the saddest story I've ever heard. I can't bear it. Did she cry a lot?"

"She cried for about a year."

"I don't understand why everyone calls her bad bad. Shouldn't it be *sad sad*?"

"You'd think so, wouldn't you?"

"Then what happened? Tell me more, Gran. Tell me everything. I have to know."

Azaria was in two minds about how much to share. It was better for the child to know the truth rather than to keep perpetuating misinformation.

"Astrid began to have some counselling for her grief. She wasn't coping at all well."

"Did she miss her baby? Did she regret giving her up?"

"Truth be told, I don't think she thought about the baby much. She was too grief-stricken about Rory. You have to remember, Astrid was still a child herself when she gave birth. She'd have barely had two menstrual cycles before she was pregnant. I imagine it was a huge shock to her. And, her marriage to Rory had been a simple affair. Just the two of them, and registry office staff as witnesses. Due to Astrid's age, she'd been granted judicial permission because of her pregnancy. So much had happened to her in a short space of time."

"Did the counselling help? Did it make her better? Was she happy again?"

"If only that was the case. No, it didn't help. It made things worse. Over the next few years she had several counsellors, and then…"

"What, Gran?"

"You see, Astrid fell in love with her counsellor."

"Did he love her too?"

"Yes."

"That's a good thing."

"Well, it might have been, except for the fact that he was married! His wife was expecting a baby. Derek had been promising Astrid that he was going to leave his wife, and then when she was pregnant, he changed his mind. The thing is, Ruby, he was out of line. If he wanted to have a relationship with her then he should have recommended another counsellor. It's ethically wrong to be in a position like that and to cross that sort of boundary. Astrid came to him for help. What happened was disastrous."

"Are you going to tell me? I want to know, Gran."

Executioner's Moon

Astrid phoned Derek, desperately asking if he'd meet her that night by the river. She could tell he'd been drinking, as some of his words slurred into each other, like a train ramming into a lone carriage. She watched the waxing quarter Moon disappear beneath a black cloud, and for a moment wished that she'd called her mother instead. That would have been the sensible thing to do. Car would have helped to calm her down.

Looking at her watch, Astrid counted down the minutes until he'd arrive.

Perching herself on an old tree stump, she shivered against the driving rain now lashing her skin. Perhaps they should have met in a café, but she wanted privacy.

Derek arrived on foot, and one more time

45

mentally rehearsed the news that he'd tell
Astrid: he would not be leaving his wife, as
promised, because she was pregnant. It would
be wrong to leave her under the circumstances.

Ruby was crying softly, the thought of one of the women
in her family suffering like that was unthinkable to her.

Azaria looked up at the fragile-blue sky, hoping to find
the right words.

"He told her the news but she didn't believe him.
They sat and drank a bottle of whisky, and Astrid got as
drunk as he did. She walked over to the railway track and
threatened to take her own life if he didn't leave his wife.
Derek thought she was bluffing, but as the train came
closer, he started to wonder if perhaps she was serious. He
waited for Astrid to move away from the train track. By
some miracle, Derek managed to push her off the tracks
and down the steep bank, just in time. He saved her life."

"Were they hurt?"

"In many ways they were hurt, yes. Astrid, as it turned
out, was also pregnant. The tumble down the steep hill
caused her to miscarry. Derek had no idea that she'd been
carrying his baby, and was filled with remorse when he
discovered the truth. He ended up leaving his wife, and he
and Astrid moved in together the next day."

"But it wasn't happily ever after?"

"No, my sweet child. It was not. Derek couldn't live
with the guilt—of leaving his pregnant wife, and of
causing the death of his other baby—and began to drink
more and more. He lost his job, and was reliant on Astrid
to go out and earn an income, but she was not mentally
stable at that time. There'd been too much trauma in her
life."

"Then what happened?"

"What happened was that Astrid and I began to
have a difficult relationship. She'd confided in me about

46

everything, but she wasn't very good at taking advice. She was rather headstrong, to say the least. Car and I convinced her to move back here to the mountain."

"And did she?"

"Yes, she did."

"And was she okay after that?"

"No, darling. She wasn't. I don't think she's ever been okay in her life. Until now. The Astrid we know now is a different person."

It was at this point that Azaria was reluctant to share any more of Astrid's journey. It seemed too personal. But, she wondered, was it fair to hide any of this?

"Astrid started dating a lot of men. Not for long. Usually, she'd just go out on one date with them."

"You mean like a one-night stand?"

Goddess, the girl knew far too much.

"Exactly."

Azaria sighed. All those wasted years. Astrid's life could have been so different.

"Do you know I was born near a new Moon?" she said, changing the subject.

"No, I didn't," Ruby replied.

"I was born while the Moon was in Pisces, the Dreamer's Moon, and Astrid was born the next day, when the Moon had moved into Aries."

"What sort of Moon is that?"

"At the New Moon, it's the Infant's Moon."

"Is that why you're both so different?"

"In some ways, yes. Astrid has always been like a raging infant. The sort of baby that just goes red in the face and screams blue murder. The Sun also changed signs between the day I was born and the day Astrid was born. We might be twins, but we were born with a different blueprint. Did you know your Moon is in Pisces too? You were born on the crescent Moon, the Mermaid's Moon. I was there on the night you were born."

"What does that mean?"

"Pisces is about dreams, vision, poetry, music, art, feeling everything the mother experiences, and touching the face of the Goddess."

"What about Astrid's Moon?"

Azaria sighed. "Well, it can be a very brave Moon, pioneering and courageous. But," she sighed, "it's also an angry sign and one with a tendency to be self-absorbed and not terribly considerate of others. That's why Astrid has struggled so much in her life. An Aries Moon, when unchecked, can be so fiery and volatile and self-focused."

"What happened to her next?"

"The rest isn't my story to tell," Azaria said tactfully.

Azaria sank her head beneath the water, her long silver hair floating behind her like a mermaid.

Astrid spent more than two decades of her life, moving from one one-night stand to another, from one brief encounter to another. Contracting chlamydia and genital warts, Astrid was left devastated. Ashamed, guilt-ridden, and feeling dirty, she took it as a proven truth that the Gods were punishing her. Spiralling further and further into a downward path of self-sabotage, Car and Azaria thought they'd never be able to reach her, but something life-changing happened during that dark night of the soul. Astrid took a vow of celibacy, moved to New York City, and enrolled in a degree, studying psychology. Turning her life around, she became a counsellor and helped those people whose lives had been beset by sexually transmitted infections. She also, silently, with no one but God as her witness, vowed never to hurt anyone again, including herself.

They stayed in the hot pool for another half an hour, then made the slow ascent up the mountain, walking barefoot along the dusty path.

"Gran, I'd like a ceremony for my period. Just like you had. Could you help me do one? While everyone's here?"

Azaria did a double take. "Do you want to check with your mother first?"

"No. If she doesn't want to be there, she doesn't have to be. This is for me. After all, I'm a woman now!" She smiled, and reached for Azaria's hand.

"Of course we can have one. I can't promise Astrid will want to witness it though, honey."

"She will," Ruby said assuredly. "She will."

When they arrived back at the house, Starr and Luna were on the old veranda painting each other's toenails the same electric-blue colour as the Volkswagen. Kara was talking to Bob about her latest charity work in Kenya, and Eliza-May was over at the herb gardens in a world of her own. Car and James were hanging washing outside on the clothes line, laughing. Bella was looking for phone signal, still, and muttering with disgust every few feet.

As Azaria and Ruby made their way onto the veranda, everyone came in for a glass of ginger and lime presse.

"I'm having a party tomorrow, and I'd like everyone to be there," Ruby announced, matter of factly.

"It's not your birthday," James laughed. "Why do you need a party? Isn't it enough that we all came here for Granny Car's eightieth?"

"Great-Granny Car's party was very special, and I'm glad we're all here for it. But this is different. This isn't about my birthday. It's to celebrate my Moon time."

"Your *what*?" James asked, choking on his drink. He wondered what his mother-in-law had been up to this time.

"I had my first period two weeks ago," Ruby announced, ever so proudly, "and I want to celebrate it with all the women in my family. This is a perfect time. We're all together."

"Gross!" Bella called out, stomping away, shaking her

49

phone in the air. "Gross! Overshare. *Overshare!* Mom, make her stop!"

Azaria held back her smile. Who did Bella remind her of? Ah yes, her own sister. She looked over at Astrid, who by now was looking quite curiously at Ruby.

"I'll help you, Ruby. Just let me know what you need to do." Astrid reached for Bob's hand, seeking out his support.

Azaria and Car looked at each other, barely able to comprehend Astrid's willingness to be part of such a ceremony.

"We'll help," Starr said, "Won't we, Lu?"

"Sure will. Any excuse for more food!" she laughed.

"Be serious, sis."

"I am. There will be food, won't there?" Luna asked Ruby, suddenly concerned.

"Lots of food."

"Talking of food, who wants to help me get ready for lunch?" Azaria asked, looking around at everyone's faces. This was her family, and she was so grateful to have them all in one place. All right where she could mother them without interference from the outside world and all its charms and dangers.

"I'll help!" Ruby said, wrapping her arms around Azaria's toned belly.

"And so will I," Kara said, walking up the stairs of the veranda.

The only person who didn't appear to be interested in either lunch or tomorrow's ceremony was Eliza-May. She was now sitting on the edge of the veranda, her thoughts a million miles away. Azaria decided that she'd speak to her later. It was a conversation that needed to be had in private.

The old open-plan kitchen became a hive of activity. Azaria delegated jobs, and oversaw the coming together of gorgeous food and colourful flowers. Ruby adorned salads with orange nasturtiums and renaissance-blue starflower petals. Kara made cucumber and cheese sandwiches, and Starr and Luna baked dandelion tarts.

The red Aga was in full use, and, as Azaria stood there monitoring pans, she took a moment to take in the beautiful view from the wood-framed windows.

She grew up in those wildflower meadows, a happy and carefree childhood, surrounded by the love of a gaggle of wonderful, hands-on aunties and doting parents. Every fabulous life memory was forged on this farm by friends, family, flowers, freedom, and food.

The chatter and laughter which filled the kitchen also filled her heart. *Family. Love. Home.* Her favourite words.

Potted geraniums, their vibrant-red flowers alive with an intoxicating joy dominating the kitchen, lined the wooden window sills. They were in stark contrast to the indigo blue curtains, with silver crescent moons embroidered along the bottom hem.

Azaria wrapped marinated artichokes in puff pastry, and brought jugs of iced peppermint tea from the fridge.

Astrid stood by her side, mixing choc-chip and coconut cookie dough. "Talking of ceremonies," she said quietly, so only Azaria could hear, "I wonder how you'd feel about Bob and I coming here in the Summer and getting married in the garden?"

Azaria dropped her knife, and stared at her sister. Astrid? Marrying again? She never thought she'd see the day. Words failed to come out of her mouth, despite the dozens of thoughts racing around her head.

"Would you be the celebrant?" Astrid asked. "I'd really like that."

After all these years of estrangement, and Astrid was actually inviting Azaria to play an integral role in her new life? To bless the way ahead?

She forced herself to speak. "I'd be honoured. Absolutely honoured. You've left me speechless, sis. I really don't know what to say."

Astrid's arms immediately wrapped around Azaria. "Thank you! I can't wait to tell Bob."

Just then, Bob and James walked into the kitchen. Bob knew from the look on Astrid's face that Azaria had said yes.

"Fantastic!" he laughed out loud, clapping his hands. Everyone turned to look at him. For a gentle and quiet man, his outburst was uncharacteristic.

"We have some news," Astrid said. "Where's Mom? I want her to hear this?"

"I'll get her," Ruby said, anticipating an exciting announcement. Within a minute, Car, Eliza-May, and Bella had joined everyone in the kitchen.

"I've asked Bob to marry me," Astrid announced proudly, "and he has said *yes*."

The shock was palpable. Bad bad Aunty Astrid was getting married. Again. A silent prayer went around the room: *I hope it's third-time lucky.*

Azaria sensed the apprehension, and instantly lifted the mood with her joy and endorsement. "This is such wonderful news, and we're all so happy." Azaria looked at Car. "They're getting married here, in the garden, in the summertime. Put it in your diaries, people! Time for another Lafferty reunion."

"Azaria's going to officiate the ceremony," Astrid announced. Another silence descended, but was quickly broken by Ruby.

"Do you need bridesmaids?" she gushed, anticipating only one possible answer.

"Of course I do!"

"I was hoping you and Bell would be my bridesmaids."

"Do I have to wear a dress?" Bella snarled, the thought of lace and taffeta making her giddy.

"No, you can wear jeans," Astrid laughed. "I just want my family there. All of you. I don't care what you wear, just so long you're there."

Any tension that had settled was quickly diffused and replaced by long, lingering, rocking hugs of joy. Astrid was finally happy.

Azaria smiled as she placed food on trays. So this was what Bob and Astrid had been talking about? A wedding! Her heart fluttered. That her sister was finally happy gave her a sense of rightness with the world. Her own life, despite its losses over the years, had been a good one, filled with the love of friends and a good man. Azaria's health and well-being had always been reliable, and her sunny nature carried her through many a storm. Today, somehow, it seemed as if all of life had finally come together. Dare she even say, life was perfect? She just needed to help Kara see it was time to leave her corrosive marriage, and for Eliza-May to walk robustly out of the sewer of depression. But she knew, with all her heart, that the biggest drain on her emotions was always Astrid. Finally, there could be true healing. Her sister had come 'home' to family.

"Mom, can I talk to you?" Astrid asked, interrupting a conversation she was having with Azaria about the ceremony for Ruby.

"Of course you can," she said, reaching out her hand.

Azaria started to walk away, leaving them to talk in private.

"Stay," Astrid said. Azaria turned around, and came back to where they were sitting beneath the juniper tree.

"I don't know if I can ever find the words to say how truly sorry I am for not being there the day of the menarche ceremony. I've only reached a point in my life now where I can see how good it would have been for me. My whole life would have been different. I'm sorry for the pain I caused both of you, and to Dad. I truly am." Sepia-staining mascara ran its course down her face, a rivulet of pain, undisguised. She made no attempt to brush her tears

53

away. The cleansing salt water was part of her baptism. "I am truly sorry. If I could turn back time, I would."

"Astrid, everything happened as it was meant to. If you didn't go down the path you had, you wouldn't be marrying Bob this Summer. You'd never have even met him."

"But not being there, and the hurt I caused you all, is the single biggest regret of my life. I don't know how to repair that. And I want to."

"Oh my child," Car said, her voice cracking. "Let it go. It was so long ago. We never stopped loving you, and that's all that matters."

The three embraced, the wasted years of estrangement soaking onto the earth below.

Afterwards, they planned Ruby's ceremony, and discussed what they could do to make it memorable.

"Astrid, would you invite Ruby over the threshold? Invite her to womanhood?" Azaria asked. It was a role she selfishly wanted for herself; after all, Ruby was her granddaughter, and if she were honest, her favourite granddaughter, but she recognised the level of healing such an initiation would offer to Astrid.

"Of course I will. Just tell me what to do."

As they strolled back to the house, Car asked, "Astrid, could you come to my room with me?"

"Of course."

When they entered, Car closed the door behind them. She was slower now, even though her health was quite good; gravity had worn down on her bones over eight decades. "I have something I'd like to give Ruby, but I need your permission."

"My permission? I don't understand."

Car opened her wardrobe, and removed a box. Inside, wrapped in white tissue paper, was a dress. She held it up for her daughter to see.

Astrid stood, looking at it for a few seconds, before

54

registering the significance of it. "You made this for me? This was *my* New Moon dress?"

"Yes, my darling. I sewed it for you. Every single stitch."

"You kept it? All these years?" Tears began afresh. "I won't fit into it now," Astrid laughed through her tears.

"No, but Ruby will."

"Of course! Of course she will. Can I take it to her?"

"I was hoping you would."

"Oh Mom, I love you so much. More than you could ever imagine. I just can't believe how much pain I've brought to your life. How have you ever been able to forgive me?"

"I'm a mother. That's what we do. Forgiveness is hard-wired into our hearts."

"But sometimes you didn't talk to me. I thought you stopped loving me."

"Honey, those times I didn't talk to you were about me, not you. Even a mother, with her boundless love, sometimes needs to wrap herself in cotton wool as she tends her broken heart."

"I must have broken your heart a lot, Mom."

"Yes, sweetheart, you did. You did indeed. But it only hurt because I loved you so much. I was desperate to save you from yourself."

They sat on the bed for some time while they composed themselves.

"Bob's a good man, Mom. Really good."

"I can see that." Car smiled. "I can tell a good man when I see one. I have no fears about your relationship. Just enjoy each other."

"I'm making every day count." Astrid wiped her tears, and picked up the dress. "This is truly beautiful. And you know what? Ruby will look amazing in this. That girl would look good dressed in a tea towel, but this? Oh she's going to be a princess! Hey, maybe she could wear it for

55

the wedding, too?"

"And Bell in jeans?"

They both giggled. "She won't wear jeans. She's just winding everyone up."

"Bell is more like you than I ever dare to believe. Don't count on her wearing a dress! Have you set a date yet?"

"The sooner the better. Beginning of the school holidays, so everyone can be here."

Astrid awoke early, excited to take the dress to Ruby. She knocked on the bedroom door, and tiptoed in. Bella was snoring softly, and Ruby was reading. "Hey Aunty Astrid," she said, sitting up in bed.

"I've got you a gift," Astrid said, holding up the dress.

"It's for me?"

"Would you like to wear it for your ceremony today?"

"That looks just like the one Gran told me she wore for her ceremony." She threw the blankets off and raced over to hold it in her hands.

"It is just like it. This was mine, only..."

"I know," Ruby said tenderly. "I know." She placed her hand on her great aunty's hand.

Astrid marvelled at the level of empathy Ruby possessed. "You'd let me borrow this?"

"You can keep it, and maybe, if you love it, you'd like to wear it for my wedding? I'd like it if you did, but if you want something modern, that's okay too."

"Oh no, this is perfect. I could wear this every day for the rest of my life. Can you believe Great-Granny Car sewed this all by hand?"

"Every stitch sewn with love," she whispered, the enormity of it slamming her in the chest. "She's a very special woman."

"And we came from her body," Ruby said wisely. "Even me, down the family line."

"We surely did!" Astrid tried to lighten the mood.

56

"Would you like me to do your hair? I could do braids or something?"

"Oh yes please! Could you make me a flower crown? I love wearing flowers in my hair."

Astrid felt the twang of bittersweet relief and regret. She'd never had a connection with her own daughter like this. She gave up that right the day she left her baby. The day she turned her back on the mother she could have been. Should have been. But Ruby? Ruby was open like a flower waiting to be pollinated by life itself. Just like Azaria, she thought wryly, wondering how different her life would have been had she been more like her sister.

They spent the morning playing with different hairstyles, and red ribbons. Astrid helped Ruby to put on the dress. It fitted perfectly. It seemed like a miracle, but Astrid was coming to realise that nothing was coincidence in the Lafferty family. "I'm so glad Car saved this dress. I don't know why she saved it, she had no reason to, but I'm so glad she did. You look gorgeous, Ruby. So gorgeous. I'm really glad that I'm here today to celebrate your menarche."

"I'm glad you are too. I love you Aunty Astrid. We all do. Do you know that? We all love you."

It was the tender, teary-eyed way that Ruby expressed herself that caught Astrid completely off guard.

"You're one amazing human being, Ruby Megane. Don't ever change. I couldn't bear it." She blinked her tears away, then placed the floral crown of lavender-red alpine violets upon Ruby's head as if adorning a young princess. Astrid couldn't have been more proud if Ruby had been her own child. And then, remembering how she coldly abandoned her own child, she was thankful, for Ruby's sake, that she'd had a better mother.

The ceremony was just like Azaria had described hers, with beautiful candles and the smiles of gorgeous women

57

holding her close in a circle.

Towards the end of the ceremony, the women formed two lines with their arms raised, to create an archway. Ruby had been asked to bring an item from her childhood as she stood at the entrance.

Her Great-Aunty Astrid called to her: "Who is approaching this pathway?"

"Ruby."

Astrid felt the tears rise, but continued anyway. "Dear Maiden, Ruby, it is time to let go of your childhood so that you can join our circle. When you are ready, leave your childhood at the entrance."

Ruby placed her mood ring, that she'd had for five years, on the ground, and moved forward.

The women stood in silence as Ruby walked. When she reached the end, Astrid rang a bell and threw rose petals over her. Bella took photos on her phone. Dozens of photos.

"Why are there white and red candles?" Bella asked of no one in particular.

Car whispered, "They're the colours of the deep and sacred feminine. White is for the virgin, the maiden, and of Ruby's purity and innocence. With red, we acknowledge that she is also the fertile, child-bearing woman."

"Oh."

Car smiled. Despite Bella's insistence that menstruation was disgusting, today she seemed intrigued and under the spell of women's mysteries.

Bella kept taking photos. "There's a lot of red here, isn't there?" she asked.

"Red," Car said, "is the colour of our blood; our passion, creativity, and our vibrancy. It says we're alive!"

"Oh." Click, click, click. "Rubes looks different today, doesn't she? Sort of more grown up or something. That dress is quite nice. I wonder if Astrid would let us have dresses like that for the wedding?"

"I thought you were wearing jeans?" Car said, her voice hushed.

"It might be a bit hot to wear them for a Summer wedding."

Car smiled and winked at Astrid.

In the midst of Ruby's ceremony, Azaria's thoughts drifted back, back, *way back,* to the day of her initiation into the ways of the Moontime.

Priestess's Moon

The full Moon, a time of culmination, rising in Scorpio

Car and Azaria wandered through their hillside garden, gathering herbs and flowers for the celebration that evening. Azaria's eight aunties were busy in the kitchen preparing a feast.

As she placed foliage into her basket, Azaria could hear their laughter from the kitchen, and was overjoyed at the celebration which awaited her. Today she would be welcomed by the ladies in her community to walk the path of womanhood. She felt heady with anticipation. None of her friends had celebrated menstruation in this way. Instead, their initiation had been a time of secrecy, a curse, a darkness, and fear.

She sat with her mother beneath the slender branches and short grey-green needles of a Rocky Mountain juniper, taking shade from the midday sunshine. Neither of them said a word about Astrid. Surely she'd be back soon? She couldn't have really meant that she wasn't coming to the ceremony.

Car had put the final touches to their *New-to-the-Moon* dresses, and hung them on the clothes line to air out.

"Let's go to the hot spring for the afternoon," Car said, standing up. "My sisters have everything covered."

They made the familiar walk to the medicinal waters, and chatted about menstruation, and the gifts of the Moonflow.

"In some languages," Car said, "Moon is another word for menstruation."

"Most of my friends won't talk about their periods. They're repulsed by it."

"They have been taught, usually by unspoken means, to keep this part of womanhood hidden. Our blood is sacred, Azaria, and the ground you walk upon is now holy because you're a woman," Car said, smiling at her. "Today, you will sit before women who have walked this path before you, and they'll share their stories of being a bleeding woman. One day, you may even share your story with your daughters."

Just before sunset, they began the trek up to the homestead. Bats flitted in the twilight, as if guiding them back up the mountain.

Awaiting them, was a ceremonial circle rich with as yet unclaimed ritual. On the lawn, beneath the apple trees, red candles burned in old glass jam jars.

Four of the aunties had gathered rosy, Indian paintbrush blossoms, a pretty wildflower which their ancestresses, Native American Indians, ground and drank in small amounts. The story down the matridonal line was that it regulated the menstrual cycle. Today, however, its sole purpose was to provide a beautiful garland for each of the twins. The vibrant and flamboyant auburn-red blossoms would sit, like crimson crowns, upon their heads. And later, Car would show her daughters how to shape the crown into a heart to hang above their beds.

Two garlands waited patiently upon a small altar, and the garden area was adorned

61

in red scarves, ruby fabrics, silky maroon cushions, and burgundy and claret-coloured satin ribbons.

Bowls of cherries marked out a circle on the grass, creating an identifiable ceremonial space.

Azaria tiptoed inside to get ready. Slipping into the beautiful, hand-sewn white dress, she admired how it swung at her ankles, and this simple swish reminded her that she was on the verge of womanhood. With careful movements, Azaria brushed red lipstick onto her naturally ruby-red lips. She'd never worn make-up before, but somehow today it seemed right, and she was pleased Car had bought it for her. After all, she was being celebrated as a woman, and throughout time women have adorned their faces. She stood for several minutes in front of the mirror, admiring her femininity and graceful curves.

Through her bedroom window, she could hear soft chanting, and as she left her room, she shimmied along towards the sweet sound of voices: her circle of women. Before Azaria joined them, her father called her into the kitchen.

"I wanted to give you a gift, my love, to say that although I won't be in the ceremony tonight, I will be with you in my heart." He reached into his pocket, and brought out a small box.

"Dad?" Azaria whispered.

"Open it," he smiled, passing the navy-blue velvet box to her. "It was my grandmother's. I know she'd want you to have it."

Azaria tentatively lifted the lid of the small

box, until it opened wide. She held it as if she was the caretaker of a prized possession. She gasped, and carefully took out the silver, ruby-encrusted locket.

"It's so beautiful," she said, her words barely audible.

"Just like you, Azaria. Just like you. Now, I believe there are women waiting for you."

She hugged him tightly, and smiled as he wiped away the tears from her eyes. "Go on and have a lovely time, sweetheart," he said.

The guests had gathered beneath the apple trees, and each woman was dressed in scarlet hues. It was clear that the ceremony would have to begin without Astrid. Car felt her heart sink, but kept a smile on her face for Azaria. Car would make sure it was a beautiful evening that she'd never forget.

The garden was bathed in moonlight, the full Moon spreading her milky gown across the galaxy like a regal Queen addressing her loyal subjects. Dozens of white and red candles mimicked her luminosity.

As Azaria reached the circle, she was invited to sit on a throne of red cushions. Each of the women introduced themselves and the women in their family line.

Car began by saying, "My name is Car, and I'm the daughter of Angelina and granddaughter of Adahy and Jane."

By the time each woman in the circle had introduced herself, many were reaching for tissues, such was the power of invoking the ancestral line. Car bathed Azaria's feet in warm lavender-water, and the women crowned her with the garland.

63

Aunty Alisha spoke first. "Your experience of first blood prepares you for life as a menstruating woman. How you walk through today's initiation will affect you for the rest of your life. Your thoughts and feelings about your body will shape how you experience birth, and later on, menopause. The menstrual trinity is all connected. We call it the triple spiral. Today, at the Altar of Menarche, we invite you into the Temple of Womanhood."

Azaria looked over at the small altar which had been created: a vase of red paintbrush flowers, a red candle, a statue of a fertility goddess, a triple-Goddess necklace. She noticed how much care Car had taken to choose each item, including a cauldron, chalice, feather and hand-sewn, cloth menstrual pads.

Shivering a little as the mountain fog blew in from the valley below, Azaria listened to the small fire as it crackled and hissed. Car added another log inside the circle of rocks. Between the branches of the old apple trees, red cloths trembled in the evening air. Sage sticks and a bowl of spring water lay between the garlands of flowers.

Several women shared wisdom, including a short treatise on the elements.

Air, to honour womanly wisdom, thoughts and ideas.

Fire, to acknowledge sensuality, passion and drive.

Water, holder of dreams, intuition, insights and visions.

Earth, to provide stability and practicality.

Car led the singing, beginning with a song from her ancestresses, one that had been taught to her on her grandmother's knee.

River she is flowing, growing
River she is flowing to the sea
Carry me my mother
Your Child I will always be
Carry me my Mother to the sea
River she is flowing

Car proffered a small clay bowl of wildflower honey. "Taste this, my daughter. May you always taste the sweetness that life has to offer you. You are a woman, now, Azaria, but never lose sight of the little girl who lives within you. She will always be there."

Aunty Aviva invited Azaria to come forward, and offered to paint her hands with red henna.

Breathing in the scent of the lavender sprigs which had been scattered around the circle, Azaria's body was painted in henna.

As the henna dried, and her aunties shared their own stories of first blood, Car walked around the circle sprinkling red rose petals over everyone.

Azaria lit a candle, and accepted the blessings of the circle.

Afterwards, there was much feasting. The aunties had created an entire meal from red foods: watermelon balls, red-currant jelly, red-capsicum soup, sun-dried tomato bread. For dessert, cherry tart and rhubarb ice cream.

Azaria skipped to her bedroom that night, her heart filled with the love of her community of women, yet teetering, always, on sadness because her beloved sister had deliberately stayed away. This should have been *their* day. After all, they were twins. Nurtured together in their mother's womb. Sisters of the silver Moon. Azaria wondered if the Moon had let her down. Had let them both down.

Carefully hanging the beautiful gown in the antique oak wardrobe, she crawled into bed, naked. The sheets, sensual and cool around her body, felt like an old friend. Lingering awhile around her widening hips, her fingers searched further until they reached to her blossoming breasts. Yes, she was a woman, and the women around her honoured those changes, and paved the way for a lifetime of celebrating her femininity.

Her thoughts kept coming back to Astrid. Where was she? What was she doing now? Her gnawing dull ache gave way to the sensations those exploring fingers elicited. A delicious tingling demanded her full attention.

Her previously slumbering nipples, the colour of rose-wine, hardened, standing bolt upright, and Azaria delighted in the unfamiliar pleasure rapidly coursing through her blood. It was as if her body, her newly discovered woman's body, wanted to dance. She moved her hips from side to side. To her surprise, she thought of Jake, the new boy in town who had caught her eye more than once. As Azaria conjured his perfect face into her mind, the memory of his dimples and plump lips made her face blush — even under the cover of dark — and so her frisky fingertips travelled, silently and secretly, across her sweet skin, igniting feelings of joy and mystery. Was this the honey of life that Car had talked about?

At the start of her upper thighs, Azaria felt a wave of sensation rush over her entire body. *Oh, that felt so good!* She had known the pleasure of tasty food, a starry sky, the warm water of the secret hot pool, and love of family, but she had never experienced anything like this. That her own body was able to give her this clandestine adventure made her smile. A hidden pearl of bliss, flourishing in a sea of moisture, beckoned her, calling those fingers to keep coming back. More. Again. Faster, now.

Breathing rapidly, the movements took on a life of their own as her back arched gently, meeting an unknown need. Jake's face was there, the whole time, smiling shyly and encouraging her to take the path to the mountain top. Each moment, a step further. She could almost feel herself at the summit, arousal gripping her entire body, as the Moon navigated the heavens. Who knew that a woman's body could do this? Azaria wondered if her mother's body held the same secrets. And what about her mother before her? Did she know the truth? Unselfconsciously, she moaned as the intense pleasure grew and grew, until, finally, it peaked, and there...there at the top, she could see below. The world around her was, indeed, beautiful. Azaria was reluctant to come down, and that night, and for many nights afterwards, she revisited the mountain, revelling in the ecstasy of self-love.

Leaving

Kara was the first to leave the old Lafferty homestead, early the next morning, citing functions she had to preside over. She was remarkably dry-eyed when she hugged her mother goodbye at sunrise, and barely made eye contact with the other women in her family. Perhaps she's just tired, Azaria thought to herself.

With her boutique overnight bag safely on the front seat, Kara started the car and drove away without so much as a wave or beep of the horn.

Odd, Azaria thought, shaking her head.

It was always Eliza-May that Azaria had worried about in recent years, not Kara. Sure, Kara's husband left a lot to be desired, but Kara had made a life she appeared to be happy with; one that was busy with various social engagements. Kara didn't have a job, but a busy schedule as a doctor's wife — a doctor who came from old Boston money — facilitating charity work and fundraisers. She had expressed no desire for children, but Azaria often wondered if that was more about William's desires than her daughter's. She made a mental note to call Kara as soon as the house was empty.

Kara dropped off the rental car at the airport, and waited patiently for her flight back to Boston. Her thoughts turned to her life, and how empty it felt. Meaningless. A charade. Being back with family had given her hope. Family, to her, was everything. Why couldn't William see that? Why was he so adamant that there was no place for children in their life? She thought of preparing his favourite meal, chicken teriyaki, and decorating the table with candles. He was due to be home early from work tonight. She'd ask him again then. The last time Kara had attempted a discussion about trying for a baby, he threw his dinner plate across the room, smashing the three-hundred-year-old, gold-framed mirror. She replayed the scene over and over on the flight home. Kara spent years walking on eggshells, allowing for his volatile temper and stubborn ways. It was a shame his charming bedside manner at the hospital—the one that attracted her to him in the first place—never made it into their home. Many times she'd packed her bag, ready to leave. Ready to start a new life. And every time she unpacked it as she heard him come in the front door. Don't be silly, she'd tell herself. No one has a perfect marriage.

In Boston, she caught a cab through the vibrant cosmopolitan streets, garlanded by ornate Victorian townhouses. Tick. Tick. Tick. Her watch, one staccato second at a time, marched her life away without a note of empathy or apology. He'd be home in about three hours. Kara got out of the cab at her local delicatessen, and picked up some ingredients from the produce section. His favourite meal. That's what she kept bringing her thoughts back to. Feed him and satiate his appetite. Talk about how wonderful the family reunion had been. Tell him how quickly her nieces were growing into beautiful young women. And then ask him about having a baby. Kara stepped out of the shop, and as the sunlight fell upon her skin she thought to herself: no, I won't ask him. I'll tell him! Unsure where this new inner resolve was coming from, she felt a lightness in her step. If there was anything she was certain of, it was that she wanted children in her life. She wanted that more than anything. A little voice asked: do you want it more than your marriage? She stopped walking for a few chaotic seconds, shaken by the thought. Kara contemplated hailing another cab, but then decided to walk the two blocks back to their apartment. The setting Sun was so beautiful that she wanted to feel those rays on her skin just a little bit longer. Her life was about more than obligatory dinners with the wives of other doctors. It had to be. She'd spent years dressed in boutique clothes. Suddenly she found herself wanting to wear jeans and t-shirts, and sit in a sandpit with a child. She wanted to be draped in ice-cream kisses, and deafened by rambunctious laughter. Her manicured nails needed gritty grains of sand beneath them. The feeling overwhelmed her. Was it a vision or an overactive imagination? Whatever it was, it jolted her from everything she'd known her life to be. There was more to her than what other people saw, but somehow the life she had carved out for herself left her looking as if she were, perhaps, shallow in some ways.

Kara noticed a small bird on the branch of a cherry tree. Its apricot-pink chest caught her eye, and its gay tune made her smile. And without warning, it flew away. She admired its freedom. That faith in its own wings, rather than upon the branch it had been resting.

Ironic, she laughed, that the best part of twenty years had been spent married to a man who gave her a life where she'd forgotten she had wings.

Stopping in front of the apartment, she put her overnight travel case down alongside the shopping bag, and fetched her keys from her handbag. A quick look at her watch — that cursed keeper of time — showed that she'd need to hurry up if she wanted to have the meal ready before he came home. Life waits for no one, a voice whispered into her ear. She looked around. Despite being alone, she suddenly felt as if she had a companion by her side.

Kara placed the shopping in the kitchen and decided to have a quick shower. It had been a long day in transit. She mentally scanned the wardrobe. Did she even own jeans? She laughed as she walked down the hallway to the bedroom. A strange sensation gripped her in the gut. Was there an intruder? Something seemed different, but she couldn't pinpoint what it was. Gently pushing the bedroom door open, her legs turned to jelly. It took several seconds for the scene to fully register in her brain. Disbelief, shock, anger. How was this even possible? He was supposed to be working at the hospital. With her fingers shaking, Kara took a step backward. She found herself wanting to scream, but no sounds came from her mouth. This was simply not possible!

William, her husband of twenty years, penetrating a man about half his age from behind, shallow-groaned with each thrust. Kara watched as they climaxed together, her husband's body mounted over the young man like a dog, their grunts intermingling as he pushed himself further inside. Was the other man even an adult yet? That's what she wondered, as his heavily tattooed body moved back and forward too expertly for his age. He was pulling against the headboard, his knuckles white. Then, he collapsed in satisfaction beneath her husband.

Her *husband*.

My silk sheets, she thought.

Our bedroom.

But he doesn't even like sex, she thought, watching them as they laughed.

"Got a smoke, mate?" the man-child asked. "You're good, for an old fella, you know!"

Did they even *know* each other? Too many thoughts for a small moment in time, she felt the contents of her in-flight meal rise to her mouth. Instinctively bringing her hand over her lips, she closed her eyes. This was too much.

Kara didn't bother closing the door. She simply walked to the kitchen, collected her handbag and overnight bag, and walked away. Doubting her legs could carry her, she stopped for a take-away espresso while she gathered her thoughts and jittery nerves, and developed a plan of action. Kara walked five long miles that night around the city. The only thing she was certain of was that she was walking out of her life. Her mind amplifying every last detail of the scene she never expected to see, she found herself starting to shake. *Don't lose it, girl. You're better than him. You always have been. Get a grip. This is your 'get out of jail' card.*

Enough, she whispered to herself. *Enough.*

Kara stopped in Avery Street, and booked herself into the Ritz-Carlton hotel. The luxurious suite offered a temporary sanctuary. With views across the historic city, the living room featured French doors which led into the master suite. Tempted by the handcrafted bed linen, she was instead swayed by the full marble bath. As the steam rose, and the scented oils lingered, she placed two fluffy, Egyptian towels next to it, and prepared to soak. Calming her mind, as Azaria had taught her to do years ago, Kara put a plan into action. Yes, she told herself, you can do it.

Sometime later, she settled onto the opulent, king-sized bed, and pulled out her smartphone. If a bloody ten-inch bird can fly, so can I, damn it! She chuckled at the high-speed internet access. A bit different to being at Mom's, she thought, and smiled at how infuriated Bella had been.

Within three hours, with flights booked, a new life waited eagerly for her to embrace it with both hands. If there was anything she was particularly grateful for right now, it was that she'd spent two decades putting savings away each week. She'd never touched them before now. Today they were her passport to a new life. Her flight left in nine hours. That gave her enough time to sleep, and buy some jeans. Though, she reflected, smiling for the first time since seeing William screwing the Tattooed Wonder, it'll probably be too hot for jeans.

But first, she said to herself, you have to tell Ma. She knew Azaria would be devastated at her first-born child living so far away, but that she'd be secretly pleased William would no longer be part of the family. Not that he ever was. He studiously avoided every social gathering that involved the Linden family.

Dear Ma, By the time you receive this letter, I'll no longer be living in Boston. In my heart, I know I should phone and tell you the news, but leaving is so much easier without having to witness your tears. Wish me well. I'll be in touch, Love always, Kara.

***

When the twins left the old Lafferty homestead, a billow of dust trailed behind them as their VW raced down the mountainside. Azaria and Car laughed. The joy of youth! They were happy, ambitious, content young women, who always had time for each other, friends, family, and were committed to their careers.

Luna, a primary-school teacher, with a passion for working one-on-one with children who needed extra support, had been headhunted by the school after Starr had written an article for the New York Times about the difference her sister had made with an autistic boy. Luna had freaked out at the publicity, but Starr revelled in it. She was so proud of her sister, and this was her way of showing it: shouting it to the world.

Luna had received dozens of job offers, and could pick and choose. Her final decision rested on the fact she didn't want to leave Denver, and intended to stay living with her sister. In her mind, it was incomprehensible that they'd ever live apart. The new job meant a longer commute, but the rewards were worth it. Employed by a Montessori school, she had seven children, with varying disabilities, under her care. Working in an educational system which honoured a child's character, values and self-image was important to Luna. Azaria had always placed them at the core of her parenting, and this instinctively led Luna to seeking them out in her working life.

One of her skills was thinking outside the educational box and implementing a whole-body approach to their care. Where possible, she encouraged her students to take responsibility for their part in Nature, and the Universe. The foundation of her work was humility. Working closely with the parents, she made suggestions around nutrition, exercise, animal therapy, floatation therapy, homeopathy, and sometimes drew on her mother's vast knowledge of psychological and medical astrology to work in ways that best suited each child. At twenty four, she had the wisdom of a sage, and balanced it beautifully with being a young and effervescent woman.

Denver, a city of artistic ambience, held their hearts. The sunny, sprawling city was the backdrop to their diverse interests. Home was a loft conversion overlooking a street of vibrant, hip cafés, nightclubs and restaurants. They both had bedrooms, like havens of beauty, in the attic. Its A-framed pine ceiling featured hanging beds, held securely by strong chains.

They lost count of the number of parties which had been held there, and were always in demand to host wine and cheese evenings for their arty friends who were launching books, art exhibitions, and poetry evenings.

Starr had worked on the Denver newspaper for eight years, having earnt a cadetship after winning a writing competition whilst still in school. Ambition with compassion was her guiding light, and she often submitted articles on a freelance basis to newspapers and magazines around the world. Her mother once said she could always pick out her articles, even if they didn't have a byline. There was something about Starr's writing style, the way she always dug a bit deeper, and asked questions of her subjects that no one else was willing to go near.

Despite their different careers, the twins shared a deep passion for making a difference in the world: for leaving a footprint behind that would inspire other people long after they left this world. They often talked about how they'd be remembered, and then laughed it off with that self-proclaimed right to immortality that youth inevitably brings.

Azaria couldn't have been prouder. It had been tough watching her twins go their separate ways during the years that Luna was at university. They had expected to study together, and even imagined sharing a dorm at university. Starr's offer of a cadetship was like a bolt of lightning, but they managed to speak on the phone every day, and Luna would spend her weekends at Starr's tiny flat above a bakery.

Those years were well behind them now, and apart from work, they spent most of their time together either hanging out in their spacious loft, playing guitar, baking cakes, or hiking up the mountains. A few overseas holidays had made Starr restless for adventure, but for Luna it just made her pine for the comforts of home.

They were back at the loft just over an hour after leaving their Mom's house. Starr instructed Luna to make them a cup of tea, and then ducked into her writing room to check emails. "Yes!" she high-fived herself upon seeing the long-awaited reply. "Yes, yes, yes!" The rain splattering against the window panes muffled the sound of her excitement from reaching the kitchen, where she could just make out Luna singing the John Denver song *Take Me Home Country Roads*.

Starr stepped back out to the open-plan kitchen, poker-faced, with her heart smiling. Barely able to contain herself, she ate five gingernut cookies in a row.

"I thought you'd gone sugar-free?" Luna asked.

"Oops. I forgot!" Starr laughed.

***

Eliza-May cried as she held her mother close. "We'll see each other in the Summer, honey. Okay?" Azaria tried to

75

reassure her. She knew these tears were about so much more than goodbye.

"Eliza-May, come on. Get in the car," James said lovingly, but with a hint of impatience. He was starting to wonder if it was such a good idea coming here for the weekend. It reinforced everything she hated about city life.

"In the Summer," Eliza-May repeated after her mother. "In the Summer." She reluctantly let go of Azaria, as if she were leaving behind a life raft. The pain in her eyes ripped right through Azaria's heart, but what could she do? Eliza-May was a grown woman with a family of her own, capable of making her own choices. Or was she? Had she become so used to following everyone else's plans and dreams that she'd lost sight of who she was and what she really wanted?

Azaria reached out her hand. "Come back before then, if you want. Anytime, honey. For as long as you want or need. This is still your home. It always will be."

James's face darkened, but Azaria ignored it. Right now she was fighting for her daughter's life, and she knew it. They all knew it. "Anytime."

Eliza-May lumbered over to the passenger side and let herself in, covering her face with her hands. James reached over and touched her shoulder. "Come on, time to go," he said softly.

"Bye Gran! See ya, Great-Granny Car!" Ruby yelled out with a passion that could light up a city. "See you in the Summer. I can't wait!"

Bella looked up sheepishly when she realised her attention should have been on goodbyes rather than checking for phone signal. Waving briefly, her chin dropped to her chest as she scanned the small screen on her lap. Damn. No signal.

Upon fighting their way through busy New York streets,

the discord of taxi horns and emergency sirens was a rude shock after a weekend in the sweet heart of rural Colorado. They traipsed along the corridor of their highrise, Manhattan apartment, dragging their suitcases.

James was grateful for their return to civilisation. He went into his study and caught up on legal briefs for a high-profile case that was looming. Bella headed to her bedroom, headphones on, and smiled at the unlimited Wi-Fi. *Home sweet home*, she laughed, jumping onto her bed. *Thank you, God!*

Eliza-May went to her bedroom. Just for a quick nap, she said.

Ruby stood at the lounge-room window, watching the traffic below. *I hate this place*, she said out loud. *I hate it. I will do anything to get out of here. Anything at all.*

She looked around the room. This was family: a mother too disinterested in life to be bothered even being awake. A father so focused on work that he didn't even know he had a family half the time. And a sister whose only thought was: *boys, phone signal and skinny jeans*, as if they were all one and the same.

Ruby sighed. She missed her grandmother's cooking already. For five minutes she stood with the fridge door open. There was one thing she was certain of. Her sister and her parents wouldn't be making dinner. At about midnight, her dad would wander out and call the Chinese take away to deliver. Just like he did every night of the week. Except Thursdays. On Thursday night, it was Indian. Without skipping a beat, she picked up the phone and dialled. "Gran, we're home. Can you talk me through how to make that red pepper tart?"

Writing down the ingredients, Ruby then collected some money from the jar above the refrigerator, and headed down to the delicatessen.

Red peppers, onion, cream cheese, fresh basil, walnuts.

Counting the money in her hand, Ruby reasoned that if

she made two tarts, she'd have enough for school for the next couple of days. If there was anything she detested, it was canteen lunches. No, right now, the only food she wanted to eat was anything which reminded her of Azaria Linden.

***

Azaria and Astrid embraced for the longest time. It was surreal. A relationship begun in the womb, a cellular bonding for life, and yet fate had separated them on many occasions. Now they were together again, a healing balm to their hearts, it seemed impossible to let go and say goodbye.

"Stay in touch, okay, sis?," Azaria said, tears pricking her eyes, then, gently withdrawing, added: "Don't be a stranger, okay?"

"I promise."

Azaria bit her bottom lip, unsure whether she should keep it to herself. "And one more thing. Will you eat a bit more? You're all bones."

Astrid nodded, and then walked away, reaching for Bob's hand. "See you in the Summer," he called back. "Thanks for having us. It's been lovely. Simply lovely. Perfect. Just what we needed."

Astrid barely said a word on the flight back to New York. She was deep in thought about her past, and how her actions had shaped her life in ways that she regretted. Bob was her pot of gold at the end of the rainbow, but she was unsure how she deserved such a love. Thinking of all the pain she'd inflicted on her family, she wondered how they were still able to embrace her with so much love. It unsettled her that they could be so forgiving. And then she winced at the fact she still hadn't told them her secret. The timing wasn't right. But when would it ever be right?

As if picking up her thoughts, Bob gently squeezed her

hand. "My darling, the only thing we truly have is this present moment. Let go of the past, and stop worrying about the future. Whatever is before us, I'm there with you the whole way."

Stifling her tears, Astrid spluttered the words out: "I don't deserve you."

"Rubbish!" he laughed. "That's rubbish. You and I fit together like a hand in a glove. We're made for each other."

"I'm so sorry, Bob. I didn't mean for this to happen. I wouldn't have fallen in love with you if I knew. I really wouldn't have. I just want all this to go away. Why can't we be forever together? Life's just not fair!"

"We're here together now. That's all that matters. That is more than enough for me. Enough with those tears. We've got a wedding to plan! So, bohemian, vintage, 70s rock, modern?"

Astrid couldn't help but laugh. That was what had made her fall in love with Bob Gentle in the first place. Gentle by name, gentle by nature. He'd made her laugh so hard that she'd forgotten she was his counsellor. She knew within seconds of their first meeting that she couldn't continue working with him in a professional capacity, and that she'd have to refer him. The electricity between them was too strong. They both knew they had no hope of ignoring it.

"I have that effect on women," he'd laughed, when she let him know of her dilemma.

In a dream-like world, they lived their days like young lovers, making up for all the years of their lives they'd not had together. But now, the future stood before her like a closed door. All she wanted to know was not what was on the other side of it, but if Bob would still be with her.

"We're soulmates," he said, kissing the top of her hand. "Nothing gets in the way of that. I promise you."

79

Appleseeds Health Store

Fate's Moon

Azaria took the sack barrow out of the van, and then stacked several wooden crates on top of each other, like Lego blocks, so they fitted neatly. Standing in the main street of town, she took a moment to look around her. The late-May sunshine brought out the best in everyone, and she couldn't help but smile to see the tourists being enchanted by the vibrancy of this artisan community. Pushing the barrow, she headed into Appleseeds Health Store.

"Hi Marion," she called out, waving to her from the other side of the shop. "I've brought you this month's order."

"I'll be with you in a minute!" Marion yelled over, with a brief wave, and then finished unpacking boxes of black rice noodles, kale-and-smoked-ricotta pesto, and liquorice tea.

Appleseeds was the hub of the community, even for those who weren't actively interested in health. Marion stocked an assortment of vegetarian pasties and pies from an organic baker five miles away. Locals congregated here over the lunch hour, grabbing cans of elderflower presse and dandelion-and-burdock iced tea, or something from the fresh juice bar. The tourists studied every corner of the shop, breathing in the heady scent of Nag Champa incense, and buying handcrafted greeting cards and Fairtrade gifts. The local wood-turner also supplied his handmade wooden toys here: a collection of people, about 10cm high, and painted in bright, bold colours. Children couldn't keep their hands off the fascinating characters.

Azaria's produce took up the whole left wall of the shop. She began to unpack the crates. Bundles of baby sage and cedar, tied in purple ribbon, were particularly popular with the New Age community. Car had packaged them beautifully, Azaria thought, as she placed them on the shelves. Alongside these were dozens of bottles of sage shampoo for those with silver hair.

Sage essence, in amber bottles with droppers, helped women transitioning through menopause. A dozen clear cellophane bags of sage tea would be bought by those who wanted help with sore throats, as a menstrual tonic, to heal burns, liver issues, and as an antidepressant. Her small glass bottles of raw sage juice were rumoured by locals to heal tumours, skin cancer and warts. Azaria made no claims, but quietly observed the changes in people's lives when they consumed it regularly.

Marion came over and helped unpack. "Best day ever out there, isn't it?"

"Feels like Summer has finally arrived." They worked together, chatting and laughing, and unpacking items to display. The first ones to be shelved were those labelled *Made with Love at Azaria's Mountainside Apothecary*. Chamomile-and-mint tinctures eased indigestion and nervousness, and catnip helped to heal the throat. Garlic and pumpkin seed paste was proven to remove worms in children, while fennel helped those suffering from obesity.

Russell Jackson arrived with several crates of fresh organic fruits and vegetables. Marion arranged them into the large wicker baskets that were on display. Panflute music played softly in the background, and Azaria unpacked the items labelled *Azaria's Apiary*. Each item had been handcrafted. Jars of royal jelly, with purple cotton covers over the lids, featured labels suggesting the jelly would help with high cholesterol, breast cancer, liver repair, osteoporosis, skin conditions, and improving brain function. Marion placed them into the chilled cabinet. No wonder any doctor who tried to set up practice in this town rarely lasted longer than six months. It had never

81

been Azaria's intention to compete with conventional medicine, but she did make it her mission to educate people that the body always wants to heal, and just needs to be given the right nourishment.

Pure, raw propolis, straight from the hives, was packaged in dark-green hexagonal jars: the ultimate elixir for healing high blood pressure, easing a tooth abscess, for treating prostate and colon cancers, improving bone health, and killing bacteria. This was, by far, her most popular product.

Vitamin and mineral-rich bee pollen was stored in the freezer to protect its many healing properties. Menopausal women, from miles around, stocked up on this vital supplement.

Eighty jars of amber honey, all labelled *raw, organic, wildflower*, were lined up on the tranches of roughly hewn wooden shelves. They were right at home in Marion's rustic health store.

As Marion arranged the non-edible bee products on the shelves — beeswax pillar candles and tealight candles — she confided in Azaria. "I've put the shop up for sale."

Azaria felt her stomach fall. She loved this shop. She loved Marion! For years Marion had put her heart and soul into creating this gem of a place. It was the local treasure, and even had a couple of comfy sofas so people could stop and rest for a while if they wanted.

"I suppose you couldn't do this forever, could you?" Azaria said, trying to put her feelings of disappointment aside.

"I work seven days a week, as you know, and I just feel like a rest!"

"Well, good for you! Just do me a favour. Make sure I like the new owner!" she laughed, placing the empty crates back onto the sack barrow.

The Summer

The Lover's Moon

A warm tear threatened to wreak havoc on Azaria's mascara as she watched her sister walk barefoot across the soft mossy grass of their childhood garden. How many tears had been shed between them, no one could possibly count. But today's tears? They were priceless. So much healing, growth and transformation had touched their lives recently. Bob had been such a blessing to all of their hearts, not just Astrid's. Today, she blossomed. There was the flush of young love across her pink cheeks. For some time, Azaria had wondered if something wasn't quite right in Astrid's life. Ever since the night of Car's eightieth birthday party. It was such a relief that the only problem was that Bob wanted her to share their special day with family, and heal old wounds.

The gathered friends were few, but each of them had a place in her life. Her dress was simple and elegant, and eloquently matched the words of her ceremony. Azaria had spent many nights crafting just the right images and meanings, always phoning Astrid the following morning to get her blessing.

Azaria noted the unfettered tears tumbling across Bob's freshly shaven jaw line. This was his dream come true: marrying the love of his life. A soft, stolen sob left his mouth, and he restrained himself, regaining a sense of equilibrium.

"My love," he whispered. "You look stunning."

Their hands gently caught each other, and together they turned to face Azaria.

"We are gathered here today, as witnesses to this love." Thanking everyone for their presence, she invited them to come closer and gather in around the couple.

Granny Car watched the ceremony unfold, her two

beautiful daughters, radiant in their Autumn years, like the luminous Moon, the love of all those around them shining in their eyes. *It was a perfect day to go to Heaven.* That was her thought as she watched Bob lift Astrid high off the ground to the whoops and laughter.

"Yes, you may kiss the bride!" Azaria laughed, realising she was a little off cue and that Bob was not waiting for anyone's permission.

Bella and Smudge stole away from the wedding celebrations, and raced up behind the beehives to the neglected old barn. The building was nothing more than ten old weathered telegraph posts, with a rusty tin roof.

It had been torture hanging out with the olds all day. They had only one thing on their mind. Smudge wasn't sure how much longer he could contain his horniness. Bella had been promising for months now — months! — that they'd have sex. Tonight was the night. All the adults would be so caught up in the carnival atmosphere that no one would notice their absence.

Bella felt her heart race. They'd petted heavily before, very heavily, but she knew there was no stalling now. She couldn't go back on her word, not after he'd travelled from one side of the country to the other. Excitement. Nervousness. Fear. Anticipation. So many emotions were racing through her body. Did he bring condoms? Should she be on the Pill? Azaria had tried to have 'the conversation' with her, but Bella had dismissed her quicker than Azaria could say 'penetration'. "Overshare, Gran. *Overshare!*" she'd yelled, blocking her ears.

Azaria knew without doubt that Eliza-May would not have made time to educate her daughter about the complexities of sex, love-making, and relationships.

In the hayshed, far from the wedding crowd, Bella breathed in the sweet scent of meadow hay. A dozen childhood holidays all emerging from that one earthy

85

smell almost made her forget how frightened she was. *Almost.* Smudge pulled Bella down against a hay bale. "Are you ready, babe?" he groaned, pulling down his black trousers.

"Yes," she mumbled, quickly wondering what she'd got herself into. Now that they were finally alone, it didn't seem like a good idea. All she wanted to do was go back and be with her family. Not feeling safe, she hesitated, unconsciously biting her lower lip.

"Take your dress off, Bell. Come on. We can't be up here all night."

Tentatively tugging at the hem of her dress, she carefully pulled it up over her shoulders. Sitting on the itchy bale, she felt vulnerable in her underwear.

"Get 'em off," he motioned, not bothering to help her get undressed.

Smudge whisked off his shirt and bow tie, and threw them by his trousers and shoes.

Bella wanted to laugh at the sight of him, naked, wearing nothing but socks, but the shock of seeing his towering erection jolted her laugh right back down her throat. She'd felt his penis before, beneath his jeans, but this…this was a whole different story. And she didn't like how it was going to end.

Not for one second could she imagine it — that! — inside of her. For a moment, she thought she might vomit. With all her heart, she wished she could go back in time and listen to Azaria. To savour each word of wisdom. To ask questions. To share fears.

"You told me you were ready for this! What's the problem?" He didn't seem as friendly now. He was agitated, annoyed and unable to hide his anger. When Smudge saw the look on her face, he said: "Come here babe. Come and sit next to me." He reached out his hand, and Bella made herself a space next to him. The hay under her bottom itched. She wished they were on a bed. In a

86

moment of sensitivity, Smudge reached for his shirt and said 'Here, lie back on this."

"Thanks," she murmured, closing her eyes in the hope the whole situation would vanish just like waking up from a bad dream.

Rubbing his hardness against her, Smudge groaned. Drawing himself up onto all fours, he climbed over her and then changed his mind. "I know what will help you feel more relaxed. Come and suck on this." He laughed at the look on her face.

The thought of that red, large rod in her mouth terrified Bella.

"It doesn't bite! Come on. Don't be a baby. If you want to be all grown-up and have a boyfriend, this is what you do."

"Okay."

She swallowed hard, and closed her eyes. Smudge pushed himself deep into her mouth.

"Oh yes, baby."

Involuntarily gagging, she tried pulling away from the stench of what was reminiscent of the old Stilton cheese she'd once found in the back of their fridge.

"Don't do that!" he snapped, forcing her head towards him. "Jeez, you're not very good at this!"

At that second, she wanted to sink her teeth right through him and then run away. Far away. Instead, she gently grazed her teeth against the head of his penis as a silent warning.

"What's the matter? You told me you were totally up for this. I travelled from the other side of the country so we could do it."

"I know. I know." Bella cried softly. "It's just that…"

"Never mind. Lie back on the shirt."

She did as she was told, stifling her sobs.

"You're being silly, Bella. What happened to the sophisticated girl at my gym who was always coming

87

onto me? Where has she gone? You've turned out to be a real disappointment. And frankly, you're really ruining the mood by being so childish. But let's be clear. I am not leaving here with nothing but a faulty blow job."

"Okay."

"Looks like I'm going to have to teach you. Okay, then," he said, raising his eyebrows impatiently. "You really are a beginner, aren't you? Open your legs, and at least pretend you're enjoying yourself. Can you do that?"

"Yes. I'm sorry, Smudge. I'm really sorry. Anything you want, just tell me. I'll do it. I'm so sorry." Bella looked away, ashamed, and focused on the view: a trio of pine trees, their branches waving gently in the Summer breeze.

Using both hands, he pushed her legs open wide, and then lowered himself down on both knees. He'd never been with a woman so young, and was thrilled at deflowering a virgin. This would be a great story to share with his mates. He groaned as the head of his penis pierced her tightness, and then used the fingers of both hands to coax her to open wider, and gain leverage,

Smudge said, exasperated, "Come on, open up for me babe."

"I'm trying. It hurts." She winced, squeezing her eyes closed. "I don't like it."

"You have to relax." Removing one hand, he spat onto his fingers, breathing in her musky scent, then brusquely rubbed them against her clitoris for a few seconds to warm her up. Then, without further warning, fully penetrated Bella to the sound of her shocked gasp. Within four full thrusts, he came, exploding his load deep into her gloomy, claustrophobic cave. His half-hearted grunt was the only suggestion that intercourse had just taken place.

Bella barely registered the moment, for she was caught up in the discomfort of her dry labia being stretched and pulled in unfamiliar ways. Stinging sensations brought tears to her eyes.

She wanted Azaria. Right now, even her mother would do.

Smudge stood up and got dressed, spat into his hands, and raked them through his hair.

"What are you doing?" Bella asked. "I thought you wanted to have sex."

"That was it. It's all over, babe. Not as bad as you thought, hey? We should have done it months ago," he chuckled. "Come on, get dressed. Let's get back to the party."

With all her might, she tried not to whimper. "No," she said, suddenly finding her strength "You go back. I'll join you in a moment."

"Fair enough," he said, humming a tune as he left the barn.

Smudge carefully entered through the back door of the house, grabbed his backpack, and without attracting attention, scrawled a brief goodbye note, then headed off down the mountainside to hitch-hike to the airport.

Bella cried into her dress. She'd never felt so humiliated and hurt. Oh why, oh why, hadn't she listened to Azaria?

She doubted the tears would ever dry. Carefully reaching down between her legs, she winced at the torn skin. The odour of semen wafted from between her legs like the pong of raw potatoes. In that moment, she hated the smell of her body. She needed a shower. Now. She wanted to wash him off her. Out of her. She wanted to scream. Why didn't she just say 'no' to him?

I never want to have sex again, she cried on her walk back to the homestead.

For an hour and a half Bella stood in the shower, sobbing, reaching between her legs in disbelief. Why did people say sex was so amazing when it was painful, quick and not at all romantic or beautiful? Why had she been lied to about it all?

A gentle voice called from the other side of the shower room door. "Honey, it's Gran here," Azaria said. "Is there anything I can do for you, love? I haven't seen you outside at the party for a while. Do you need a towel or something?"

"I'm fine, Gran." She lied. "I'll be out soon."

Azaria knew that she was anything but fine, and sensed that the evening had not gone as her granddaughter expected. "I'll be in the kitchen when you're ready. How about I put on the kettle for a mug of hot chocolate? Would you like that?"

"Yes, Gran."

Azaria heard the crying continue, and steadied her breathing. She'd been so grateful that her daughters had survived the trials of teenage sex relatively unscathed, but knowing her granddaughter was enduring a harsh lesson hit her hard. She kept telling herself that she was Bella's grandmother, not her mother. That she was not responsible for keeping her safe. But the voices wouldn't go away. Guilt pounded at her heart.

It was 2am when Bella finally showed up in the kitchen. The party had died down about an hour earlier, and there wasn't a single sound in the house.

"Come on love, come and have that chocolate I promised you." Azaria wrapped a thick terry-towelling robe around Bella's shoulders. "Marshmallows?"

Sobbing, Bella sank into the comforting bosom of her grandmother. "I thought I loved him. I really did. But I don't. I don't want anything to do with him. How was I so stupid?"

"Sweetheart, we all make mistakes." She held Bella close, and rocked her until the crying stopped.

"I thought sex was special. It's not. It's awful! It hurts. And it's over before it even starts. I hate it. I'm never having sex again! Why didn't I listen to you?"

90

Azaria didn't know where to start. How could she begin to explain the nirvana of lovemaking to someone who'd just been treated so poorly? Tonight wasn't the night for explanations, just for cuddles. Grandmother cuddles.

"It stings down there, Gran. I can't pee without it hurting. When is it going to stop? Do you have any herby things to help?"

"Yes, darling. I do. Come to my bedroom, where we won't be disturbed."

Azaria turned off the kitchen light, after motioning to Bella to carry the mugs of chocolate. They headed up the hallway to the master bedroom.

"Did Granddad do that to you? Did he hurt you when you had sex?" Bella asked, desperate to know how a woman could ever love a man.

"Never. Not once." She was honest and kind in her reply. "Another time we'll talk about the difference between sex and love-making, but not tonight. Right," Azaria said, pulling a carved wooden box from her wardrobe, "let's find you a tincture or two. Take this first. A few drops on your tongue. It's crab apple. It'll help you stop feeling ashamed of your body."

"How do you know I'm…" Bella cried. "I love you so much, Gran. I know I don't show it, but you're one of the kindest people I know. You never judge me, either. How do you do that? When you know what I've just done?"

"It's not my job to judge you, honey. It's my job to love you. That's what grandmothers do. Now, this ointment, it's calendula. You'll need to rub that in where you've torn your skin. Are you okay to do that on your own? I'll look the other way while you're doing it."

Azaria busied herself in the 300-year-old wooden merchant's chest where she stored some of her tinctures, potions and lotions. There were a few flower essences which called to her. Her mind wandered back to the day when she harvested the wild corydalis flowers. They were

91

five-feet high, growing in the alpine meadows behind her home. The dense spires of fragrant pink flowers, with fern-like leaves, were known traditionally to substantially reduce pain. Yes, she'd give that tincture to Bella.

She was slightly distracted for a moment, as she heard Bella whimper. Oh how she wanted to tend to the grazes herself, but Bella was a teenager and that was not an option. She became aware that Bella needed something powerful to restore her inner circuitry after such a huge physical and emotional shock. *Musk thistle*, she whispered.

"I hate myself, Gran. I hate myself!"

"I have just the remedy for you," Azaria replied, trying to remain detached as she chose the right one for her patient. "It's called sneezeweed, or in my world, Hymenoxys hoopesii."

"Sneezeweed is much easier to say." Bella tried to make light of the name. "Will it make me sneeze?"

"No, but it will help you to stop judging yourself. Take a few drops. It will release you from self-loathing."

Azaria made a few scribbles into her notebook, mentioning patient, time, date and remedies. She did this as a matter of course, whether the remedy was for a family member, a stranger or herself.

"Fancy sleeping in my bed tonight? Just like the old days?"

"There isn't anywhere else in the world I'd rather be," Bella cried. "I'm so sorry, Gran. You must be so disappointed in me."

"Never. You could never disappoint me. Now, hop into bed."

Azaria pulled back the eiderdown, and plumped up the pillows. It was a king-sized bed, the four-poster frame hand-carved by her late husband. The embroidered curtain surround was hand-stitched by Car as a wedding present many years before.

They lay in silence for about half an hour, a hooting owl

calling out in the distance, with Bella nestled against her grandmother's side, and just as Azaria was falling into a deep sleep, a voice asked: "Will you tell me about the first time you had sex?"

Azaria willed herself awake, fighting against the delectable draw to the deep world of blissful sleep. There was plenty of time for that. Sleep would come later. But now, her granddaughter needed her more than ever. She needed her more than tinctures and lotions. She needed the truth. The whole truth.

As the words formed in her mind, they both stayed still and silent at the spine-tingling howl of a wolf from nearby the old homestead. As if on the hunt, he bayed and yowled around their bedroom window. Bella reached for Azaria's hand.

"I've never had sex. I've only ever made love," Azaria said, her voice soft upon the deep dark night. "And that lovemaking has only ever been with one man. Your grandfather. I've only known gentle hands. His hands. Hands that held me like I was a Goddess. I was young, but when the time came, I was ready. How did I know? Because the love I felt in my heart for Jake consumed me night and day. I knew I wanted to have children with him one day, but it was more than that. His hands were kind, and his words were soft. Jake was different to all the other boys. He never needed to prove himself or act tough. He just smiled, and he had the best hug in the world. It always felt like a safe place to be."

"But it's not like that for every woman?"

"No, it's not."

"So how do you know? How can you tell if someone is right for you?"

"You have to close your eyes. You see, it's not what someone looks like, it's how they feel. It's how you feel when you're around them. Sure, it's nice if they're good looking and you find them attractive, but it's about so much more than that. If you had to go through your whole life with someone and never be able to see their face, how would you know what they were like?"

"By the sound of their voice?"

"Yes."

"And how they made you feel?"

"Yes, honey. That's right. Jake always made me feel like a princess. He cared about how I felt, and what I thought."

"I want to be with someone who treats me like that."

"Oh honey, you will. I have no doubt about that."

"Do you miss Granddad?"

"With all my heart. He was the one true love of my life. But, you know, in other ways, it's like he has never left. I feel him all around me. He's with me when I tend the beehives, or take a dip in the hot spring. I feel Jake when I'm lying here in bed. He made this bed for us. It's like he is in every part of this house. In all the woodwork, and the rock walls he mended over the years. He's in the flower gardens. Jake's with me when I sit on the veranda each morning sipping tea."

"He was a lucky man, being married to you, Gran."

"No, honey, I was the lucky one."

And with those words, they fell asleep. Somewhere between Earthside and Dreamtime, Jake was standing in a doorway of the homestead. He had a knapsack on his back and was waving goodbye. Azaria didn't feel sad, but had a sense she'd see him again. She followed him a little way as he wandered down the track. He turned to face her and smiled again. "I love you!" he called back, and walked away one last time. She stood, smiling, grateful for a lifetime of love, and then when he was out of sight for the final time, she noticed he'd left a crate of apples on her front lawn. "What's this?" she called after him, but sleep closed in and took her to a place that time forgot.

The Rebel Moon

"Mom," Starr called across the lawn that stifling hot Summer morning.

Azaria took a moment to register what felt odd. Ah yes, that was it. She wasn't used to seeing only one of the twins. They were inseparable.

"On your own, sweetheart?" Unsure if it was Luna or Starr before her.

"I need to talk to you about something. I wanted to run it by you before I tell Luna. Is that okay?"

"Have you taken the day off work?"

"Yeah, I pulled a sickie. It was the only way I could escape," she said, sheepishly. "You know what I mean!"

"The joy of being the older twin. Such a responsibility!" They giggled and hugged, then went up onto the veranda. "Hey Granny Car," she smiled, and then reached over for a cuddle.

"I'm just off to hang a bit of laundry," Car said. "I'll join you in a little while." Picking up the oval willow basket, she disappeared around the side of the veranda.

Seating themselves around the table, Azaria lifted the teapot to pour. The bergamot tea had steeped to perfection, the scent of oregano citrus dispersing itself tantalisingly in the air.

"No honey, thanks, Mom. I'm cutting back on sweeteners."

"This isn't ordinary honey, you know."

"The best honey in the world. Nothing else like it. I know! We've had it ingrained since before we could talk!"

"So, are you pregnant?" Azaria asked, determined not to let the suspense last a second longer.

"What?" Starr laughed. "No! Not at all. I'm on my period right now, if you must know."

"Well I can't think of what other news would cause you to not only call a sickie but that you'd want to keep from your sister."

She looked her mother right in the eye, knowing how much she liked directness. "I'm moving to Australia."

"Australia?"

"Yeah, that place on the other side of the world where the kids ride kangaroos to school."

They laughed, and it instantly released the tension and unexpected panic Azaria felt building up in her heart.

"Moving? Not just going for a visit?"

"Remember Sasha, my penpal from first grade? She's going on maternity leave, and her boss said I could take her position for a year, if I wanted it. He'd seen my piece in the NY Times. How could I say no? It's a dream come true to work on a newspaper in another country. You know that's been my goal since I completed my cadetship."

"When do you start?" Azaria asked, her mind more focused on Luna's reaction than the reality of the situation.

"Next week. I can fly out on Friday, and start the following Monday. Sasha would guide me around the newsroom and introduce me to other reporters for a week, then I'd be on my own. It's just a small paper, but it covers a large area."

"I think it's wonderful."

"Will you miss me?"

"And you have to ask that question, why? The thought of you being so far away does terrify me, I must admit. But I'd never stop you from doing something you love. You know that. Life is too short not to live your dreams."

"But Ma...Luna? I can't bear to break the news to her. She's already suspecting I'm up to something. I've paid rent for the next six months so she doesn't need to worry about a new housemate for a while, but she's gonna kill me, Ma."

"It's going to take some adjusting to, there's no doubt

about that. But sweetie, she loves you. She loves you with her whole life. She'll want this for you, just as much as I do."

"The thing is she might want to try and get a teaching job out there, which would kinda be nice, because I know I'm going to miss her like crazy, but I feel I need to do something for me. I want to be Starr Linden. Just Starr Linden. Not Luna's twin sister. Not the daughter of the amazing Azaria Linden. No offence, Mom." She laughed. "I want to find out who I am when I'm away from family. Don't get me wrong. I love all of you. Desperately. Passionately. And I think that's my point. I need to get a sense of perspective about me. About life. About the world."

"You don't need to justify your choices to me, sweetheart! I'm on your side."

"But Luna?"

"Just tell her straight out. Like you told me."

"You make it sound simple."

"She might take it better than you expect."

They both shook their heads and laughed.

"No, she won't!" they said in unison.

7pm that night

"Mom!" Luna cried down the phone.

Azaria had been expecting a call for the past couple of hours. Either that, or a visit.

The words wouldn't come out for all the sobbing.

"I'm here, honey. Anytime you want to talk. Take all the time to cry. It's okay."

"It hurts. I can't bear the thought of her not being here."

"I know, honey."

"Can I come and stay the night?"

"Sure, but what about work?"

"I'm taking a few days off."

97

"I'll get your room ready. See you in an hour or so. Drive carefully."

"Mom?"

"Yes?"

"I want to sleep in your bed."

"Of course."

Azaria smiled to think of all the nights she'd shared sleep with her daughters and granddaughters. Jake had made the bed under strict instructions that it needed to be able to fit a whole family of children in there, if it had to. It might have seemed like a piece of luxury furniture to an outsider, but to Azaria it was an absolute parenting necessity. The family bed, she'd called it. Her best mothering and grandmothering usually involved all-night talking sessions in there.

They chatted deep into the night, watching the cheeky Moon rise over the mountains like a naughty schoolgirl, teasing them relentlessly with Starr's upcoming adventure.

"Tell me again the story about the night we were born."

"For the millionth time?"

"I never get sick of it, Ma. Never."

"You know, you could tell me the story. I'll bet you could recite it backwards."

"True. But it sounds so much sweeter when you tell it," Luna said, snuggling into her mother's side. It didn't matter that she was twenty-four years old. Tonight she needed her mother. Tonight she needed to be a young child.

Azaria smoothed her hand across Luna's chocolate-coloured, long hair, offering the soothing gesture as a precursor to the story.

The story that had been told hundreds of times, not just in this bed, but around the local community. She breathed deeply for a few moments, conscious of how Luna was always the more sensitive one of the twins. Starr was the adventurous, go-getter. Luna waited in the wings. Always waiting to see what her sister was up to.

"It had been a beautiful Summer's day, and Jake and I had pottered around the garden for a few hours. Mostly I'd been deheading faded blooms, and planning what to plant the following Spring. Jake did all the heavy wheelbarrowing. I felt fantastic, but tired. I'd probably overdone it a bit in the garden but the sunshine was simply amazing. Siobhán, the midwife I'd had for Kara and Eliza-May's births, had just retired, so Jake and I thought 'what the heck, let's be our own midwife'. I had thought about birthing under the apple trees like I did with your sisters' births, but there was something about this pregnancy that felt different. I couldn't tell you what it was exactly. Jake and I had made the bed up with fresh sheets, and I had my essential oils ready. I even took a basket of post-birth items out under the apple trees. But even then a little voice inside me said I wouldn't be giving birth there. For a second, just a nano-second, I wondered if perhaps something wasn't right and I'd have to go to hospital. I dismissed the thought and just trusted that I'd be wherever I needed to be.

Jake asked if I wanted him to put a fire under the hot tub and maybe relax in there for a bit. I said that I'd have a cup of tea and then think about it. I was rather sleepy, and thought I'd just go to bed instead. No sooner had I poured the tea than a huge contraction ripped through me. The baby's coming, I said. The baby is coming now. There's no time to do anything. This baby is not waiting for us.

Jake asked me how long I thought it would be. I shook my head, and told him to grab the basket under the apple trees and just follow me. And it's the strangest thing. I don't even know where those words came from. It was late. I stepped out onto the veranda and followed Jake to the apple trees, but on the way, with another sweeping contraction, I stopped and looked at the sky. I could never remember the stars looking so incredible. It was as if God had pinned them up there just for me.

Suddenly, I knew that, yes, I wanted to be outside, more than anything. I wanted to see the stars. And I'd name my baby Starr. It all happened in a microsecond. And then my legs just started moving. Jake asked where I was going. To the hot spring, of course. He laughed and said: how are we going to get back up the hill with a new baby and this basket? And the baby will be cold when you get out of the water.

I smiled, and said there was a blanket and flannels, and even matches. Light a fire, I said.

He grabbed my hand, and that's how the journey to your birth started."

"But you didn't call me Starr," Luna interjected.

"No, we didn't. But oh how beautiful those stars were. Jake ran inside and told Car to look after Kara and Eliza-May, and then grabbed a couple of torches, before catching up with me. Of course I knew the track down to the spring and could walk it with my eyes closed, but he wasn't taking any chances. When we arrived, I stepped into the water. It's always so deliciously warm. Jake found some twigs and branches, and set to building a small fire on the granite rocks. I laboured gently to the soundtrack of crackling, popping, and hissing. The water soothed my belly, and about ten minutes later Jake got into the pool with me. The baby is nearly here, I said.

I squatted while my baby, my beautiful baby, came Earthside. I leant forward and caught her, and Jake helped me as I brought her up out of the warm water to my breast. He then got some flannel cloths and a small towel, and draped them over the baby's shoulders while she suckled. I wished, for a moment, that my parents and other daughters had been with us, but it was perfect with just the two of us to witness our baby's birth. Jake started singing. It was beautiful, and so perfect. Just the three of us, beneath the starlight. Warm, safe, loved.

Why am I so starry eyed
Starry eyed and mystified
Every time I look at you
Falling stars come into view

We laughed and cried so much, and fell in love with our baby Starr, and with each other all over again. Would you believe there were five falling stars that night? We did a whole lot of wishing."

"But that's not the end of the story, is it Ma? Tell me more. Please tell me more."

"Okay, if you insist." Azaria tried not to cry as she continued. She had told the story so many times, and each time it was like the first time. Luna soaked up every word. "The Moon rose over the tops of the Colorado pine trees. I don't know if the Moon had ever spoken to me so tenderly and profoundly as she did that night. And with a strong tug of my uterus, I thought: what on Earth is going on? It was like an earthquake in my belly!

Jake told me it was afterbirth pains, and to try and breathe through it. I did, but it was rather intense. I need the toilet, I said. Just do what you need to do in the water, Jake said. And that's when I realised…I had another baby in my belly, and she was on her way out. Twins? *Twins?* I must have said that word about one hundred times in the few minutes between realising you were on the way, to holding you in my arms.

When Starr finished suckling, Jake held her while I pushed you into the world. Truth be told, you didn't need any pushing. You were coming at lightning speed. I looked up at that Moon, and breathed in all her wisdom, power and strength. My last thought before looking into

101

your eyes was that if the Moon can move tides and shift tectonic plates, then she could surely help me birth you, and be the mother of twins. I called out and asked for the Moon's help. I found so much sustenance in that moment. The milky light of the heavens bathed your arrival. I could hardly call you Jane or Susan. There was only one name for you, my love. Luna. Blessed Luna."

Azaria held Luna as she gently cried herself to sleep, dreading the day Starr would leave the country, as much for herself as for Luna, but if there was anything Azaria knew about life it was that you have to follow your heart no matter what. She leaned in closer to Luna. It didn't matter what brand of exotic shampoo her daughter used, she still smelt the same as the night she was born: a unique mix of moonlight, Rocky Mountain juniper, and fresh country air. It was Luna's depth of empathy for other human beings that made her such a beautifully sensitive person. Azaria wondered many times over the years how she could 'bottle' her daughter's beautiful soul, and make an essence to share with the world. If there was anything the world needed more of it was people like Luna, whose love and kindness erased all sorts of maladies.

Azaria thought of the night Jake died — an untimely death caused by a falling tree as he checked the beehives one stormy night — and how Luna held her hand the whole time whispering. "It's going to be okay, Mom. We'll look after you. We'll all look after you. We'll never leave you. I promise we'll always stay with you."

At the time, the words of a ten-year-old kept her going. It provided the ballast against a grief so raw and painful that she thought, had it not been for her parents and children, she might just die herself. But Luna, especially, was her rock. Always there, like a shadow, ready to hold hands or make a cup of tea. Gently humming *Starry Eyed* from the corner of a room, or playing the tune on her piano. Other times, her actions were more overt, like placing her hands over Azaria's heart and instructing her to breathe.

Azaria watched Luna sleeping, the Moon casting a milky light upon her olive skin. *My beautiful child*, Azaria whispered, a lump climbing up her throat. *You're free to fly away too, you know. Don't let me hold you back. Ever. Not ever.*

She Laughed

"Linden Herbs," Azaria said, answering the phone with joy. She adored the possibilities that Monday mornings brought with them. And even though last night had been another emotionally raw evening with Luna's crying, today was a new day. And every new day deserved the benefit of the doubt. But Mondays, they were special. *The day of the Moon.*

"Azaria Linden?" the mellifluous voice asked down the phone at 8 o'clock that hot Summer's morning.

"Yes, I'm Azaria. How can I help you?"

"Hi, I'm Isaac Jameson. I've just bought Appleseeds Health Store. Marion may have mentioned me?"

"Yes, I was aware she was selling. Have you taken over already?"

"In a week or two. Just wanted to introduce myself. Marion said you're the go-to person for herbs and honey. Are you likely to be in town in the next few days? If not, I'm happy to drive up to your land. Marion said it's worth it for the view." He laughed, the warmth sending a tingle down Azaria's face.

"She's right. The view is spectacular. I will be in town, but if you're happy to come by why not come and have a bite of lunch? Then I can show you the beehives, and where I make my potions and tinctures. It's always good to understand the working practices of your suppliers, don't you think?"

"Indeed. How does Wednesday suit?"

"Perfect. It's a date then?" she laughed, wondering where such silly words had come from. One thing was for sure: it would be a nice distraction from Starr's impending departure.

"It's a date!"

She hung up the phone, and noticed a skip in her step. Just because he has a warm voice, she told herself… Don't be silly!

But when Wednesday morning rolled around, she realised the voice matched the face perfectly. His amber-coloured eyes and short, spikey silver-butterscotch hair were as warm as his personality. Highlighted by his glowing tan, she couldn't remember ever seeing a man of his age looking so youthful and healthy. She liked him immediately, and felt as if they'd always known each other. The laughter lines around his eyes told her more than any words could ever do. This was a happy man, who lived with a smile in his heart.

"Marion tells me you're something of a Bee Whisperer," he said, placing a wooden crate of apples on her veranda as a gift. "Do you charm them with that beautiful smile?" he teased gently as he shook her hand.

"I suppose I do have that reputation. Shall we see the hives first, and then I'll show you where I extract honey?"

"Sounds great. How long have you kept hives?" he asked, walking by her side as they left the homestead and followed a path out of the flower-filled garden.

"Car, my mother, tended bees her whole life, and her mother before that. You could say it's in my blood. I come from a long line of shamanic women."

"Marion said there's a chap who drives 200 miles to get bee products from you. Is that true?" Isaac asked in disbelief.

"You think he's just coming for honey, right? Something he could get anywhere?" Azaria smiled. "Here, put this on," she said when they stopped by the covered porch area of the old barn. Isaac slipped into the white overalls and placed the netted hat on his head.

"Cute," she laughed.

"Why aren't you wearing a hat and face protection?" Isaac asked as she led him from the barn.

"Bee whisperers don't need them," she winked, feeling cheeky.

"Seriously?"

"I suppose it's a huge risk, but I don't have an antagonistic relationship with the bees, so there's no need to protect myself from them."

"But I do?"

"I have no idea what your relationship with them will be like. I'm not taking any chances."

He loved the way she smiled, and how the lines around her eyes rose upwards as if reaching for the Sun.

They walked for several minutes, across wildflower meadows, through a wooded area, and then through an orchard with trees almost as old as Azaria. The grasses were high, and Isaac was grateful for the freshly mown paths, as it made walking easier.

"How often do you check the bees?" he asked.

"Every day. Sometimes my mother comes up for me, if I'm busy doing other things. But one of us is always up here."

She talked about how calming she found it to spend time in the sunshine, the bees dancing around her.

"Some of my greatest spiritual learning has come from watching the bees," she confided. "They spend their lives working, creating, being of service. And even though they work individually, the whole time they're part of a collective force. Their work blesses us with gorgeous honeycomb fit for the Gods. The women in my line taught us how important honey was for our health, but also that it held secrets of the divine feminine." She watched closely to see if he'd raise his eyebrows or mock her in any way, but he didn't.

Isaac listened, thoughtfully, intrigued by everything she had to say.

"Maybe it sounds silly, but shamanically we work with ancestral healing. Somehow, the beekeeping connects us

106

to our ancestresses. The one thing we definitely have in common down the family line is the use of pollen and honey in ceremonies and consecration."

Isaac looked at her curiously. "What do you mean?"

Azaria could tell he was genuinely interested, and she was no longer afraid to hold back the depth of this work that had held so much meaning for her over the years: and was the reason why someone would travel 200 miles for her honey.

"It's believed that bees are able to travel between this world and the next. Because of that, if a beekeeper is in tune with the bees she's able to connect or act as a bridge, if you like, between here and the spiritual realm."

He looked at her, not smiling, but intently. Curious. Keen to know more.

"Do you think I'm nuts?" she asked, tentatively.

"No, I think you are the most interesting woman I've ever met."

"Well, then wait till you've met my mother!"

They shared a gentle laugh, and with each step Isaac felt he was moving closer to Azaria.

She was wearing bleached jeans, a sheer, see-through floral blouse, and walked barefoot through the grass. Her silver hair, blowing gently in the breeze, brushed away from her tanned, heart-shaped face.

"I really like the way you look, Azaria. You're a picture of beauty."

"Thank you." She wanted to dance a jig. It had been a long time since a man had paid her such a compliment. For quite a while, she'd felt like an invisible middle-aged woman, and not just because she was known around town as a widow.

"Here we are," she said as they circled some trees and turned into a new field.

Isaac stood still, taking in the breathtaking scene before him. It was astonishing. There were dozens of hives, many beneath a grove of Lodgepole pines. So many of the steeple-roofed hives were painted, and each a work of art with murals, spirals and symbols. Hanging between the trees were colourful Tibetan prayer flags gently flapping in the breeze, a courteous hello to the stranger now in their midst.

The whole field was like a shrine: an outdoor temple to the bees. Humbled by the dancing bees, all he could do was smile. Eventually, he pointed to seven hives somewhat away from the others. "They're so colourful. What's that about?"

"Fun!" she laughed. And then, more seriously, "Well, some of those hives over there were painted by school children. The local schools do field trips up here, and we spend the day showing them how to extract honey and render beeswax. All the hives are painted using natural earth-based pigments, such as violet, malachite, yellow ochre, lapis lazuli, red carmine. These ones here represent the colours of the seven human chakras. It makes me smile whenever I come up here. It's a visual reminder to me to live my life in balance. That I'm not just my physical body, but a spiritual being too. Red is for being grounded. Orange is for creativity. Yellow is for power. Green is for love. Blue is for communication. Indigo is for intuition, and white is for connection to the divine."

"It made me smile to see all this. I have to be honest, I was overwhelmed. It's like a different world here. Mind if I look around?"

"Go for it," she smiled, and stayed where she was while he walked mindfully around the meadow. Azaria knew what an other-worldly experience it was, and that it was best undertaken as a solitary walk.

Conical skeps, an olden style of hive, were braided from straw by Car's very hand, and sat in hollows in a stone wall. Others, all top-bar hives, stood on small posts amongst a riot of wildflowers, while a handful of others

108

sat, snugged up to one another, on shelving by a tree.

Isaac wandered around for some time. There were various altars to Goddesses, with shells, flowers, and sculptures. He suspected she'd probably made them from clay herself. It was more beautiful than any cathedral he'd ever been in. Whatever it was people bought from Azaria's Apiary, they bought so much more than a jar of honey: but an ancient tradition.

As if reading his mind, Azaria said: "In our family's tradition, we talk to the bees. They hear of daily stuff, but they always hear of the big changes, such as deaths, births, marriages and so on. One of the most important things to tell the bees is if their main beekeeper dies. If you don't, the bees will all leave."

"Really?" He looked shocked.

"It makes sense. The bees are an important part of our family's life."

"May I ask what all the altars are about?" he asked respectfully, aware he was on hallowed ground.

"Sure. They're offerings to the bees. We leave food, flowers…just simple items as a sign of respect, and to honour the work they do for us, and the land around. Did you know that if all the bees of the world died out, humanity would be gone in under four years?"

"I had heard of that statistic. It's shocking, isn't it?" He thought for a moment, then said "tell me more about the shamanic way."

"Well, according to my foremothers, those of us who work with the bees must tell the bees about what we know of magic so they can retain this knowing for future generations. If I'm ever stuck in my life, or need help with a major decision, I come to the bees. I ask the bees."

"And they tell you?"

"Never let me down yet. If I'm ever up here, planting herbs or adding new wildflowers, the bees come by to check me out."

"Can't blame them," Isaac smiled, winking at her.

The feeling's mutual, she thought, admiring his sculpted cheekbones, and the way the sunlight reflected in his eyes. *Eyes the colour of honey*, she noted.

"One of my favourite things in the whole world is when the bees swarm. Sometimes there'll be 30,000 of them swarming all around me, the sky filled with the beating of their wings."

"I can only begin to imagine. And you're out here without protective gear on?"

"They don't call me a bee charmer for nothing!"

"Do you ever get scared?"

"Not at all. I learnt to walk in this field, barefoot around the bees by the age of one. I grew up to the sound of swarming. It's so loud, but oh my, there's nothing like it. It's a powerful and vibrant expression of a healthy bee colony. The sound can be overwhelming but the feeling of being around it is indescribable."

"It would scare most people to be near a swarm of bees," he added.

"Yes, but that's because they don't understand what swarming is about. Most of the colony in the hive has been built up by late Spring, and the combs are filled with nectar. They've also stored a fair amount of pollen. For the bees, this abundance means a guarantee of raising their brood in the summer months or when nectar flow is down. Swarming is a bit like when humans have worked hard all their life, and then when their mortgage is paid and everything feels safe and comfortable, they decide to go off traveling. Swarming bees are content, and gentle. It's highly unlikely someone would be stung by such creatures. Swarming rejuvenates the bees. It's a natural instinct, and they shouldn't be denied the pleasure. It's like a relaxing dance. You want to know why someone drives two hundred miles to buy my honey? Despite using hives, I have created a place which honours bees. I

110

don't use toxic paints on the hives, or antibiotics or other mainstream medicine. I allow my bees to swarm. And, most importantly, I don't change the queen each year, which is a common practice amongst beekeepers. My bees are loved, and I always leave them plenty of honey in their hives."

"What's that?" Isaac asked, seeing a special glass jug on one of her altars.

"It's sacred honey water. I use it for gratitude ceremonies, and as a way of giving back. I pour a libation over Mother Earth. It's made from honey, pollen and water."

To her great surprise, he said "That makes sense."

Rarely did she share the deeper mysteries and teachings with people who came here. As a matter of course, she kept her teaching rudimentary, leaving the spiritual realm completely behind closed doors.

They headed back towards the homestead, and she showed Isaac around her barn. It was spacious, with an upstairs loft which had been made into luxurious self-contained accommodation to rent out during the Winter to holidaymakers keen to hit the ski slopes. Built of local stone, the inside of the barn featured half-a-dozen cruck frames of naturally curved wooden beams resembling the A-framed structures used in shipbuilding. Beautiful, he murmured. Simply beautiful.

Isaac marvelled at the immaculately tidy work space, and how everything was in its own place, clean, practical and efficient in the rustic barn. In amongst this, were pieces of artwork and poetry on the old walls bringing flair and artistry to this small artisan business.

Intrigued by the trio of old merchants' drawers, and the thousands of tinctures, lotions and potions which had all been handcrafted, Isaac found himself lost for words in a world that brimmed with creativity, love, art and joy.

"I use water from the waterfall for my essences. I'll take

you down there sometime," she promised.

A life-sized oil painting of the Indian Bee Goddess, Bhramari Devi, in an ornate gold frame, overlooked pine dressers filled to the brim with glass jars of amber honey.

He stood looking at the painting for several minutes.

Azaria said "Her name means bees, and she makes her home in the heart chakra."

"That's beautiful," he said, aware of just how deep her reverence for this world was.

A saffron-dyed piece of cotton featured a reference to the Rig-Veda, India's ancient sacred text, which contained many references to honey and bees.

"These ancient texts are important to you?" he asked.

"I grew up with most of these teachings. My mother did a pilgrimage out there before she got married. It influenced her in many ways. My yogic practice is based on some of these texts."

"In what way?"

"Well, the Great Goddess Shakti is believed to awaken within the base of our spine an energy which is like the buzzing of bees. This sends an energy up the spine to the crown chakra. Am I speaking another language?" she asked.

"I know what chakras are," Isaac smiled. "Though I never thought about them in relation to bees before, I have to confess."

"The buzzing's vibration realigns the brain, body and nervous system by the way it vibrates the vocal chords. It only takes a few minutes each day, but it's amazing for how it calms the mind, lowers blood pressure, and eases mental tension."

Unselfconsciously, Isaac read out a poem, from A Dictionary of Alchemical Imagery, which had been handwritten and stuck with a pin to a wooden beam.

*The sting of the bee
and the dart of cupid
both signify the secret fire,
the mercurial solvent which
destroys the old metal or
outmoded state of being.*

"Powerful imagery," he said, admiring Azaria and wondering what she was thinking about. He couldn't help but think about the cupid arrow now sitting firmly in his heart, and the fire surging through his veins. If he could make love to Azaria right now, he would.

Aware that he was probably flushing due to his sexual thoughts, he turned back to the rows upon rows of honey jars, and read through their descriptions. "How do you know what flavour the honey is?"

"I taste it," she laughed, as if it should have been obvious. "Here," she said, passing him a thick book.

Inside, he found long hand-written descriptions of honey from every year dating back decades.

Summer of 1984, he read, flicking open to a random page. *Harvested during the Maiden's Moon. The colour resembles olive oil, but is a bit lighter, like Grandfather's apple juice. It's orange and muted sunflower yellow. It smells of maple syrup and is quite resinous, and tastes of mother's cherry brownies.*

He looked up, smiling, and asked, "Did you paint the logo?" It was of a beekeeper, flowers at her feet, with a clay skep in the background.

"Yeah, I did it in high school for an art project."

"Wow. You're so talented."

Azaria showed him the various products he'd be able to stock in the health shop. She explained that wax was bee sweat, and that traditionally the wax was often used in funerals, and in boat building, as well as for sealing containers. There were drawers filled with medicinal salves: a mix of herbs and honey. "This is particularly good for healing open wounds. Highly antibacterial. Your clientele includes a lot of mothers. They buy this stuff like it's going out of fashion."

Azaria then explained how she rendered beeswax from honeycomb, and how most frames yielded about 10 to 15lb of honey. She said how mesmerised the school children were when she spun out the liquid gold into the filtering buckets.

Isaac breathed in the sweet scent of honey and beeswax. He would forever associate the heavenly scent with Azaria Linden.

"And this," she said, leading him into a room separated by a stained-glass door, "is my secret chamber. Follow me!" She smiled mischievously.

"Should I be worried?" he laughed, following her in there without any hint of hesitation.

"Not at all. This is where I store the mead. You have to be over 18 to come inside."

"Pretty sure I don't need to show ID."

"Mead has a long tradition in our family, having been known to fill my foremothers with ecstasy. Legend has it that nymphs lured men away with the taste of fermented sweet honey and milk. They trapped men with them for all of eternity. Want to try some?" she teased.

He laughed, then noticed the large cauldron in the corner, with mead bubbling. "Sure smells good."

"Tastes even better. Just have a mouthful, though. You don't want to be driving later with too much alcohol in your system. It's pretty potent. I'll show you the candles." And without waiting for him to finish the shot of mead, Azaria walked back into the main area of the barn. "My mother taught me how to divine using beeswax."

"You're a regular white witch, aren't you?"

"You've only just worked this out, then?" she smiled, turning to the beeswax work station in front of her. Reaching up, she checked the dozens of candles that were

114

dipped just a few days before.

"Is it like tea-leaf reading or something?"

"Yeah, pretty well. I pour the wax into this enamel dish of cold water, which sits on the querant's head. What happens is that when the wax sets there are bumps underneath it. It's really about looking for images and symbols like lightning, fire, eggs, and so on. Boy, sure is warm today," she said, feeling her temperature rise as she caught his smile. "Let's go back to the house and get a drink and some lunch."

They chatted for quite some time, sharing stories about their lives and quietly getting to know each other some more. Azaria loved how effortless it was to be with him.

Just before lunchtime, Azaria peeked her head around the bedroom door to see if Luna was planning on getting out of bed. "Are you awake, honey? Do you want to join us for lunch? Car is in town, but I've got the new owner of the health store here. He's lovely. *Really* lovely!" She swooned, hoping to get her daughter's attention.

Luna moaned. She'd barely left her mother's bed in the past few days. She just wanted Starr's leaving to Australia to be postponed. Forever. "I'll have a shower and be there in five." And then, with some force, placed the pillow over her head again to block out the harsh reality of life. A life without her sister: her best friend.

Azaria found herself sharing everything about her life, and then, without warning, felt herself welling up as she shared about Starr's big overseas adventure.

"Could be the making of both girls," he said, gently reaching to wipe a tear off her cheek. That one simple gesture reminded her of what it was like to be in a relationship with someone who truly cared for you. An act of kindness that words could never imitate. It was so tender, so intimate. He smiled gently before removing his hand. Azaria found herself wanting to hold his hand

115

there. Close. Safe. Within kissing distance.

"That's what I'm hoping. I never had that depth of bonding with my twin like they have. I can imagine what they share, but it's still light years away from my experiences."

"I can't wait to meet them." He smiled, taking a mouthful of honeycomb into his hands. "This stuff is good!"

She laughed, and guided him to the sink so he could wash his hands.

"You know, you say your mother had her big overseas experience to India. Is it so much different your daughter wanting to see the world and spread her wings?"

Azaria pondered on his words, reflecting on just how much Car's life changed when she entered the sacred Hindu temple and lived there for a year.

She set the table with pottery bowls, hand-carved wooden spoons, and a glass jam jar with wildflowers she'd picked on their walk to the hives. Isaac carried out the pot of soup. "Smells terrific. What is it?"

"Moroccan chickpea and apricot."

Luna dragged herself out of the bedroom, her eyes bloodshot. The spidery red hues didn't dampen her natural beauty, however it did put Azaria and Isaac on high alert. This was a young woman in pain, and she needed tender care.

"Good to meet you, Luna. Your reputation goes before you. Marion showed me the article your sister wrote about you. I'm really impressed."

"It's my job," she said humbly. "It didn't warrant an article."

"People like you, people behind the scenes, are the ones who change the world. Every day we see horrible images on the news, and yet the real news is what we don't see."

They chatted over soup and sourdough rye bread, and Isaac listened with care as Luna talked about how devastated she felt.

"Have you thought of going overseas? I don't mean following your sister to Australia, but some other place? There are always charities looking for people like you. People who really make a difference."

She looked up at him, her eyes big as the Moon on the night of her birth, as if it was the most obvious thing in the world. Why hadn't she thought of that? She'd spent so much time crying, that she didn't think beyond Starr's departure on Friday.

Isaac continued. "It's always harder for the people left behind. They have to continue their life as normal, while the person who has left is having all sorts of adventures. Perhaps if you had some of your own life-changes it would make the separation more bearable."

Looking at Azaria, Luna asked: "Ma, what do you think? Could you cope with two daughters overseas?"

At that moment, Azaria wasn't sure whether to kick Isaac Jameson or kiss him. She knew he was right.

"You need to be free, honey, and if that means seeing the world, then yes, do it. This isn't about me." Her heavy heart thudded to the ground, landing near her numb feet.

Luna's face lit up at the possibilities. Suddenly, it was like a door had opened. "Where would I go? Would I teach? How do I even decide?"

Isaac didn't miss a beat. "You could google Volunteer Services Overseas, or apply for a paying job. There's no limit to what's available. All it takes is a willingness to say yes."

She reached for another slice of sourdough bread. The afternoon carried itself away on dreams, possibilities, and freshly brewed coffee. Isaac talked about his son, Martin, a marine biologist lecturing at Bangor University, in Wales. He'd lived on Roatan Island, in Honduras, for many years, integral to some amazing work there, and became a world expert in his field.

"When Martin's wife left him for another man, he was stranded with two boisterous young sons to raise. They were just starting school, but needed someone there in the afternoons. I sold my peach farm in the Okanagan in Canada, and moved to the Island. It was one of the best things I ever did. By the time the boys were teenagers, they barely needed me. I still had plenty of money to live off, because the cost of living down there is so cheap. I woke up from a dream one morning with the word Colorado spoken to me as clear as day. And here I am! There was no logic to it, but I felt like the time was right to move on with my life, so I started searching for business opportunities. Appleseeds was a perfect fit for me: thriving community, rural living, beautiful scenery, and a lifelong interest in health and well-being."

Lunchtime soon became dinner, and Car arrived home from her day out.

"Marion *couldn't* stop speaking about you," Car said as she introduced herself to Isaac. "You've made quite an impression on her."

Isaac was mesmerised by Car's beauty and vivaciousness. He had never met a woman quite like her, apart, perhaps, from Azaria. At eighty, Car wore her silver twisted locks of hair like a royal crown. Inspired by the Hindu holy men of the East, she'd been the keeper of dreadlocks for sixty years. She had consciously taken the vow of purity, and followed the seventy-seven commandments associated with the spiritual rules of devotion and sacrifice to the Deities. By the time she returned to America, she had modified the teachings to be practical in the life she would live, but the dreadlocks remained. Known as the town hippie, the locks of hair became a trademark beheld fondly by the locals.

She moved, not with the body of an old woman, but as someone who walked graciously and reverently upon the Earth. A keeper of time and wisdom.

Hours after Luna and Car had gone to sleep, Azaria and Isaac sat on the porch swing, their thighs lightly brushing each other, while sipping her sacred mead elixir. It had been a good day. The best day. It was a day Azaria Linden never wanted to forget. And she wouldn't.

The Sun rose over the valley, bringing life and hope to a new day. Azaria and Isaac were still snuggled on the porch swing, a long night of fascinating conversation and many episodes of laughter now behind them.

"I don't want to go home," Isaac said softly, placing his hand on Azaria's. "But it's probably time I did."

"I don't want you to leave," she smiled. "Breakfast?"

He nodded, and his beaming smile lit up his whole face. Azaria wanted to brush her fingers over the three-day-old silver stubble. *Oh, that chiselled jaw*, she crooned beneath her breath.

"I like your name," Azaria said as she invited him to follow her to the chicken coop. Putting several fresh eggs into the basket, she said "It reminds me of the Bible."

"It is from the Bible. It means 'she laughed'."

"Well, I've certainly laughed a lot since you arrived in my life yesterday morning. Has it really only been a day since we first met?" Azaria felt herself longing to put her arms around him and kiss that delicious smile of his right into her body. Instead, she shooshed a chicken from her feet. "Come along Henrietta, go up to the meadow with your friends."

"Do they all have names?" Isaac asked.

"All 34 of them. But I still can't tell the difference between Phoebe and Fleur! A bit like my Starr and Luna, actually."

"Marion was so keen for me to meet you," Isaac confided, taking the egg basket from her. "I can see why." His smile made her heart skip a beat.

"Did Marion also tell you that she's my cousin?"

119

"No, she omitted that detail."

"Marion is a matchmaker from way back. Don't pay any attention to her."

They walked in silence back to the homestead, and while Azaria cooked the eggs, Isaac squeezed oranges for fresh juice. It felt perfectly natural to work side by side, and Azaria found herself wanting to share every morning with this handsome stranger.

"Marion's parents died young, and Car raised her. In many ways, she feels more like a sister to me than my twin does. She's a dear friend, as much as a relative."

They sat at the oak kitchen table, side by side, eating breakfast, talking about Marion, as well as Isaac's plans for Appleseeds Health Store.

It was 10am when Isaac reluctantly parted and drove away from Azaria's hillside home. He tooted the horn, and waved as the red truck slowly went down the hill. Azaria hoped, with all her heart, that he'd be back for breakfast before too long.

To Wish Upon A Shooting Star

In just six hours, Azaria, Car and Luna would be at the airport wishing Starr all the luck in the world. Azaria felt her heart drop, but knew, with all her being, that she had to support Starr in this choice. The world was waiting for someone like her, someone who could inspire people with her passion and her words. It wasn't Azaria's job to stand in the way. Mothering, for Azaria, had been about empowering her children to stand on their two feet so they could face the world, and all it had to offer, with enthusiasm. Azaria couldn't change her mind now. She was disappointed that Eliza-May and Kara weren't here to wish Starr well. After all, who knew how long it would be until they were all reunited. It was a sobering thought, and Azaria felt a wave of nausea.

The grief of their potential goodbye was overwhelming her. Isaac's face came to her mind, and she wished she'd taken him up on his offer to drive them to the airport. If only she'd said yes. His grounding presence and gorgeous smile was just what she needed right now. It surprised her how quickly his warmth and positive nature had won their way into her life. *Into her heart.* The truth was: she barely knew him, and yet…and yet it was like they'd always known each other. Familiar, comforting, nurturing. Disturbed by the sound of the mailman at the front door, Azaria wandered from the kitchen to see what bills were in the post.

In an instant, she recognised Kara's handwriting on the trademark pink envelope she always used. Maybe she'd find out what the heck Kara was up to and bring an end to the mystery of her missive.

Dear Ma, I hope my brief note didn't scare you too much. I'm

121

safe. I'm fine. I'm happy. Happier than I've been in a very long time. I'm excited about the life that awaits me, and feel more alive and vibrant than I have for most of my adult life.

I've been working for many years to raise funds for a charity that's close to my heart. Now it's time to get involved at a grass-roots level. It's no longer enough for me to raise funds. I want to get my hands dirty. I want to be part of the lives of the children we work so hard to help.

There are hundreds and thousands of forgotten children in South Africa. I am living on a 700-acre nature reserve in the heart of Zululand.

"What the heck?" Azaria gasped. "Zululand?" Her head spinning, she kept reading.

Part of my work involves retaining some of the land as a wildlife sanctuary, at the same time as creating a strong community for HIV mothers, orphans and poor street children. Not only will we keep these children safe, but our work will take them out of poverty and help them to reclaim their heritage. I am finally using my degree for something useful: to help develop training opportunities for the poor and for youths, and empower them with life skills and the ability to earn an income. Mom, please don't worry about me, and for goodness sake don't send out a search party if you don't hear from me for a while. I need some time to settle in and find my feet. When you think of me, imagine me in my new life here: smiling and playing with children. Only ever think of me as being happy. After all, that's how I think of you. I love you, Mom. You're the best. I'll write soon. Love, Kara. P.S. Just a reminder, please don't contact William.

"Zululand," she said out loud once again. Kara had been there several times as part of the charity work she was part of, but to move there? Azaria sat down, right there on the veranda, barely able to take in the news. And today, of all days. It was the last thing she needed to hear.

"Kara? Oh my Kara." The dyke that was regulating her emotions crashed down; the pressure too much for Azaria. Who was she kidding? She wasn't strong. She wasn't able to deal with one daughter moving to the other side of the world. How on Earth would she cope with two of them living so far away?

A gutteral howl climbed up from the crater of angst that was churning her belly, hurtling out into the world without warning.

This is what giving your children wings to fly really meant: they literally flew away. All Azaria wanted to do was hold all four daughters and both granddaughters close, and to protect them forever. To ease their pain from life's bumps and grazes. "My babies," she cried. "My babies."

Grateful to be on her own, Azaria sobbed. The truth was that she wasn't ready to let her daughters be so far away. Not yet. Maybe in a year or two. Or ten. But not now. Not today!

The distant sound of a vehicle at the bottom of the hill drew her from the eruption of tears. She wasn't expecting anyone. Car had spent the night at Starr and Luna's loft to help keep them settled. Marion had phoned to wish them all well. Sienna, Azaria's best friend, had popped in briefly to bring flowers and chocolate.

And there, there in the dust, she saw the red truck. And inside was the man who had quickly become a happy memory for her. *Isaac*, she whispered. *You came.* Quickly wiping her tears, she ran her fingers through her silver hair. The last thing she wanted was for him to see her so distraught. He was, after all, a customer who'd be buying a lot of products from her.

How was she going to keep a professional boundary when they'd already been unable to tear themselves away from each other?

The pickup truck pulled into the clearing at the front of the old homestead, Isaac's smile already lightening her heart.

"Tough day, hey?" he asked softly as he closed the driver's side door.

"Tougher than I ever imagined," she answered, trying to keep some semblance of control. She passed him the letter from Kara. Isaac read it, and then placed it back in her hand. "Come here," he whispered. "Come here."

"Our working relationship is getting off to a great start, isn't it?" she said sheepishly, but the words were barely out before she fell into his arms and opened her heart completely to him. It was impossible to keep track of the tears. His bear-like embrace gave her permission to let them all out.

"Maybe I didn't come into your life to buy honey and herbs. Maybe there is a different reason for it."

Azaria barely registered his words, so filled with distress was she, but they lodged themselves discreetly near her heart. She'd tend to them another time, and in another place. For now, all she could deal with was the seismic upheaval about to take place in her life.

Kara had left home more than twenty years ago, and the twins had been in the city for a number of years, so she was used to them being away from her, even though it was only an hour by car. But this, this was so much bigger. Oceans between them. No domestic flights to be taken at a moment's notice, but huge long-haul expeditions to separate their days and nights. And possibly, she hated to admit it, years.

"Have you heard from the twins this morning?" Isaac asked tenderly.

"No, I thought I'd leave Car to manage them. I should probably head down soon though. Who knows when I'll get to be with Starr again?"

"I'll drive you. I can stay in the airport car park when

you say goodbye, but let me take you. Azaria, let me be there for you. I'd like to do that." She was still safely in his arms, and then realised he'd been stroking her hair softly.

"I'd like that too. I really would. Thank you." Azaria breathed in his scent, evocative of a forest, pine needles and fresh air.

Where did you come from? she wondered. *You came into my life at just the right time, Mr Jameson.* She kept her thoughts to herself, but gave a little prayer of thanks to the juniper trees which were looking on curiously.

The journey to the twins' city loft went by quickly. Azaria shared what she perceived to be an unhappy marriage between Kara and William, but that she had no idea what had triggered her daughter's abrupt departure. Isaac listened in that thoughtful way she was quickly getting used to. It seemed there wasn't anything she couldn't tell him.

The voice over the tannoy announced: *Final call for passengers on Flight JZ909. This is the last call for passengers on Flight JZ909. Please board now.*

With a slow hug, and a huge rush of panicked emotion, Azaria, Car and Luna then stepped back and allowed the inevitable separation to happen. Luna wasn't sure she could even breathe. Isaac reached for her hand, and said "You'll get through this. I promise you. All three of you will."

Starr had insisted that Isaac come into the departure lounge. She knew her mother would need all the support she could get. And as for Luna, Starr was acutely aware of the lifetime of guilt ahead of her where she'd feel like the worst sister in the world. The guilt was ripping her apart.

"I'll write, I promise, and I'll Skype. All the time!" They were the last words they heard as her beautiful long hair disappeared from sight.

Isaac's arms went around the trio. Three generations

of women mourning a life which was just about to begin. "Learning how to cry is the hardest part," he said. "Don't ever feel you can't grieve for your loss. But I promise, the anxiety you feel now will be dwarfed by the happiness you'll experience when Starr starts sharing her new life with you. It will get easier. You just need some time."

Adventurer's Moon

Tales from The Outback

Starr wiped her brow, still adjusting to the sweltering heat of Australia, and made herself familiar with her temporary lodgings: Kununurra Backpackers, a budget-accommodation guest house. As soon as possible, she'd find a flat to rent. But for now, this was home. The buildings were situated around large garden areas with water features, dining areas, a swimming pool, barbecue area and hammocks. Dozens of photos were taken of the scenery, known as Kelly's Knob. It was stunning, with its colours always changing.

Tomorrow, she would start work at her new job on the local newspaper. This morning, she rested. Jetlag had knocked her sideways, but the last thing she wanted to do was sleep. There'd be plenty of time for that. After a few laps in the palm-tree-fringed swimming pool, she decided to head into town and look around. Staying in a four-bed dormitory was all the impetus she needed to get out and explore. Freedom was her middle name.

It was Starr's first visit to Australia. She couldn't have chosen a more out-of-the-way destination. Kununurra, a small town in the far north of Western Australia, was situated at the eastern edge of the Kimberleys.

Dressed in a simple, vintage-style sundress, and sandals, Starr walked through the scorching 40C morning, looking in shop windows and trying to get a sense of the town and a feel for the people and their way of life. She'd spent as much time as she could researching the area, a lively booming town. The newspaper covered the areas of Kununurra, Wyndham, Halls Creek, Warmun, Fitzroy Crossing, and Timber. One thing she was sure of, there'd be a lot of travelling involved. This was one of the wildest places on Earth, and she was thrilled to have the opportunity to live and work here.

Beads of sweat trickled down her spine. Escaping the scorching heat, she stepped into a retro-style café, and sought relief in the soft ambient New Age music that was playing. In the heart of Kununurra, the Wild Mango Café served exotic coffee, and offered a well-balanced breakfast menu and varied lunch options. Service was friendly, and she found herself relaxing while her food was prepared. An ice-cold, fresh mango nectar brought quick relief from the heat.

Chatting to a young couple at the next table, Starr learned that the name Kununurra meant large river. Having lived here for more than a decade, they were keen to describe the gorges, waterfalls, streams, creeks, tidal rivers and Lakes Kununurra and Argyle. She jotted down the names of all the places they'd recommended, including the ranges, gorges and cliffs. Enjoying their companionship, her ears quickly adjusted to the lazy Australian drawl. More than anything, she wished she had Luna to share all this with. Their whole lives, they'd shared every detail of their experiences, and now Starr was alone. She'd chosen this, of course, and kept reminding herself that. Coming to the other side of the world was a way of finding herself.

Sunday morning was spent reading magazines, and feasting on hot corn fritters with fresh coriander. Sated, she sat back making plans of everything she'd do outside of working hours. The next place on her list was the Zebra Rock Gallery and Café. Located on the upper Ord River, just 20 minutes out of Kununurra, she looked forward to its promise of resting under the mango trees while overlooking the river and enjoying a cool mango smoothie. But first, she had to get into work mode.

At 8 o'clock the next morning, she walked along Pruinosa Street to meet her new editor, and get to know the journalists in the newsroom. She knew that the tone and topics would be hugely different to what she was used to on a city newspaper, but was looking forward to the challenge.

In no time at all, a few weeks had passed, and Starr found herself in her spacious and airy flat, cutting out the newspaper clippings of all the articles she'd written. There was the feature piece on the Indian sandalwood plantations, and the spotlight on the global market of the local chia-seed farm.

The crash at the airport held a heavy note, not just in her reporting, but across the whole town, yet the tragedy was contrasted by the two-part piece on the local high school's media department. Her favourite pieces involved the great outdoors of the Kimberleys. She'd become best friends with Tobias, the photographer who'd accompanied her on most of her reporting jobs. They spent evenings under the stars, laughing, talking, and getting to know each other. He was great company, and in a short time her guilt about leaving Luna started to ease. She still skyped Luna most days, but life felt full and her thoughts were less about what she'd left behind, and more on where she was now.

They both had the following Saturday rostered off work, so Tobias invited her to the Kununurra Markets at the White Gum Park. Soaking up the friendly atmosphere of the crowded market, they feasted on fresh food, and took plenty of time looking at each stall. Tobias carried her string bags, which brimmed over with fresh organic fruit and vegetables.

"My legs are going to snap if I don't sit down soon," she said, spying the stall selling organic brewed coffee. Not only did she have enough produce for a month, but somehow Tobias ended up carrying bags of arts, crafts and preserves that Starr just had to have!

When she invited him into her flat that afternoon, they both knew this was the start of something special.

Relationships between staff members at the newspaper were forbidden, so they continued to deny the blossoming feelings and played the role of workmates to perfection. But Starr Linden had a skip in her step, and no one could take that away from her.

The Cloaked One's Moon

The next few weeks were a daze for all three women at the homestead.

Life felt strange without Starr's laughter, and her excitement about the various articles she'd be working on. Azaria couldn't quite get used to there not being daily phone calls or random texts.

The time zone played havoc with the sense of rhythm she associated with mothering her adult daughters.

Azaria was busy in the kitchen preparing a meal when she heard Car on the veranda with her guitar. The kettle had just boiled, so she brewed her some tea.

Quietly walking to the front door, Azaria stood and listened while Car strummed. Her richly melodic voice was as honest and angelic as ever:

> *You gave them moonbeams, daydreams,*
> *Wings from the start*
> *Now they're flying, and you're crying*
> *Don't be breaking your sweet heart*
>
> *Just as the trees release their leaves*
> *And pretty petals fall*
> *All will go on, with them gone*
> *As they must heed life's call*
>
> *They'll see the same Moon, the same Sun*
> *They'll see the same stars*
> *We'll wish on every one*
> *We will get by, you and I*
> *Under the same beautiful sky*

Azaria, tears flowing down her cheeks, cried as she sat

down beside Car.

"You're right, Ma, we will get by. I don't know how, but we will."

Luna took some extended leave from work so she could come to terms with the major life change which had been forced up on her. During a visit to the old homestead, Isaac reminded her that change is always easier if we instigate it ourselves.

"When do you take over the health store?" Luna asked him.

"Next week. Marion and I are just finalising the changeover. I'm really looking forward to it. The regulars seem like such great people. It must be so hard to give it all up."

"She has lots of hobbies. I'm sure she'll be fine," Azaria smiled, pouring them all another cup of tea.

Car said "As you say, Isaac, change is so much easier when we instigate it ourselves. That's what Marion is doing. The time is right. I think it's a lot easier for her knowing that her shop is going to someone like you. She couldn't have just sold it to any old person."

He smiled at the compliment.

Each day since Starr's departure, Isaac had come to the homestead, fitting visits in-between learning about Appleseeds Health Store, and meeting other local suppliers. Visiting Azaria was his priority, and their friendship was the first thing he thought of when he woke up each morning. That, and how she smelled of jasmine and honey. And how, when she laughed, her cheekbones rose and he couldn't think straight. Friendship? *You fool!* This is love. Unmistakeable love.

Of the many conversations he'd had with her, the one thing he hadn't established was whether she was ready for a new relationship. He'd learnt about Jake, and that they'd been soulmates, and the incredible life they'd created up there on the hill. It wasn't that Isaac doubted himself. If he knew anything, it was that he shouldn't compare himself to the memory of a good man. But he valued the relationship he was building with Azaria just as it was, the one they were creating together through laughter, emotional intimacy, kindness and respect; and he wasn't prepared to jeopardise it simply because he wanted something more.

Isaac was imagining being naked in bed with Azaria, her long silver hair tumbling around his face, when Luna stood up and said: "I have something to share. I've been thinking a lot about what you said, Isaac, and you, too, Ma, about having my own overseas experience. Maybe the time is right. Maybe I shouldn't keep dreaming about it. Would you be devastated if I went overseas, too? It wouldn't be forever, Ma. I promise. Just a few months. Six months, tops. I think it would help me to shift this heaviness I feel. I just find it so hard to go back to the loft and not have Starr there rattling on about her latest article ideas. But if…if I do something completely different my life won't feel so empty. Say something, Ma. Something. Anything."

"It's a great idea. Honestly. Yes, do it. I'm one-hundred-percent behind it." Though the tears trickling down her cheek were kind of a giveaway that her heart was breaking all over again. Feeling Isaac's hand reach hers under the table, she looked at him and smiled.

"So, where you do have in mind?" Isaac asked, diffusing the difficulty of the information Luna had just shared.

"Actually, I was really inspired by what you'd shared about Honduras." Luna's face lit up, and she looked like she did in happier times: her smile bright and captivating; her olive skin glowing. "I've been doing my research. There's an amazing charity there that has touched my heart." She spoke rapidly, her mind full of possibilities. "I've also been thinking about Kara, and her work with

133

orphans. It's so meaningful, and really makes a difference in people's lives. That's what I want to do."

"Dare I ask when you're going?" Azaria enquired, feeling Isaac's hand squeezing hers just a little bit tighter.

"I've not booked flights. I wanted to check in with you first. Make sure you were really alright about it. It's one thing telling me to have an overseas adventure, but it's a different story saying goodbye, isn't it Ma?"

Azaria smiled. What could she say? Three daughters out of the country at one time. Her work might have been about the community, but her real work, her true life's work, was about being a mother and creating a place they could always come home to. A place where they could phone any time of the day. Didn't they need her anymore? Who was she if she wasn't Ma?

"I've been doing lots of research. I've been in contact with the charity. All I need is your blessing, Ma."

Car spoke up. "Of course you have her blessing. That goes without saying. We only want the best for you. This is your one precious life. Make the most of it. Just one thing, Luna…"

"Yes, Granny Car, what is it?"

"I don't Skype. Postcards. I want good old-fashioned postcards to hang up in the kitchen. One every week. I want images and words of your adventures that I can look at when I'm on the veranda. I want to savour your experiences, second-hand. Postcards," she said firmly. "Can you promise me that?" Car asked, letting her tears flow.

"Of course I can!" Luna laughed, taking time to hug each of them. "You know, it's so much easier going knowing that Isaac is here to look after you two."

Azaria was about to protest, when Isaac said "Nothing would give me more pleasure."

134

The Storyteller's Moon

Granny Car had six postcards to pin up that morning. "We need a new wall," she said to Azaria, smiling.

Azaria was baking a batch of gluten-free raspberry muffins, and Isaac was washing up after her. Car read out each postcard, stopping every few seconds to wipe her tears.

Dear Car, Ma and Isaac,

Roatan Island is amazing! I start every day by riding my bike from the papaya plantation down to the beach. The water is incredible. I swim for half an hour, then go back to my cosy one-room hut and have papaya for breakfast. The flowers here, Ma. The flowers! You would love them so much. I do hope you can come and visit me here sometime. I'd really love that. Love to you all, Luna

Car pinned the pretty picture of a hibiscus flower onto the wall next to the map of Honduras. The farmhouse kitchen wall was now a shrine to her gypsy granddaughters.

Kununurra is incredible. Every day there is something new to see or do. Still not used to the heat. I'm drinking four litres of water a day, and am still thirsty. Nearly stood on a snake today! Wowzer! Tobias and I are working on a feature about Outback Holidays. We've been to all sorts of places. So much fun. I've even slept under the Aussie Moon when I went camping the other day. And guess what? This is amazing: my new editor loves my work so much he's put my name forward to a friend of his who runs a city paper. He's hinted that there's a syndicated job being offered! Love, love, love, your Starr. P.S. Your Wild and Free Starr! xxx

The postcard from Zululand featured a hippo in wetlands. Kara wrote:

I danced till three in the morning. Can't remember ever having so much fun. We'd feasted on our usual staples of cabbage, tomatoes, onions and corn, but there was something magical in the air, and they tasted incredible. Our orphanage chef had prepared us a feast, and the way the chilli, turmeric, nutmeg, cinnamon and ginger infused through the onions was incredible. He wouldn't give me his recipe!

Five of us from the orphanage sat around the fire talking, and then Bago brought his drum out, beating it under the moonlight. It reminded me of Car, and how the drum was always integral to any ceremony or party we had when I was growing up. Strangely, I felt rather homesick! Love, Kara

The next postcard featured a scene of waving grasslands. Kara wrote about the subtropical sunshine and the rolling emerald hills.

This morning I walked through lush, waist-high grasslands. The landscape was draped in acacia trees. I love this place so much. I feel so at home. I am having the time of my life. Big hugs to all of you, K xxxx

Azaria felt her heart clench. *Home.* Kara felt at home there? That was not the word she wanted to hear. Would her daughters ever come back to America?

"Glad our passports are up to date," Car laughed. "I'm starting to get the travel bug!"

Azaria smiled weakly. She'd done her share of travelling, but her favourite place in the world was home. She'd be happy if she never travelled anywhere again.

The Life-Giver's Moon

Bella approached the fitness suite in downtown Manhattan nervously. She hadn't spoken to Smudge since the wedding. Today she wasn't wearing lycra, but jeans and a singlet top. She looked around the room. Five personal trainers were there, working one-on-one with clients. Ralph was at the kettle bells with a fifteen-year-old girl. Asher was urging a plump middle-aged man in skin-tight purple lycra to run faster on the treadmill. Hector was massaging a cramp from the hamstring of an elite athlete, and, if Bella didn't know better, was perving at her butt. Polly was demonstrating an advanced form of the plank to a newcomer.

Brent, a personal trainer from London, looked over at Bella and said "Hey Bella, haven't seen you in here for a while. School holidays stopping you coming in?"

"No, I've just been…busy." She looked around the room once more. "Is Smudge in?"

"Smudge? No, mate. Didn't he tell you?" he said, his jovial cockney accent somewhat out of place amongst the New York ones. "He's moved to Tahoe. Two weeks ago. Maybe it was Tennessee. Heck, it could have been Toronto. Sorry, can't quite remember!" Brent laughed. "Sorry. That's not very helpful."

"Did he leave any contact details?" she asked, a sense of urgency forcing her to confront her deepest fears.

"Afraid not. He left in a hurry. The rotter didn't give us any notice that he was leaving. Just left one afternoon and said he was off."

"I really need to talk to him. It's important." Bella began to cry.

"Yeah, you and 20 other girls. Several of them are up the duff, you know! Didn't anyone ever tell him about

137

condoms? I know you had a crush on him, but you're better off without him. He's a selfish prick. Only ever thought of himself. Wasn't that nice to chicks, if you don't mind me saying. Not sure why everyone found him so hot. He was an idiot. Don't know what's going on, but he didn't leave a forwarding address. Why don't you leave me your email, and if we hear from him I'll let him know you were asking after him."

Devastated that Smudge had been unfaithful, Bella let out an involuntary cry. Embarrassed at such a display, Bella scuttled out of the fitness suite, stopping by reception to cancel her monthly membership. Her life flashed before her eyes, and blinded by tears, she headed to the nearest park.

"Oh God, please help me. I know I've never prayed to you before in my life, but I really need your help. I have no idea what to do. I'm scared. I'm really scared."

She gave him exactly five minutes, but when God didn't answer, Bella pulled out her phone and pressed the first name in her emergency contacts.

"Gran?"

"Bella, honey. Are you okay? You sound like you've been crying? Are you okay? Is Eliza-May okay? Is it Ruby? What's wrong, sweetie? Tell me. Please."

After several minutes of sobbing, Bella found the courage to speak.

"I'm late...very late."

Azaria sat down on the chair by the telephone. For the first time in her life, she was unable to find a single word to say. The go-to lady for everyone in her community, as well as her own family, she now found herself so shocked, that any wise words evaporated before they were even formed.

"Gran? Are you there? Say something. Please. Don't hate me. I need you. I need you more than I've ever needed anyone else in the world. Are you there?"

138

"Yes," she croaked, summoning up the strength to be present. "I'm here. Of course I'm here. I was…just listening. How late is your period?"

"About nine or ten weeks."

"Have you told Smudge? What about your parents?"

"You, Gran. Only you. You're the only person who knows I'm pregnant."

The burden of being the keeper of Bella's secret lay heavily on Azaria's heart.

"What am I going to do, Gran? I'm terrified. I'm too young to be a mother."

Azaria looked out of the window of the kitchen, hoping for an answer. Such a sunny Summer's day, wildflowers waving in the breeze without a worry in the world, but inside her heart it couldn't have been darker. Pregnancy was a time for rejoicing and celebrating new life. She was going to be a great grandmother! Bella was way too young to be facing all the responsibilities that parenthood would bring with it.

"I don't want to be a mother! Smudge had sex with other people, not just me! I don't want his horrible baby!"

Azaria reeled back at the words being thrown at her.

"I hate him. I hate this baby. Have you got some herbs or something I can take? I want to get rid of it. Now!"

Azaria thought of the traditional remedy for bringing on a late period: inserting fresh parsley into the vagina. She admonished such a thought. The irony, Azaria inwardly hissed. Hundreds of women had turned up at her door over the years wanting herbal treatments for infertility. In all but one case, each woman went on to birth a healthy baby.

And now, right here, a woman in her family line — *her family* — wanted to erase the life of a baby. It jolted her.

Something deep and primordial woke up within Azaria, and she found her voice. With a sternness she rarely ever used, she spoke firmly and clearly to her angry, terrified

139

grandchild.

"That baby hears every word you say. Make up your mind. If you don't want that baby, then do something about it. But I'm not being involved in the destruction of that life. But if you do want to keep the child and take responsibility for your actions, then I don't want to hear another negative word spoken. If you think you're old enough to have sex, then you have to take responsibility for the outcome one way or another. I will support you in every way I can, whatever decision you make, but I will not hear you talk about your baby in that way. Have I made myself clear?"

There was a long silence as the words slowly sank in.

Azaria had said her piece, and now it was time for Bella to face her future.

"Gran?"

"Yes, honey?"

"Thank you. Thank you for being honest with me. I didn't know who else to turn to."

"That's what I'm here for. Do you want me to come to New York?"

"I'll have a think about it. Gran?"

"Yes?"

"Do you think Aunty Astrid would be okay if I went and stayed with her for a few days while I think things through?"

"If there's anyone who could give you guidance at a time like this, Astrid is probably the person." Azaria wondered where the words came from. Astrid? Pregnant at fifteen? A mother who'd not spent more than one day with her own daughter? What was she saying? "Astrid will have a good idea of what you're going through. Give her a call, and remember, if you need me, I'll catch a flight over and help you talk to your parents."

"I love you Gran."

"I love you more," Azaria said, reluctantly hanging up

140

the phone.

"Shit!" she yelled as she walked across the kitchen, and then headed out to the veranda to see Car. "Shit!"

"Oh dear. What's happened? Not like you to swear." Car smiled cheekily, wondering what had set her daughter off.

Azaria looked her mother in the eye and said "How do you feel about becoming a great, great grandmother?"

"Old."

Overwhelmed by the shock, they both laughed out loud. Once again, life had changed and put a new path in their way. They wondered where the road would lead them, and how a new baby would impact on their cosy and comfortable lives. And, more importantly, what choice Bella would make. If Smudge wasn't on the scene, and Eliza-May not functioning well on a day-to-day basis, then Bella had no support for what is rarely an easy journey: motherhood.

"Is Aunty Astrid there?" Bella asked when Bob answered the phone.

"She's taking a nap. Who's speaking?" he asked kindly, sensing a vulnerable soul at the end of the line.

"It's Bella."

"Of course. Sorry, love, I didn't recognise your voice straight away. Astrid's a bit unwell, love. Can I get her to call you back when she's feeling brighter?"

Bella started crying.

"Oh dear, are you okay? Is there something I can help you with?" he asked, concern in every careful word he spoke. "I'm a good listener. I really am."

"I'm..." she snuffled, then wiping the mucus from her nose said, "I'm sorry. I didn't mean to disturb you."

"Love, you're not disturbing me. Honest. I was just here having a cup of tea. I've got all day to talk with you. Remember, we're related now. What am I? Let's see, does that make me your Great Uncle?"

She laughed a little. "Yes, my Great Uncle Bob."

"Right, well then, your Great Uncle Bob isn't going anywhere. How can I help you?"

"You can't. No one can. It's my problem to deal with."

"You must have thought Astrid could help you. That's why you phoned, isn't it?"

Feeling a little safer now, she said "I thought she'd understand, that's all."

"Sweetheart, are you pregnant?"

Bella started crying all over again. It was impossible to speak. She felt so safe with Bob, like he really cared. She'd never had that experience with a man before. Her dad was nice, but he was always at work, and when he was home, he was too busy working on cases to spend time as a family.

"Love, I don't want to wake Astrid, but if you get a cab to our place I'll pay for it when you arrive. Have you got our address?"

"Yes, Gran gave it to me." Bella blew her nose. "Bob?"

"Mmmm?"

"Can I stay a few nights?"

"Of course. I'll see you in about forty minutes. Bella, you're going to be okay. There are a lot of people in your family who love you. We'll look after you. See you soon, love."

Bella scribbled a note and left it on the kitchen table. She snuck out before Ruby could notice that she'd even come back home. With nothing more than a backpack and a few clothes, Bella headed out the door and hailed a cab.

That baby hears every word you say. Her grandmother's words kept replaying themselves like a CD on repeat.

The cab driver tried to make small talk, but Bella just kept thinking about the life growing inside her. Without realising it, she placed a hand gently over her belly. "I'm sorry," she whispered. "I'm sorry for saying those mean

142

things."

"What's that?" the cab driver called back in a thick New York drawl. "You say something?"

"No," she replied, suddenly feeling protective of the passenger she was carrying.

Bob welcomed Bella with open arms, and hugged her for the longest time. "We're all here for you, Bella. Don't ever forget that. We're family."

"When can I see Astrid?"

"Later. I promise you can see her later."

Bob prepared them a delicious meal: cauliflower biryani. He invited Bella to help him make a chocolate and orange ganache tart.

Bella placed dates in a bowl and made a mixture with coconut oil, ground almonds, desiccated coconut, and honey that Bob had brought back from Azaria's Apiary.

Bella pressed the crust into a tart tin. Her fingers were brown, and the sweet scent of raw honey reminded her of Azaria. A warm feeling filled her heart.

Scraping the chocolaty mix onto the crust, Bob took their creation and placed it in the fridge while they ate their dinner.

"You're a good cook," Bella said, licking the last of the chocolate from her fingers. It had been years since Eliza-May had cooked a family meal. The only time Bella had such delicious food was when she was staying with her grandmother.

For a few hours, they listened to music, and then Bob showed her the photograph album from the wedding. Bella started to cry. "I didn't mean to make you sad, love. I'll put it away. I'm sorry," he said.

"It's not that," she cried. "It's just that it's a happy memory for you, but that's the night I had sex. The only time I've ever had sex, and now my life will never be the same again. I'm so scared!"

143

Bob held her as if she were his own daughter, and let her cry. He didn't mind that his t-shirt was now sopping wet. "Of course you're scared. But here's what we can do. If you keep telling me everything you're scared of, we can talk about how to get through it. If you face your fears, they won't seem nearly as big and frightening. They'll become smaller."

"Really?"

"Really."

They were interrupted from their conversation by Astrid walking into the room.

"Bella? What are you doing here? I wasn't expecting you."

Bob stood up, smiling, and helped Astrid walk to the sofa. "Isn't it lovely? Bella's come to stay with us for a few days."

Astrid looked at Bob as if to say are you sure that's a good idea, and why the hell is she crying?

"Aunty Astrid, you look terrible. I mean, really ill. If I'd known, I wouldn't have come over."

"Hush," Astrid said, waving her hand as if to dismiss the idea. "You're welcome here any time. It's lovely to see you. I'd have got dressed and put on some make-up if I knew we were having a visitor."

"Astrid, your hair. What's happened to your hair?"

Astrid looked at Bob, and then Bob looked at Bella.

"Astrid is having chemotherapy. She's just a bit unwell at the moment."

Bella gasped, and shook her head in disbelief. "You've got cancer? You're dying?"

Astrid took a deep breath. This was not how she wanted her family to find out. Damn!

"Yes, I've got cancer. But am I dying? It feels like it some days. The chemo is a nightmare. But I'm going to fight this as best I can."

"Gran doesn't know, does she? How come you've not

told Gran?"

"You know what she's like! She'll want me to come off the medication and treat me with all that herbal stuff."

"But she's really good at it. She cured a man in the town who had lung cancer. The doctors gave him four months. Incurable, they said. That was fourteen years ago!"

"I love Azaria, but we've got too much baggage between us. And besides, it's not fair to expect her to be a carer or provide some miracle cure. She's my sister, not my doctor. Bob is more than enough for me. And, to be honest, I feel safer in the world of conventional medicine. Your Gran knows me well enough to know that."

"But Gran is the best. You know three doctors left the town and moved on because there wasn't any need for them. With Gran, people simply don't need medication."

"Bella, thank you for you concern, but I have made up my mind. Azaria isn't a magician. She can't make this go away."

"Will you at least tell her?"

"Yes, but not yet."

Bob interrupted. "Bella has some news of her own, Astrid."

"What's that love," she asked as Bob arranged some cushions behind Astrid's back and put a woolly throw over her emaciated legs.

"I'm having a baby."

"Oh." That's all Astrid could say. "Oh."

"I thought…I thought you might understand and be able to tell me what to do." Bella looked so vulnerable and frightened, that for a few minutes Astrid forgot she was dying, and was suddenly a teenager again reliving her own fears.

"Did Azaria send you here?" Astrid asked, suddenly feeling suspicious.

"No, it was my idea. I…was it a bad idea?"

"Not at all. Who am I to give advice? Look how horribly

145

my life turned out."

Bella looked up at Bob. "I think your life gave you one of the best things ever: love."

Astrid welled up. "Yes, you're right. I was feeling sorry for myself. I've been blessed so much. And I'm very thankful!"

"It's been a long evening," Bob said. "How about we all get some sleep? Come on Bella, I'll show you to the spare room." He smiled, and then led the way.

Bella gave Astrid a hug and said "I'm so sorry you're ill. You don't deserve this. You really don't. It's not fair."

"Sometimes life doesn't seem very fair, does it love?"

"No, it doesn't."

Bella lay in bed for hours thinking about her life, and the unseen life growing rapidly inside her by the second, and about Astrid's life, and about how life would be for Bob when Astrid died. It all seemed so wrong. She scrolled through the 476 text messages she'd sent to Smudge, and then sent one final one: *I'm pregnant. I'm having this baby. And I never want to hear from you again.* She then deleted his contact details, and sent a private message to Azaria on Facebook. "Gran, you should come to New York. Now. Don't ask questions. Just come. I'm staying with Aunty Astrid and Uncle Bob. If ever you were needed, the time is now. Please don't delay."

The Dancer's Moon

Luna felt like she'd woken up in paradise. How quickly life could change.

For three weeks she'd been immersed in the tropical landscape and pristine beaches just forty miles off the northern-Honduras coastline. Several days had been spent diving in the world's largest coral reef. Each night, she posted dozens of photos onto her Honduras album on Facebook.

Today, walking hand in hand with Patrick, they explored verdant mountains, and palm-fringed beaches. They'd met at the papaya grove where she rented a small one-bedroom hut. He was having his big overseas experience before heading back to Tucson to begin work as a park ranger. That was, until he met Luna, and he knew life would never be the same again.

Love had been instant for both of them, and the only impediment to their relationship was his rapidly expiring visa. Beneath the shade of banana and mango trees, they planned their life together. A wedding in the Spring, and babies—dozens of them—in the years that followed.

Luna had never been in love before, and hadn't had a boyfriend, either. Starr, however, had had dozens of boyfriends, and Luna lived her love life vicariously through her twin sister.

Pinning an exotic gardenia flower in Luna's hair, Patrick bent down on one knee that day and said "I want to spend the rest of my life with you, Luna. You are everything I've always dreamed of. I don't want us to be apart any longer than we have to."

She laughed, she cried, and she said yes. *Yes!* Everything about their relationship had been uncomplicated.

Logic would suggest they take more time getting to

know each other, but neither of them cared about that. It just felt right to be together. Why wait?

The heart of the island of Roatan beat to the sound of love that afternoon, and the world was a little brighter because of their union.

When friends and family logged onto Facebook that week, it wasn't the photos of the island's rustic charm that caught their eye, or the unpaved roads, or the lush jungles teeming with tropical plant life. It was the smile on Luna's face as she shared photos of her and Patrick, eating papayas; riding bareback on horses along white sandy beaches; kayaking; hiking up mountains; and eating in restaurants. Everything ended with: #love

It seemed like a lifetime ago that Luna's heart was breaking at the departure of her sister. Now they chatted almost daily, regaling each other with stories of their new lives. Luna was in love with Patrick, but she'd also found her spiritual home on the lush tropical island. In her heart, Luna was clear that she never wanted to leave this island. But she had a dilemma: she'd promised Azaria that she'd only stay for six months. How was she going to break that heart-led promise to her mother in order to be true to her own needs?

When Patrick made love to Luna for the first time, it was beneath a coconut tree one lazy afternoon. She wept at his tender touch. Luna had never experienced such exquisite beauty and pleasure, and his lovemaking lifted her into a world previously unknown. His caresses were so faultless, that somehow it seemed she'd never be able to share the beauty of them with her sister. Words — Starr's only currency — would ruin the experience. Luna tucked her happiness deep inside her heart, in a place that defied human language. Feeling as if she'd touched the face of The Great Goddess, Luna bent down on her knees in reverent prayer. *I believe*, she whispered to the Moon that night.

By the light of a flickering candle, Luna spent a few hours writing postcards to friends and family so she could share more of her life with them. Captivated by the tropical flowers, she was sure to send a new postcard to Azaria each day featuring local flora: hibiscus, bird of paradise, butterfly bushes, gardenia, roses, pink and red ginger, shell ginger and bougainvillea.

Dear Ma, I think I'm going to explode with happiness. Don't get me wrong, my life was already wonderful. I had so much to be grateful for, but now I feel like I've found myself, and I really like who I am. I suppose, if I look back, it's like I never really felt free. Like I was always a bit scared to move forward and to be someone who was a person in their own right, and not just someone's twin sister.

It wasn't all play on the island, though. Luna had begun work as a volunteer for a charity which built beds for orphaned children who lived on the streets. She'd learnt, from an old carpenter, how to nail together a simple wooden platform so that the children no longer had to sleep on dirt.

Luna felt her heart growing and expanding. Life had never held so much meaning for her, despite the wonderful career she'd already had. Perhaps that was why it was so simple to fall in love with Patrick. The time was right. After a lifetime of living in Starr's shadow, always waiting to see what she was up to first before committing to a plan, idea or project, now Luna was creating a life that she'd never known possible.

At the end of each day, as she fell asleep in her ramshackle hut, wrapped in Patrick's arms, Luna gave thanks for her life. Her one, beautiful, amazing life. Who knew it was possible to be so happy and content? As she drifted off that night, her last prayer of gratitude was to her mother: *thank you for giving me the wings to fly, Ma.*

149

Early next morning, Luna packed up her postcards to take to the local post office. She smiled as she looked at the ones she'd written for her nieces, Ruby and Bella, telling them all about the colourful history of the island, and how it used to be inhabited by Maya Indians, and that it was a refuge in the 17th century for British pirates. She remembered how much Ruby loved history at school. And there was a postcard for Isaac, too. Her hands hadn't been able to write quickly enough as she described how she'd met someone at the marine sanctuary who remembered Isaac's son, Martin, and they'd had a long chat. The research centre had initiated a dolphin-discovery programme. Luna was excited at the possibilities for children with handicaps, and had put her name down to volunteer when her time working with the Beds for Orphans charity had ended. In Luna's heart, she knew she'd never leave the island again. This was home now. At some point, she'd need to consider paid employment, too, but for now she had plenty of savings.

Living on the papaya plantation brought its own charms, and she balanced her charity work in the town with plenty of pampering. A favourite treat was *lodo*, a healing medicinal mudbath. Those particular self-portraits generated lots of comments on Facebook. Before travelling, she'd never given much time to social media. It was always Starr's thing. But now, it was like instant contact with everyone she loved, and she never felt they were that far away. With a growing awareness, like the morning Sun rising over the hills, Luna discovered a hidden part of her personality coming to light, and that she didn't mind being seen. For so long, she was the one on the sidelines content to watch her sister. But now, she was the lead actress: centre stage. A leading lady with her own script!

That evening, lying in a hammock between two papaya trees, Luna smiled as Patrick brought them their evening meal: beans and tortillas, to be followed by papaya and pink-ginger ice cream. "Are you happy?" he asked, knowing the answer.

"Deliriously so. It isn't actually possible for me to be any happier." She climbed out of the hammock, and took her plate over to a seating area beneath the trees. "I can't wait for Ma to meet you. It's not the same on Skype. I want her to really meet you. She'll adore you. I know she will."

"Let's get my visa sorted before we set a date, okay?"

"Of course."

"No reason we can't plan the wedding, though, is there?"

Luna's face lit up again.

"How would you feel if we married on the beach beneath the trees? You know...the place where we first made love?" he asked.

"Perfect. That would be perfect."

They held hands for some time, leaving their meal to one side.

"Barefoot. Everyone needs to be barefoot. Shall we marry at sunset?" Luna asked, but the image was already firmly in place in her mind.

"Absolutely," agreed Patrick.

Azaria promised to come for the wedding, not that a date had been set. Isaac offered Azaria and Car the use of Martin's old house. It was used as a holiday let by his friends. Isaac still had the keys. Azaria hoped he might come with them, though he'd already taken more than enough time off work.

In Azaria's mind, the wedding was also an opportunity to discover the native flora: around 6,000 species of plants, about 630 of which were orchids. She never got sick of the postcards arriving in the mail. There were several each week, for her, Car and Isaac. The only downside was that she started having cravings for papaya. It seemed there wasn't a meal went by where Luna didn't describe her breakfast or dessert or the dozens of ways she'd eaten the fruit. Azaria could recite Luna's description of their taste, word for word: deliciously sweet with musky undertones and a tender, butter-like consistency.

Little Sister's Moon

When Azaria knocked on the door of Astrid's New York home, she expected to find Bella in a state of distress. What she saw, instead, was her granddaughter with a smile on her face.

"Come in, Gran. About time! Never thought you'd get here."

"Your message had me worried. Are you okay?"

"I'm fine. We're fine. Me and the baby…we're fine." She smiled, and then hugged her grandmother. "Thank you for reminding me to speak kindly to the baby. I've been trying to do that all the time now."

"Does your mother know?"

"Not yet. I thought we could go there together, but first…. Never mind, come inside."

Azaria's first thought on seeing her Astrid was: what on Earth have you done to your hair? Why would you shave it off? It took about 8.3 seconds for Azaria to realise that it wasn't Bella who needed her, but Astrid. Her little sister.

"Why didn't you tell me?" she asked, distraught, as the dots began to connect.

"Because I know what you're like! This isn't something you can fix with herbs, Azaria. I've had a total hysterectomy, and still the cancer keeps eating away at me. They can't keep cutting away and burning off my insides. I'm dying. You don't need this in your life. Go back home, Azaria."

"I want you in my life, Astrid. I always have wanted that. Come home with me. You and Bob will be comfortable in the barn. You know it's palatial and luxurious. Let's put it to good use, hey? You don't need to think about meals. Car and I can take care of that. If you want to continue with chemo, then do, but at least come home and have some extra care. You can't expect Bob to bear the weight of all this himself."

"I don't mind," he interjected.

"It's a full-time job being a carer. You'll need to make sure you get rest. If you're at home, then there'll be three of us caring for Astrid. And Marion can help, too. She's got a bit of time on her hands now."

"I'd be a burden," Astrid argued.

"Rubbish. Absolute rubbish."

Astrid looked at Bob, then at Bella. "You can't save the whole world, Azaria. Sometimes people just have to find their own way. I know being a clucky mother hen comes naturally to you, but sometimes you have to let people be." Astrid was kind, but firm.

"I want to love you. That's all I'm asking. Give me the chance to do that?"

"I'll think about it. We'll think about it. I give you my word. First things first, though. We've got a new baby coming into the family. That's what we should all be thinking about." Astrid said, holding Bella's hand tightly. "It's time to tell your Mom, sweetheart."

"I don't want to," Bella said. "She won't care. Dad won't care. And Ruby, Queen Ruby, will go nuts. Little Miss Perfect will not be supportive."

"They have a right to know," Azaria said. "They need to know."

"Mom doesn't even have the energy to pack us school lunches, she's hardly going to be interested in being a grandmother."

"Well then she better get interested," Azaria said, feeling her blood boil. "Maybe this is the wake-up call your mother needs."

Azaria sat with Bella in the lounge room of her New York apartment waiting for either Eliza-May to get out of bed or James to come home from work. "Where's Ruby?" Azaria asked.

"At Mary's. She's spent most of the school holidays there. They go up to Martha's Vineyard at the weekends, and during the week go horseriding, to the movies, and help out in Mary's dad's Fairtrade shop. I've hardly seen her."

"What on Earth has happened to this family? I can't understand it. Eliza-May was always such a good mother; so attentive, caring and kind. It's like the person she was has just vanished."

"What do you expect?" Bella argued, vigorously defending her mother. "She married the love of her life and she never sees him. He's always at work. She hates the city, and barely leaves the apartment."

"But she has children!" Azaria stormed back and forward across the lounge room. In the end, she couldn't stand it any longer. Walking into Eliza-May's bedroom, Azaria was taken aback by the darkness and stench. She edged her way carefully towards the window, and pulled back the heavy, thick velvet curtains. "Get out bed Eliza-May. Get out now."

"Ma?" Eliza-May covered her eyes from the blinding light, cowering under the bedclothes. "What are you doing here?" came her muffled voice.

"You'll soon find out. Now, get out of bed. Get yourself in that shower and clean yourself up. You look like you haven't bathed in weeks. Doesn't James see to it that you at least wash yourself each day?" As soon as the words were out, she spied a few dreadlocks in Eliza-May's hair: the consequence of not brushing her hair for several weeks.

"He sleeps on the sofa. Comes in late. I'm tired. I need to sleep."

"Shower. Now. Get dressed, and then come into the lounge. You don't have a god-damned Prozac deficiency, Eliza-May. You're deficient in life! You need to get out of bed. Now do it, or I'll drag you out!"

Eliza-May couldn't ever remember seeing her mother

155

so angry. Surely she understood how life was for her daughter? That she felt like a fish out of water? That she was a country girl at heart, and never bonded with the city?

It was about half an hour later when Eliza-May cautiously came into the lounge room. Azaria had made a pot of fresh tea, and with Bella had baked some coconut cookies from the few ingredients in the pantry.

Azaria shared with Eliza-May about the amazing adventures her three sisters were enjoying overseas. They seemed such a stark contrast to Eliza-May's paltry existence living in her pretty prison.

"Surely you didn't come to New York just to rub their wonderful lives in my nose, mother?" Eliza-May had never spoken rudely to Azaria. Not once. Not ever. But she was in no mood to hear how happy everyone else was. She'd been dealt a rotten hand, and it was about time her mother just accepted that, instead of thinking it could be wished away or wafted into thin air with a bunch of potions.

"Bella's pregnant." Azaria didn't mince her words.

"What?"

"I'm having a baby, Mom."

"Don't be ridiculous! How…how did this happen? Not that personal trainer chap? I thought you'd stopped seeing him? How far along are you?"

"Enough with the questions," Azaria said, halting her daughter's interrogation. "The only question is: are you going to support her? Because, if you are, then you damn well have to get your butt out of bed each morning."

"You don't understand Ma! You can't possibly know how I feel. You have the perfect life up there on the hill. You have the life I want! The life I dreamed of having my whole childhood. And what do I have? This shitty existence in a city filled with pollution. All I hear all day long are sirens and noise. There's always so much noise. Noise. Noise. All the time. Everywhere. I hate it here. I

156

hate the smells. I hate the sounds. It terrifies me to go out into the street. Can't you comprehend that? I hate New York!"

Azaria wondered when her daughter's dreary depression morphed into agoraphobia.

"No one is forcing you to stay here, Eliza-May. It's a choice."

"I don't have a choice! For God's sake, I'm married to James. He'll never leave New York. He's worked too hard to get where he is."

"If his work is more important than his marriage, then maybe you should ask yourself what exactly you're staying for. Are you going to support your daughter, or not? Just answer me that question. She could stay in school, and you could raise the baby. Bella could raise the baby herself, or she could adopt it out."

"I'm not giving my baby away!" Bella said, indignant at the thought. "It's mine."

Hoorah! Azaria cheered inwardly. Finally, some fierce motherly protection towards the unborn child.

"I want to raise the baby myself. I don't know how I'll do that on my own, but I don't want to be in school or college and have someone else watching my baby get its first tooth or learn to walk. That's my job!"

"Well you can't live here," Eliza-May said flatly. "Your dad couldn't cope with a screaming baby when he works so hard.

Azaria raised her eyebrows. "Would you stop putting his needs first? Look where that has gotten you."

"You're being unfair, Ma, and I don't like it." Eliza-May said.

"I'm being honest." Azaria turned to Bella. "If you're sure you want to raise this baby, then there might be a solution. The flat above the healthstore is vacant because Marion has moved to a small homestead out of town. My friend Isaac, the new owner, was going to live in there but is going to buy a house instead. He's said you could rent it really cheaply, if you want to. You've been in there plenty of times, so you know how nice it is. It has those lovely views over the mountains, and it has that courtyard downstairs so the baby would have somewhere safe to play when it starts toddling around. In time, you could even do a bit of part-time work in the healthshop. If you want to, that is."

Bella's eyes lit up. For the first time, she was starting to feel as if there was a light at the end of the tunnel. As if she might just cope with the new path life was leading her on.

"He wouldn't mind? This Isaac fella?" she asked tentatively, still in disbelief at the offer before her.

"Not at all. It was his idea."

"I'd be near you and Great-Granny Car. That'd be cool. If the baby ever got sick, I'd feel good knowing you could help."

"So if you have all this worked out, why did you come here?" Eliza-May demanded. "You made it sound as if you needed me. You don't need me at all."

"Not while you're like this, I don't." Bella snapped. "I need a mother who bothers to get out of bed and wash herself. I need a mother who gives a toss. If you want to be that mother, then yeah, I do need you."

"I don't need this crap in my life," Eliza-May said, walking away and back to her bedroom. She pulled the curtains closed, and crawled back into bed.

Azaria stood in disbelief. What had happened to her daughter? Eliza-May used to love life.

"So," Azaria sighed, "do you want to wait for your father to come home, or shall we go back to Colorado tonight?"

"Don't see the point in waiting," Bella said, though she was surprised how happy she felt. It had never occurred to her that living in rural Colorado might be good for her. But right now, she couldn't think of anything better. With her grandmother and great grandmother by her side, Bella felt safe and strong, like she finally belonged in the family.

Azaria wrote a long, thoughtful letter to Eliza-May and James. She also slipped a love letter to Ruby inside her pillow case. Despite the tense relationship between Ruby and Bella, the loss would hit her hard. Now she really would be all alone in this high-rise apartment.

Darling Rubes, One day, you can come too, Azaria promised her in the letter.

The Autumn

The Counting Moon

Summer whispered goodbye, not wishing to make a fuss. The heady scent of hay meadows and colour explosion of late wildflowers were usurped by the undeniable smoky, crisp smell of Fall in the mountains, and the distinct change of light.

Agitated, Azaria paced the kitchen. Autumn had crept up, not leaving time for her to adjust to the change of season. So much had happened in the past few weeks, that her work had been neglected. Herbs needed harvesting, and yet the days just whizzed by. She hadn't checked on the beehives in days. Her priority had been to settle Bella into the flat above Appleseeds. With Car's help, they'd sewn new curtains for each room, and made a pretty patchwork quilt. They'd tidied up the courtyard garden, and brought in terracotta pots brimming with herbs. In the kitchen, they stuffed the pantry with Kilner jars filled to the rim with fruits, vegetables, pickles and French jams.

Azaria taught her granddaughter how to make natural cleaning products from scratch, not only to protect the environment from harsh chemicals, but also to keep her and the baby safe and away from hazardous substances. Bella soon become familiar with the intoxicating scents of eucalyptus, thyme, tea tree, neroli and rosemary oils. She felt like a queen, and with her bump beginning to really show, settled into her new life with ease. She helped Isaac out in the shop most days, and in the evenings he'd drive her up to Azaria's, where they'd all share a meal by the woodstove.

Azaria stood for a few minutes gazing at the calendar. She flicked back the pages, month by month, Moon by Moon. It had been a year since her last menstrual cycle.

For a number of years, the idea of a Crone Ceremony

161

appealed to her. Now, she wondered if she even had time to gather her close female friends for such a thing. She thought it oddly ironic to wear the crown of the wise crone at long last. If anything, she felt far from wise. Eliza-May hadn't been in contact, not once, since that day Azaria had yelled at her to get out of bed and start living. James had sent a terse email in which he expressed nothing but shame and disgust at Bella's pregnancy.

The brutal wind outside kicked up the leaves, hurling them against the window pane. Unease gripped her deep in the gut. She couldn't pinpoint it, but knew herself well enough to consider it a warning. Something wasn't right. The wind was calling her, saying: pay attention! Nothing Azaria could think of made sense. Three of her daughters were having the time of their life. It was just Eliza-May to be concerned about. And Ruby, of course.

Ruby phoned every night, in a flood of tears. If Azaria could whisk her out of there, she would. She'd caused enough of a rift by bringing Bella back West, but there wasn't really any other option. As it turned out, Bella was thriving here and making the most of earning some money before the birth of her baby. She'd made new friends, too. If Azaria didn't know better, she'd think Callum, the lifeguard Bella met at aquanatal classes, fancied her. She kept her nose out of it, but Azaria could recognise attraction like that didn't come along every day. In many ways, their 'friendship' reminded her of when she met Jake all those years ago.

Change. That's what I need, she thought to herself. I need some change. And with that thought, Azaria decided to redecorate the lounge room. For years, the curtains and cushions had been cream coloured. Something about the cold Autumn drew her to maroon: a strong, stable brownish-red colour spoke of hidden mysteries. Softer than burgundy, but not as melodramatic as red. Carefully placing Car's sleek black vintage Singer sewing machine

162

on the kitchen table, Azaria stopped for a moment to sip her tea and admire the machine that had been instrumental in the creation of many clothes for decades. Made in 1923, it was ornately decorated in gold patterns, and featured a serial number embossed in a stainless steel silver badge.

Azaria rummaged through her collection of scrap fabrics until she gathered an assortment of hues in the desired colour.

The old homestead was built around the spacious farmhouse kitchen, but the lounge room held its own charm. Rustic, with massive wooden beams, its features were evenly divided between the large stone fireplace, and the cathedral ceilings which framed the awe-inspiring floor-to-ceiling triangle window, with sweeping views across the valley and mountains. The billionaire's view, visitors called it.

Azaria walked around the room, deciding what additions it needed, and what cushions should be recovered.

Several new cushion covers later, she already felt a difference in the energy of the room. Her life was changing, and her home needed to reflect that.

Tomorrow, she'd head into town and buy more fabric.

The phone's shrill ring startled her from daydreams. She waited for Car to answer the call, and then realised she must have been outside. Hurrying over, she picked it up.

"Mrs Linden?"

"Yes, how may I help you?" she answered, not recognising the voice at the end of the line."

"My name's David Hudson. I'm the headmaster at St. Ursula's Girls' School, New York. I understand you're Ruby's grandmother."

"What's happened? Is she okay?"

"No, she's not. I'm unable to locate her parents. You're down as her third next of kin."

"Tell me what's happened!"

"I'm afraid I can't do that. You'll need to come into the school!"

"Don't give me that bureaucratic bullshit! I live in the West. Just tell me what's wrong!" She shocked herself at the use of language and the harsh way she responded, but the truth was she was frightened something truly awful had happened to her beloved grandchild, and she was in no mood for games.

"I'm afraid Ruby has been expelled. We simply can't tolerate such behaviour. This is a school for young ladies!" he said. Azaria could almost see him looking disdainfully down his nose.

Ruby. Beautiful, precious, dainty Ruby. What could she have done to warrant expulsion?

"She has punched two girls in the face. One of them is in hospital with a broken nose. I will have to call the police. Don't be surprised if the parents press charges. Ruby is in my office with me, but I need a responsible adult to come and collect her. Have you any idea where I might be able to get hold of her parents?"

Azaria didn't know whether to laugh or cry. Ruby had promised she'd find a way to get to Colorado. Surely she didn't mean like this? Was this her last-ditch desperate attempt to leave home?

James and Eliza-May wouldn't stand for both their girls leaving home. Or would they?

"I'll send my brother-in-law around to fetch her. He's not far from the school. Thank you for your call. I'll try and track down her father."

Azaria phoned Bob, and he agreed to collect Ruby and get back in touch when she was safely at his house. Azaria laughed at the irony. It wasn't that long ago she didn't even know Bob, and Astrid wasn't part of their lives. And now, she was counting on them to help her family.

The landline at Eliza-May's apartment kept clicking

164

to the answering machine. Azaria had left several urgent messages. She'd messaged James, and had no reply. Useless, she muttered. Useless bloody parents. She then phoned the law firm where James worked.

"I'm sorry. He's out of town working on a case. He'll be back next Friday." The secretary said. "Anything else I can help you with Mrs Linden?"

"Please ask him to have the decency to phone me as soon as he can. Tell him I'm bringing Ruby to Colorado if I haven't heard from him by tomorrow morning."

Bob and Azaria agreed Ruby should stay with him and Astrid for the evening, and then he'd arrange for her to take a flight to Denver in the morning.

"It's all working out for the best, honey," Car said kindly as she served up a brew of lemongrass tea. "Those girls haven't had parents for some time by the sound of it. Having them here, with us, it's a good thing. Might not be what we had in mind, but they need us. They need some security. Look how well Bella is doing. She's like a new person. Have you noticed how she barely looks at her phone now? It's like she's looked up and realised life is going on all around her."

"Mom, that's called love. She's smitten with that young man. And I dare say he's tripped over his feet a few times in front of her, too. It's just a matter of time!"

"And you don't think the baby will deter him too much?"

"Oddly, not at all. After all, if it wasn't for the baby she'd never have ended up at the swimming pool doing aquanatal fitness classes five times a week! Gotta count our blessings where we find them, hey? But Ruby, oh my goddess, what are we going to do with her?"

"You could homeschool her, like you did with the twins for all those early years."

"She'd love that, wouldn't she? Glued to me 24/7. No,

she needs to have a life away from me. If she's going to apprentice with me when she's eighteen, then she can at least be somewhere so she can forge some friendships first. This place will be isolating enough if she does go ahead with becoming a herbalist. At least the local school will be more suited to her nature than that ridiculous all-girls' school."

"No doubt about that."

They sipped tea, then Car went back to pinning postcards to the wall. "Five more from Luna today. I don't think she'll make it to Spring before she gets married. That girl is so loved up, she'll be walking down the aisle by Christmas. I wish she'd get married here, though," Car confided. "You know what I'm like with flying."

"You'll be fine, Ma. And besides, we'll have Isaac's son's house to recover in. It's right on the beachfront."

Ruby woke from her nap, and made herself comfortable in the seat, smiling as the stewardess checked she was okay. This was her first airplane flight without a parent. Flight 764 from New York to Denver was circling over the city, waiting for permission from the air-traffic controller to land.

Admiring her bruised hand, she couldn't help but smile proudly. She owed her best friend Josie big time. How many friends would agree to let you break their nose for a mere three hundred bucks just so you could leave the life you hated? Ruby thought about all those years of being stifled in the girls' school, driven to academic success when her only goal, her only dream, was to apprentice with her grandmother Azaria, and become a herbalist and beekeeper. Algebra left her bored rigid.

"Quite some damage you've done to your hand," said the elderly lady next to her.

"It's the best thing that's ever happened to me," she

said confidently, unable to stop grinning. Of course, she'd have to face Azaria's lectures, and there would be a stern talking to—no doubt about that—but if there was one thing she knew about her grandmother, forgiveness was always just a hug away. In no time at all, they'd be working side by side in the barn, rendering honeycomb, storing tinctures, and showing schoolchildren around the beehives and orchard. They'd sip mead together, too, for quality-control purposes.

Ruby barely had a foot in the front door of the homestead when Azaria gave her about twenty rules which could not be broken, or she'd be sent straight back to New York. Ruby figured she could live with most of them, because, if nothing else, she knew with absolute certainty that there'd be a delicious meal on the table each night, and people around who cared for her. There'd always be someone to ask how her day had been. If it meant she had to walk down the mountain at seven each morning to catch the school bus, then so be it. She wasn't exactly thrilled about having to walk up the mountain each afternoon, and with Winter looming it would be dark and freezing. But if that's what Gran was insisting on, then she was not going to argue. Right now, she was the happiest girl in the world. First meal on the table: a spinach and tofu lasagne, with a rich garlicky wild-mushroom sauce. She savoured every mouthful, and ate way too much.

School turned out to be wonderful, and Ruby fell in love with her teachers. Everything about Aspen Falls High School seemed magnificent to Ruby. Within a week she had a glow to her cheeks and a smile on her face. Mr Frazer, the head teacher, phoned Azaria to say how pleased they were to have Ruby in their school, and how each teacher said she raised the bar in their classes. She was bright, popular, and funny. Azaria pondered the idea. She'd never thought of Ruby in those terms before. Bright, yes, but not popular or funny. Kind, caring, sensitive, of course, but certainly not the words Mr Frazer was using.

"I'm just delighted that she's settling in and is so happy," Azaria replied.

It was late Friday afternoon, about three weeks later, and Azaria was pottering around Isaac's healthstore, partly because she hadn't seen him for three days while he was busy doing the stocktake, and because she wanted to have a word with Bella. Her granddaughter had become so smitten with her new love interest that she forfeited her trips with Isaac to the homestead to share in evening meals. She was learning to cook, and Callum had cooked for her a few times, too. Azaria had told Ruby that morning not to bother catching the bus home, but to meet her at Appleseeds and they'd go by the fabric store and pick up some material for baby clothes, then get a hot chocolate from the Bookshop Café around the corner.

When the bells at the front door tinkled, Azaria didn't pay any notice. Customers came in all the time. It was only when she heard Bella whisper "Oh My God", that she turned around.

"Eliza-May!" Azaria gasped. "What are you doing here? Whey didn't you call?"

Azaria instinctively rushed over and embraced her.

"I thought you might still be mad at me," Eliza-May said, looking over to Bella, barely able to recognise the blossoming young woman behind the counter. She desperately wanted to touch the belly that contained her grandchild.

"I'm angry, but I still love you. You must know that."

"I've been such a disappointment to you. To all of you. But none of you could be as disappointed as I am with myself. All these wasted years! You've tried to help me so many times, and I just turned my nose up at you. I don't know why. You were right. You were always right, Mom."

"Is James with you?" Azaria asked.

"I've left James. You were right about that, too. If our marriage meant anything, then our lives would reflect that. I was in denial. I love him so much that I just didn't want to see what was happening." She lowered her voice, so customers wouldn't hear. "Mom, I've stopped taking the anti-depressants. I'm scared about what might happen. I'm going to need your help. Please say you're willing to help me."

"Never be in any doubt about that. Right, we should get you home."

"No, there's no need for that. I've rented a small house a mile out of town. I just wanted to let you know I'm here, and things are going to change."

"Looks like they already have," Bella smiled, surprised at just how happy she was to have her mother nearby.

The Winter

Grandmother's Moon

It was the iciest Winter Azaria had ever known. Each day felt torturous, and for the first time she was starting to feel her age. With aching bones, she'd do a circuit of the land, inspecting the chickens, bees, stray cats, and double-checking the herbal remedies were maturing as they should. She kept the woodstove cranked up high, and made sure Car was always warm, and kept a basket of extra blankets by the sofa. Car argued that she was fussing too much.

"I'm not feeling this Winter as badly as you are," she said, protesting when Azaria placed a second blanket over her knees.

"It just feels so dark. I really can't bear it, Mom. I have to admit I feel so envious sometimes when I log onto Facebook and see Starr and Luna with their lives in the sunshine, and the letters from Kara. That photo the other day…did you see her tan? Unbelievable. I need some sunshine."

"Why don't you visit one of them?"

"I can't leave you, Mom."

"Azaria, I've never heard anything so silly. I am capable of looking after myself."

"Yeah, but if something happened while I was away, it could be days before anyone turned up here," Azaria said.

"I'm sure Marion would be happy to pop up and check on me, if that's really what you're worried about."

"What's that supposed to mean?"

"You and Isaac."

"What are you talking about?"

"You spend so much time together, but as far as I know you haven't spent the night with him. I don't understand it. You're made for each other, and yet you're not going

171

beyond friendship. What's that about?"

"I have no idea how we went from 'I need some sunshine' to discussing my love life. Or lack of."

"Because if you just took a step closer to him you wouldn't notice how dark and gloomy it was outside." Car smiled, then said, "I think I'm ready for another cup of tea." Winking, Car picked up her knitting magazine, and then checked her stitches.

"One cup of tea coming up, then I need to pop into town for a few bits and pieces before the shops close. Do you want to come with me?"

"No dear, I'm fine. I'm determined to get these baby clothes finished before Christmas."

Azaria drove her silver, soft-top convertible Peugeot down the mountainside carefully. She should have known better than to drive in such treacherous conditions, but she figured if the school bus managed the main roads, then she should be able to get down her track. About two miles from home, the engine spluttered.

"What the hell?"

All she'd wanted to do was pick up some grains and legumes from Appleseeds. She didn't need her car breaking down. Grateful to be wearing her boots, she got out and looked under the bonnet. Who was she kidding? She didn't know the first thing about car engines. There were few tyre tracks in the snow, so she doubted anyone would be along anytime soon, and as Bella discovered on each of her visits, there was no phone signal.

"Crap," she said, and began to walk home.

Winter had disembarked on the mountain so swiftly and with such bitterness, that Azaria was taken aback by its brutality. With no regrets, the unseasonal weather blanketed the region in a carpet of snow. *There!* it said, lashing the mountains and towns with a heavy coating during a blizzard. Azaria sighed out her frustrations, and instead began to think of all the things she was grateful for. It was a game she always played with her daughters when they were growing up. If any of them started whining or moaning, Azaria asked them to share all the things they were grateful for.

I am grateful for my four beautiful daughters, and how they are managing to find their way in life.

I am grateful for my mother, who is always honest with me.

I'm grateful for granddaughters, who keep me on my toes.

I am grateful for...Isaac. I'm grateful because he has shown me that I can love again.

But let's be clear, she yelled, *I'm not grateful to be walking up this mountain in the icy cold.*

The hike up the mountain seemed long and arduous, and she admitted to herself that it was time to start giving Ruby a lift to and from the bus stop. She'd probably learnt her lesson by now, and was unlikely to punch anyone else on the nose.

It was the menstrual-red, blood sky, in vivid contrast to the white landscape, that made Azaria slow down and really look around her. This was her life. Sure, her car had just broken down, and frankly, was more than inconvenient, but her life was wonderful. It had upset her more than she could have ever imagined when three daughters moved so far away. But life had a funny way of working out, and now she had three other women in her family living nearby that she could fuss over. And Isaac. She had Isaac!

Now darkness had descended, and the full Moon lit her path as she trekked up the mountain. She pondered the idea of menopause, and how it felt to no longer have blood from between her legs each month. Her life had changed in many ways, and this inner change reflected that. It was time. Time to create a ceremony for the crone. Once she got out of her cold clothes and had a hot shower, she'd write invitations to her closest friends. She wondered if the next full Moon would be too soon. Maybe it would be better to wait until after Christmas. Ideally, she'd have had it outside, but at this time of year there was only one place to be: indoors by a roaring fire. Inevitably, her thoughts turned to Astrid, and Azaria felt ill at the thought of all the medical management that had caused her sister to have her womanly organs removed, discarded like scraps of meat at a butcher's shop. How could two sisters who'd shared their mother's womb at the same time have had such different health outcomes?

A week later, there was a respite from the icy blast, and the Sun shone again, bringing a sense of hope to Azaria. Bob and Astrid arrived, after finally agreeing to stay in the barn. It was light and airy, even in Winter, and the huge woodstove meant they'd never be cold. Azaria had decorated it in light colours, and filled the space with books, magazines, a vast collection of CDs, and brought in some lush pot plants. For a moment, she wanted to move in herself.

"This is beautiful, sis," Astrid said, noticing how much extra Azaria had done to decorate the space since they'd been here for the wedding.

"I want you to feel at home. I've got a collection of herbs, and some homeopathy, if you're interested. You don't have to take anything if you don't want. But do me a favour, and at least take this. It's an Australian Bush Flower essence called Sturt Desert Pea. I'm sure there's a lot of old grief you're still carrying about leaving home so young, about Rory's death, about giving up Victoria. This essence will help you with that."

Astrid smiled. "Will it make you happy if I take it?"

"Yes!" They hugged each other, and then Bob helped

Astrid to settle in. She spent most days in bed now, but hadn't lost her spirit.

Astrid self-medicated with various flower essences. She was curious about a tea that Azaria had recommended, but Bob said it couldn't be taken while she was on medication or chemotherapy. She'd have to choose.

"I have nothing left to lose, have I?" Astrid said to Bob one morning. "It's not like the chemo is making me better."

"No, honey, it isn't." He held her hand, while holding a piece of paper in the other and reading it out to Astrid.

"Essiac tea contains burdock root, sheep sorrel herb, slippery elm bark, watercress, Turkish rhubarb root, kelp, blessed thistle, and red-clover blossom."

"What's it supposed to do?" Astrid asked, surprising herself that she was even considering trading mainstream medicine for her sister's wacky ways.

"It makes the immune system strong, and initiates anti-cancer activity in the body. This tea has been used by Native American Indians for generations. Nothing to lose," he said, squeezing her hand and dreading that damn day when he'd never be able to hold her again.

The Prophet's Moon

It was the week before Christmas, and Azaria and Car were laughing at the latest postcards from Luna. "There can't be a single postcard on that island that she hasn't bought," Car laughed. "But what I don't understand is how she's never sent any of us the same one twice."

"That girl of ours doesn't miss a trick, Mom. She probably keeps track of it in a diary or something." Azaria grinned. "School holidays start tomorrow, so brace yourself, Mom, for Ruby time!"

"She's not going to stay with Eliza-May?"

"No, Eliza-May says she's not ready for that yet. Maybe in the new year, but not yet. She does go in and see Bella each day, so that's progress, right?"

"I guess it is."

"Bella said Eliza-May even helped out behind the counter at Appleseeds couple of days ago when things were really hectic in there, and she helped put stock onto the shelves."

Despite the bitter cold, Azaria forced herself outside early the next morning to do some yoga in the fresh air. The Winter just seemed to be going on forever and she was fed up with being so housebound. Rugged up against the ice, she stepped out and began her asanas. She noticed a lamplight coming from the barn, and smoke out of the chimney. Bob must have kept another all-night vigil. It wouldn't be long now. Maybe a month or two, at most, until Astrid left this world. Her body was weak, the medication and chemotherapy had destroyed her immune system.

Azaria did what she could with various remedies, but was under no illusions that the time was close. She had allowed herself to begin the grieving process. Mostly, it was the grief of regret. All those damn wasted years when ego ruled over compassion and tolerance. They had many conversations about the right to regret, and how there was so much they could have done or said differently. But overriding that was their gratitude to be back in each other's lives again. It was never too late to make amends.

Keeping her breathing focused, Azaria watched as the Sun began to rise. *This blessed life*, she whispered to herself. *This one, gorgeous blessed life. I am so lucky. What did I do to deserve this life?*

It was too early for visitors, but she was sure that hazy red dot in the distance was Isaac's pickup truck. It had only been last night when she'd popped by his house with a Moroccan casserole. He'd invited her to stay and share the meal, but she said she needed to get back and check on Car and Astrid. She'd clocked the disappointment on his face and vowed that soon, *soon* they'd be together.

The only thing stopping her right now was Astrid's illness. It didn't seem fair to be gallivanting around with a new love interest when Astrid was about to say goodbye to the love of her life. There was a time and a place to take their relationship further, but now was not the time. She prayed that Isaac would understand, and prayed even harder that he'd have the patience to wait for her.

Within a couple of minutes, the truck pulled into the front garden, its tyres crunching the pebbles, and disrupting the peace of dawn's early light.

She'd never seen him look so serious. Not Isaac. He was the man who was always smiling, but today something wasn't right. There was no smile.

"Is Bella okay?" Azaria asked, instantly aware something was wrong. Dreadfully wrong.

"Bella is fine. Azaria, you need to pack a bag as quick as you can. Just a few changes of clothes. We don't have time, so hurry."

177

"What are you talking about? Isaac, what's going on?"

He knew there was only one way to break the news.

"There's been an earthquake, magnitude 7.3. I don't have any more information, other than it happened 40 miles east of Roatan."

"Luna? She'd let me know if I should be worried. Are you saying we should go there? Why don't I try Skyping her?"

"There's no time. Every second counts. Tell Car where you're going. I've already phoned Marion, she'll be here in half an hour to take care of Ruby and your Mom and Astrid."

In a daze, Azaria packed together a few essential items.

"Come on, Azaria. We need to go. There are only a few flights a week from Miami to the island with American Airlines. We can't afford to miss that flight."

She sat in silence as they drove to the airport, ignoring the fact Isaac was well over the speed limit.

"It's so early in the morning. How did you know about the earthquake?" she asked, holding her hands together to stop them shaking uncontrollably. "Weren't you sleeping?"

"I still get tsunami alerts on my phone because I never disconnected from the service when I left the island. I immediately logged onto the news to see the latest reports. The quake was offshore, and lasted for about thirty seconds. That sort of magnitude causes a lot of damage. There's no word yet on the injured…" He didn't finish his sentence.

"Or fatalities," Azaria added, the reality of the situation finally sinking in. No wonder he'd looked white as a ghost.

"Bridges have been damaged, and so have dozens of buildings. Luna is probably safe and fine, but at a time like this communications go down, and when the media starts its frenzy, well, you just want to be as close as you can."

Azaria gave silent thanks for the ease with which Isaac had arranged flights, and ensured they got to the island as quickly as possible.

"You've been so kind, Isaac. How do I even begin to thank you?"

"You'd have done the same for me," he said, holding her hand as their flight began its descent to the island.

"Yes, I would have," she replied, realising that she'd do anything for this man.

Even from the sky it was obvious that the island had been badly damaged. There'd been no word of any aftershocks, and the tsunami warning was still in place.

"How do we know where to look? Would she be at the papaya plantation or with the charity? I have no idea what her timetable is," Azaria said, tears trickling down her cheek. Shock gave way to something else: determination.

"We'll find her. It's not a big place," he said, reading her mind.

"I need my daughter to be safe."

It took about two hours, after they'd landed, to ascertain that Luna was working that day at the local centre that housed orphans. She'd ridden her bike there about an hour before the quake struck. Luna had seen her fiancé off at the airport earlier. Patrick had had to leave due to visa restrictions, and Luna was now doing her last week with the charity.

The town was badly damaged. Isaac held Azaria's hand as they walked through rubble towards the Beds for Orphans building. His heart sank when he saw more than half of the building destroyed. He could see that lives had been lost, though this information hadn't yet made it to the media.

Local policemen had cordoned off the most badly damaged parts of town.

Isaac spoke in fluent Spanish, and asked for information

from the policeman on duty.

"Up here," he said to Azaria. "The policeman said we need to wait by that door and he'll radio someone to come and get us. Access is restricted, so we have to wait. I'm sorry."

"I'm scared, Isaac. How could she have survived this?" Two young boys, their badly battered bodies limp and lifeless, lay crumpled next to their bikes. Their joy of life, stopped, just like that. Azaria started crying.

"We will find her. Come on."

A policeman, on guard at the building, had been alerted by walkie talkie, and then spoke to Isaac. He ushered him into a building.

"He's telling me that we're entering at our own risk. That he can't be held responsible. He said there's a young woman matching Luna's description and there is a medic with her. She's alive."

"Oh God, please let her be alright. Please." Azaria grabbed Isaac's hand even more tightly.

"Luna!" she called out, spying her daughter's beautiful body pinned beneath a concrete pillar. "Oh honey, we'll get you out of here. Help!" Azaria yelled. "Help! We need help. Would somebody please help!"

The medic spoke in Pidgin English, and assured Azaria that they were doing everything they could despite the limited resources.

"Mom, you came. I knew you would. I waited for you." Luna drifted in and out of consciousness, her bloodied hand safely within Azaria's hands.

Speaking rapidly in Spanish, the medic spoke to Isaac, his face unable to mask the concern. In an instant, Isaac felt his heart sink. This was not news he wanted to translate.

When he was sure Luna was unconscious again, Isaac whispered softly to Azaria. His hands were trembling, and he looked at the ground before making eye contact.

"The reason they've not moved the pillar is because

180

it is keeping her alive," he sighed. "As soon as it's lifted, she won't be with us anymore. I'm so sorry, sweetheart. I think Luna was waiting for you. They're surprised she has lasted this long."

Azaria took in the information slowly, willing it to be untrue. No, it was impossible. Not Luna. Not Luna who was in love, and had a whole life ahead of her.

Luna fluttered her eyelashes, trying to focus her eyes on Azaria. "Dad said you got the apples."

"What? What did you say? Luna, stop talking. Shhh. Save your energy. I'm here with you. That's all that matters."

"Dad's here with me, too. He's waiting for me, Mom." She smiled, her breath ragged. "You know, he said it's even more beautiful where he is. More beautiful than Roatan. He said you got the apples he left you on the lawn."

"Shhh, sweetheart. Just let me hold your hand. I'm here with you. That's all that matters. Shhhh."

With all the will in the world, Azaria held back her tears. Her daughter needed her right now. It wasn't a time to be selfish and caught up in her own pain.

"I hear music. Dad? Wait for me, Dad. Don't go! Don't leave without me. I'm coming."

Consciousness was barely within Luna's grasp. Like a tug of war between two alluring worlds, Luna wasn't sure if she was coming or going.

Azaria squeezed her hand tightly. "Don't go honey, don't leave me. Stay with me, Luna. Stay with me! I'm your mother! You can't leave me."

Isaac had never felt so impotent in his life. He watched, his heart breaking in two, as the tragedy played out before him, wondering how much of this was his fault. He'd lived on the island when there'd been earthquakes. He knew the risks. Why would he ever have put the idea into Luna's mind that it was a wonderful place to visit? Would Azaria ever forgive him?

The medic walked away. He knew that his job was over. The only medicine to be administered now was love. Mother love. The only person who had a role here now was Azaria. Luna's arm was still wrapped around a three-year-old child who she had tried to protect during the quake, but had died instantly.

"Ma?" she whispered, her breathing hoarse, every gasp for air a struggle, a valiant attempt at survival.

"Yes, darling. What is it?"

"Tell Starr I love her. Tell her I forgive her for leaving me."

"You can do that, sweetie. You can do that when you see her."

"I'm tired, Ma. I need to sleep. I'm so tired. Dad's calling me. I need to go now. I love you."

Disbelief embedded itself in the rubble, and like a child tugging on an unwieldy kite, Azaria looked on, helplessly, as a beautiful light left this world.

Screaming, she yelled at the Gods for their cruelty. Pummelling the earth, Azaria beat it until exhaustion overwhelmed her. Dust, sweat and agony settled with tears, and together with Isaac, she cried long into the hollow afternoon: her wailing heard throughout all eternity.

Luna was wrong. This place wasn't paradise. It was hell!

Aftershocks continued throughout the day, but none rivalled the earthquake which had just torn through Azaria's life and ripped her world apart. Her inner terrain had irrevocably changed. Damaged. Beyond repair.

It was another five hours before the concrete pillar was removed from Luna's body. It was only then that Azaria noticed the dozens of other bodies in the area, all leaving behind families who'd mourn their loss.

Arrangements were being made for Luna's body to be taken to the local morgue. Azaria's schoolgirl Spanish

182

could just make out what was being said.

"No!"

"Azaria? Tell me what you want," Isaac begged, unable to bear her distress.

"I don't want her in the morgue. Let's...I don't know. Let's see if we can take her back to the papaya plantation. I need time to think. I don't want to leave her. I...I can't leave her. Don't you understand?" She looked at him, her words begging him for more time.

Emotionally wrung out and physically shattered, Isaac made a call to Hutti, an old friend on the island, and arranged for a van to come to the town.

Hutti and Isaac carried Luna's battered body, now carefully wrapped in a blanket, and placed it on the bed of the hut she'd rented during her time on the island. Hutti left them alone, and promised he'd be back in the morning to see what else he could do to help.

"Let me know what I can do," Isaac offered. "I'll put calls in place and do what we can to fly her home."

"I need to tell Car, and the girls." Azaria broke down again. The task was impossible.

"I've texted Marion," Isaac said calmly, though his voice was on the verge of cracking. "She has had the job of breaking the news to everyone. You've got enough to deal with right now."

Isaac made them a cup of tea, and they sat on the small sofa, numb with grief.

"If it wasn't for you..." she said, and started crying again.

This was the moment he was dreading. The moment when she'd blame it all on him, and his grand ideas about an overseas adventure. The moment when she verbalised the guilt he'd been feeling ever since he got the news.

"Isaac, if it wasn't for you, I'd never have had that last hour with Luna. Thank you. Thank you so much. It means

183

more than you could ever know."

Guilty relief set in. How was it even possible that she was thanking him?

He held her close, and together they cried. Neither of them slept that night. Instead, they listened to the pitter -patter of rain on the tin roof, while Azaria shared her memories of Luna's life. First, there was her beautiful birth in the hot pool. And her first smile. Of course, there was the day her first tooth came through. The morning, after losing her first tooth, when a bee stung her on the nose. And then there was the first time she got bucked off a horse. Luna's life, punctuated by moments indelibly etched in Azaria's heart, was shared easily.

From time to time, Azaria got off the sofa and went and lay down beside the body of her daughter, stroking her hair, saying how beautiful she was and that the world had been made a better place because of her life.

At sunrise, Azaria fell asleep beside her. Isaac came and joined them on the double bed, wrapping his arms around Azaria. As she drifted further into sleep, she thought she heard Luna calling her.

At midday, Azaria smiled as she traced her fingers over the papayas in the fruit bowl. She could hear Luna describe the taste.

On the desk were a dozen or more postcards, all written on and just waiting to be posted. There was a letter addressed to Azaria, inside an envelope covered in love hearts. She was in two minds about whether to open it.

"These are her last messages to you, I'm sure she'd want you to read the letter."

Azaria sighed, and reluctantly sat down, reading the words in silence.

> Dear Ma, I wanted to share why we're getting married on the beach. It's a lovely place, quite deserted, in a quiet cove. The

beach is pristine, and it's lined with coconut palms. I can hear Bella now saying: too much information, Overshare!; but the truth is I want to share it with you. From the depths of my heart, I want to tell you how my life has been transformed. The first time Patrick and I made love was on that beach. I'd never been with a man in that way before. I should have been nervous, but I wasn't. I knew, without doubt, I couldn't have been in safer, more loving hands.

The Moon was full, and I kept thinking of how important the Moon has always been in our lives. Not only my name, of course, but how you tend your herbs at different times depending on the Moon's phase, and speak to those pesky bees of yours in a certain way depending on what sign of the zodiac the Moon happens to be in, and how important ceremonies in the lives of the women in our family are timed to the Moon.

I often think about Starr and I, 'sisters of the silver Moon', you'd call us, and how no matter where we are on this Earth, we're never really far apart. We're always under the same sky. Always.

On the beach that night, while Patrick loved me into full being, I felt you with me. You were thousands of miles away, but you were here, in my heart. Making love is such an intimate and beautiful way to connect with another human being, and I don't know if I could have ever opened myself up to such emotional honesty if it wasn't for the way you raised us. Had I been mothered differently, it might have just been sex. But what we shared that night, Patrick and I, and all the other times since, transcends the physical body. I have no doubt Patrick and I have had many lifetimes together, and will have many more. He has to go back to the USA now and renew his visa, but my heart is full of love for him. As Car often says whenever she has a happy day: *it's a good day to die!*

Reading those words, Azaria reeled. She put the letter down, inconsolable with grief. "It wasn't a good day to die, damn it. It wasn't. It wasn't a good day for me!"

Isaac gave her the space to scream. To see the woman he loved turned inside out by a cruel twist of fate, ripped him to the core. He held Azaria as her body convulsed with pain.

It was about half an hour later before she picked up the letter to continue reading.

But Ma, it's made me think a lot about you and Isaac. Please bring him to the wedding. It would be good for you to have his company. He totally has the hots for you, so stop being a mother for a while and just let yourself be his lover. I dare you!

Azaria had to laugh at the little smiley face she'd drawn. Even in death, Luna was able to make her smile.

But those words—*stop being a mother*—slashed her heart, severing her soul. "I will never stop being your mother. Never."

The Sun was moving quickly across the sky. Isaac had to face the inevitable: telling Azaria that the body needed refrigeration so it could be sent back to the USA.

"Let's make arrangements now to fly her home," he

186

said tenderly.

Azaria looked at her daughter's lifeless body, the tears rising again, like water from a never-ending spring. "This is her home. This was her life. This place, this paradise, it made her soul sing. How could I take her away from this?"

She shook her head. Luna was gone, now, and having her body back home wouldn't bring her back. The essence, the life force, the sunshine that was Luna Mahalia Linden, was not in that body anymore. Maybe it was in the trees now, or the stars. Most definitely in the Moon. But no longer did it express itself through her tanned, toned and beautiful body.

"Let's ask if we can bury her here, on the papaya plantation?"

"If that's what you want, then yes, let's do that," Isaac said.

"What I want? I don't want her dead!" She fell into his arms, ashamed for yelling, but unable to contain the demonic anger within. "I'm sorry. It's what Luna would want. I know the family won't be happy with my decision, but it feels like the right one. I never in my wildest imagination expected to have to think about burying my child. Not this one, at least. Eliza-May, maybe. She's always been at the back of my mind, her depression niggling at me like a festering wound that stubbornly refuses to heal. That girl always had me wondering if she might overdose or something to escape the pain. But Luna? No, not her; she was always so full of life and promise."

Hutti and Isaac dug a hole beneath the trees by the hammocks, and Azaria made a small altar from the stones, candles and shells that were in Luna's hut, as they were obviously meaningful to her in some way. Azaria decorated around the burial hole in a heart shape, using hibiscus and gardenia flowers. Luna would love this, she

187

thought to herself. A beautiful and simple declaration to her life. No fuss, no fanfare.

When the time came, some of Luna's friends from the island gathered to join them. There were ten people in all, paying their last respects to Luna. Isaac was gutted that he was unable to make contact with Patrick, despite his best efforts of sending dozens of messages to him via Facebook.

Isaac began the ceremony by saying:

Naked I came from my mother's womb,
And naked I shall depart.
The Lord gave and the Lord has taken away;
May the name of the Lord be praised.
From the Holy Bible, Job 1: 21

Isaac and Azaria had spoken about what they wanted to be said today, but she just couldn't stop crying. Isaac found an inner strength, and led the intimate ceremony in mourning.

"As people who loved and cared for Luna, we are gathered together to remember all the beautiful and special things she did to win a place in our hearts. May we always remember the happy times, and how she made us laugh. Today we are sharing the pain of her death. We will all feel this pain in different ways, but it is important that we allow ourselves to cry. There are some things in this world that can't be spoken with words. They can only be expressed with tears. Grief helps to heal a broken heart."

Hutti came forward, and offered a small reading:

"You may feel cheated, and you may feel sorrow, but even though, to us, Luna has gone, she is at peace. We may no longer hear her speak, but she can hear us. When you look at the Moon, remember her, and then she'll never be gone."

When the time came to lay Luna to rest, deep in the dark womb of Mother Earth, Azaria had to force herself to keep her eyes open. As spadeful after spadeful of dark soil was shovelled over Luna's shrouded body, Azaria sang softly, the beautiful song by Mandy Bingham, that she'd heard Car sing.

Her voice kept breaking, but she forced herself to go on.

Just as the trees release their leaves
And pretty petals fall
All will go on, with them gone
As they must heed life's call

"Goodbye, my darling daughter. You will always live in my heart. No one can ever take that away from me."

As the people moved back to the little hut for tea and food, Isaac stayed behind while Azaria had a few moments more with her daughter.

From the deepest place within, Azaria screamed. She wanted the world to know she was a woman in torment, spiralling in a grief so black and morbid, and that life was unfair!

She sank to her knees and fell over the mound of earth that now separated her from the daughter she'd birthed beneath a full Moon almost twenty-five years ago. A horrible feeling overcame her. What if Luna wasn't really dead? What if they'd buried her too soon, and she still had a pulse? Maybe she was just in a deep sleep? As if sensing her questions, Isaac said softly: "She's gone, honey."

"My life will never be the same again," she cried.

Isaac was on the ground beside her, his arms around her waist.

"No, my love, it won't ever be the same again. You're a different person now."

For the next few days, they stayed close to the hut. Azaria needed to feel Luna around her. She picked flowers, ate papaya, and cried. In the evenings, she howled at the

189

waxing Moon. *How dare you take my daughter!*

On the evening of the full Moon, they walked for a few miles along the beach, eventually finding the cove that Luna had planned to get married in in a few short months.

They'd brought an oval basket with food, and some blankets. Azaria said she wanted to spend some time beneath the full Moon in Luna's favourite place. Once she'd done that, then they could go back to Colorado.

Isaac built a small fire on the beach, surrounded by shells and stones. A handsome pile of driftwood waited nearby, as if on sentry duty. They talked on and off, sometimes heading to the balmy water to dip their toes. At sunset, the Moon kissed the horizon and rose slowly, as if it were a flag at half mast, offering its last respects. Isaac bowed his head in silence.

Tears flowed freely, and Azaria poured her grief into the sand, pummelling Mother Earth yet again with an anger she'd never known.

Later, they lay together, comforting each other, beneath blankets. After some time of healing silence and gentle touch, Azaria asked: "Isaac, will you make love to me?"

Isaac wasn't sure he heard right.

"Azaria Linden, I have wanted to hold you in my arms and make love to you since the moment I first walked into your life. But, are you sure? I want to make love to you more than you could imagine, but perhaps it would be better if we waited... You're in a state of deep grief. I would be taking advantage of that vulnerability."

"Wait for what? If Luna's death has taught me anything, it's that we don't know what the future has in store. I have wanted to make love to you from the moment I heard your voice on the telephone. I need to feel you inside me. I have to know that I can still feel. That there is life beyond the raw, gut-wrenching pain that's consuming me. I want to know that I can live."

Isaac had never made love so slowly, deliberately and

190

mindfully in his whole life. The woman in his arms was a woman in pain, drowning in a quagmire of grief, and he most certainly didn't want to do anything that would cause more damage.

As their lips parted, and he tasted the sweet familiar buttery flavour of papaya, he sighed with pleasure. Azaria Linden was as delicious as the tropical fruit, and she yielded to him in every way: her body, soft and inviting.

Responding to his touch, she shivered with expectation.

Surreal yet beautiful, Azaria was shocked by the level of pleasurable intensity that coursed through her veins. How was that even possible given the heartbreaking agony she'd been in for days? Azaria couldn't get enough of this man. From out of nowhere, she thought she heard Luna say: "Look at you go, Ma. Rockin' it like a goddess! I knew you still had it in you."

If Bella had heard that, she'd have been on the other side of Azaria with her mantra: "Overshare!"

Azaria laughed. Isaac paused, mid-thrust, wondering what she was laughing at. Was he doing something wrong? Had he lost his touch? Was he a poor lover?

"What is it? What's funny?" He pulled back, reluctantly leaving the comfort of her skin.

"Don't stop!" she said. "It's not you. It's…Luna. I'll tell you later. Just *don't* stop!"

Their gentle rhythm continued for a while, gathering momentum, wanting more, wanting to stay where they were.

It had taken months to get their relationship here, and now neither of them wanted lovemaking to come to an end. As they pirouetted perilously close to the brink of ecstasy, Azaria opened her eyes, entranced by the Moon, aware that they weren't alone. Luna was right, there was something magical, something otherworldly, about this cove. She could feel Luna there, with her, saying 'Finally, Ma!"

191

Tears trickled down her cheeks, Isaac kissing them gently, one by one, sighing at the ecstasy of finally being with the woman he'd grown to love like no other. And then, he knew with absolutely certainty, Azaria was his.

The Angels of Mercy Moon

As the red pickup truck drove slowly up the mountain to the old Lafferty homestead, Azaria could see fairy lights flickering along the rails of the old wooden veranda. She supposed Car would be waiting. Maybe she was knitting.

The idea of reliving the grief with her family loomed heavy in her heart. She'd cried more in the past few days than in her whole life. And now, it would start all over again.

As they pulled into the driveway, Isaac navigated his way around several cars.

"Do you want me to come in with you?" Isaac asked, wanting to honour her privacy if she needed to be alone with family.

"I never want you to leave my side again." She looked him in the eyes, a silent plea for the future.

"That's that settled then," he said, holding her hand as they walked towards the house.

The Christmas lights on the veranda twinkled as if it were the most natural thing in the world. Azaria wondered why Car didn't ask someone to help her take them down. Christmas? Not this year. Not ever again!

Azaria stepped inside, overwhelmed by the faces before her. The room was warm from the woodstove, and cinnamon and cloves mingled in the air. Were they actually celebrating Christmas? She felt betrayal seep through her jaded veins.

Starr rushed up to her first, and the sight of Luna's identical twin overwhelmed Azaria. She dropped to her knees unable to comprehend the cruelty of the Great Creator. She'd spent a life in devotion to the Goddess of All Things, but tonight felt bereft of any relationship to the divine.

They sobbed together, as everyone gathered around. A circle formed, holding them in a place of love. Astrid stayed in her wheelchair, but Bob pushed her closer. James had flown over as soon as he heard the news, and was here, with his arms around Ruby and Eliza-May. Bella was holding hands with Callum. Marion, Car, and Kara sat behind Azaria and held her.

"I'm sorry I didn't bring her home," Azaria cried. "She loved it there so much, it just didn't seem right. I'm so sorry. Please forgive me," she said.

"You did the right thing," Starr said. "It's hard, but you're right. She was so happy there. Has anyone heard from Patrick? I've sent dozens of messages on Facebook, but there's been no reply." "Not yet," Isaac sighed. "Not yet."

Everyone settled into their armchairs and sofas, and finally Azaria asked: "Why the hell is it still decorated in here?"

Ruby stood up and walked over to Azaria, then bent down at her feet. "Because Aunty Luna wants us to." Ruby pulled out a Christmas card that she'd received in the post from her.

> "Dear Ruby, I love that you're living in the mountains and can keep an eye on Ma for me. I know she won't be happy that I'm not there for Christmas, but there's no reason not to have a lovely celebration even though I'm far away. Don't open the parcel until you're all together. Promise me! Love you, Rubes. Have a fantastic Christmas, and just know, that no matter where I am, I'm always with you all. Aunty Luna."

So, this is what Christmas Eve looks like this year, Azaria thought to herself.

"Look Gran, there's the parcel. She addressed it to me. Do you want to open it?" Ruby asked.

"You open it, sweetheart." Azaria sank back into her chair. Feeling Isaac's hand on her shoulder, she looked up at him. He was like an angel who'd walked into her life at just the right time. Suddenly, she couldn't remember a time that he wasn't part of her world. It was odd, but at the same time felt completely normal.

Ruby pulled off the ribbon, and used Car's knitting scissors to free the tape from the edges.

There were lots of little parcels wrapped up, not addressed to anyone in particular, but with a note saying "Have fun, everyone!"

Ruby unwrapped them all, one at a time, proudly displaying the contents: a cuatro, maracas, rumba-shakers, and a tambourine. There were small lanterns from the Festival of Lights, a bamboo flute, four brightly coloured hammocks to drape between the apple trees, coffee liqueur, a jade necklace, a sling for the new baby, and a book of Honduran recipes.

Azaria found herself smiling, as each gift was unwrapped. They'd all been chosen with care and love. Even in death, Luna was still giving. Her heart as open and beautiful as it always had been. Azaria would have done anything to kiss her cheeks one last time. She felt the tears welling up again, and then said, much to her surprise, "I think we need some spicy mead, and we need to make a toast." She didn't dare reveal that Luna's first liquid, after mother's milk, was mead. Sure did cure those teething pains, and bless her, she slept soundly.

Azaria rose from her seat to gather the glasses and bottle, but Isaac said "You stay there, I'll find it." Again, he was pre-empting her needs and taking care of her. It was so easy to have him around. It was as if he'd tilted his whole life to be there for her.

Within a few minutes, glasses were raised and Luna's

love and life acknowledged. "Let's sing songs, Gran. She'd have loved us doing that."

"What was her favourite?" Isaac asked, not skipping a beat and warding Azaria off at the pass.

"Jingle Bells! She said it made her happy." Ruby clapped.

Azaria couldn't think of a less appropriate song to be singing right now, but managed to get herself over to the piano just as Starr began to play.

Somehow, everyone in the room managed to sing along with gusto. Azaria thought of Luna, and how, it was true, that Jingle Bells was her favourite Christmas song.

As she looked around the room, Azaria had to acknowledge that everyone had a smile on their face. How it was even possible seemed nothing short of a miracle. When the song ended, Ruby said "Let's sing it again!"

Azaria laughed. How blessed they were to have that child in their midst. She wasn't quite sure she felt the same way when they finished singing it after the tenth time.

Car brought out food for the table, and everyone gathered to enjoy Christmas Eve dinner. Food was passed around, and people helped themselves: slow-braised red cabbage and apple with nutmeg; stir-fried Brussels sprouts with garlic; parsnips in maple and orange; fluffy roast potatoes; and the feature dish: a chestnut-and-cranberry roast. Despite themselves, they all managed to enjoy their meal. Car served a plate up for Luna, and put it at the spot she usually sat.

Isaac's hand never left Azaria's thigh. *My right hand man*, she thought to herself.

A few days later, there was a knock at the front door. The postman held a large parcel. "I'm so sorry for your loss, Mrs Linden. The whole community is in shock. Please know that we're mourning with you. She was a beautiful young lady. Such a waste of a life. If there's anything

196

anyone can do, we will. You know that, don't you?"

"Thank you. Yes, I do." God, how often was she going to have to go through this? It was kind of people to offer their condolences, but it meant the wound was always there, always raw, always open like a carcass on the roadside.

The postman then looked a bit uncomfortable as he moved from one foot to another. His weight shifted, heavy as lead, from his left foot to his right. And back again. After several changes of position Azaria asked "Are you okay?"

He looked away for a moment, down the sweep of the hill, as if summoning his strength "There's a parcel for you in the van,"

"Okay," Azaria said. "I'll come out and get it."

"It's….it's from Luna."

She sighed, wondering if Luna's love letters would ever stop. Not that she wanted them to, but it was weird to keep hearing from someone who wasn't alive anymore.

"Probably got held up with all the Christmas post," she said, trying to appear upbeat. Azaria walked over to the van, hoping he'd follow. Her boots, crunching on the ice, reminded her to be careful; not of falling, but of letting her heart freeze over in order to numb the ache. It was okay to be sad, more than okay.

Carefully taking the box inside, she wondered what it could be. It wasn't light, and when Azaria looked at the value of the stamps on the box, she gasped. It would have cost more in postage than a flight home, she muttered. And then, with a heavy heart, she asked: *why didn't you come home, my darling?*

Isaac had been in the kitchen with Car, making leek-and-potato soup, but had a hunch to check on Azaria. He watched quietly from the bedroom door as she was unwrapping the parcel.

Inside was a large box, carved from Honduran mahogany. As she opened it, Azaria smiled. It housed

197

what looked like about fifty small dropper bottles. Lifting one up, she could see clearly why Luna was so desperate to send it to her. They were essences from native Honduran flowers.

She was immersed in the booklet which described each essence and the qualities it sought to heal, when Isaac came over. Azaria looked radiant, and when she explained what Luna had sent, Isaac said: "That love you feel from her, it's always going to be with you."

"I know that, I really do, it's just how I get through daily life knowing I'm never going to see her smile again. Sometimes I find myself staring at Starr too long, trying to capture something that I don't have anymore. They might have been impossible for me to tell apart by looks and voice, but in personality they were so different. One could never replace the other, and that's what I'm struggling with so much right now. Luna's gone."

"Yes, honey. She is. And in other ways, she can never leave." He pressed his hand tenderly over her heart. "She's always with you. Hold onto that."

Life was lived in slow motion for the next few weeks. An endless marshland of unsustainable sorrow. Jack Harrer, from the local beekeepers' association, popped by every other day to check on the bees, and two of the teenagers from the newspaper shop came from time to time to see if Azaria needed help with anything. Casseroles, flowers and candles were placed by the front door with notes of affection and sympathy.

Azaria wasn't sure if Astrid was still deteriorating. She went to the barn first thing each morning and gave her tinctures and essences. Bob was ever faithful, keeping Astrid company, reading her books, massaging her feet. Ruby habitually went over each evening and chatted. For hours. Car routinely brought her basket of knitting, and sat at the end of Astrid's bed so Bob could have a break

198

and go for a walk, or drive into town.

The days, like the bees, had their own particular hum. Grief was slow: sluggish, even. At some point, Azaria had to pull herself together. But when? How? That's what she kept asking herself.

Isaac had barely been to Appleseeds, instead choosing to spend his time at the homestead watching over Car, Azaria and Astrid.

"How is that healthstore functioning?" Azaria asked him over breakfast one late and remarkably sunny January morning.

"Marion is there most days, but Eliza-May has been a great help. She's fabulous with the customers. I think she's found it therapeutic to be doing something rather than sitting at home twiddling her thumbs. It seems to have really helped the relationship between her and Bella, too."

"I love that you've been here, night and day, to help me through this, but at some time you have to go back, and I have to find my own way."

"You are finding your way. It's just that it's not at the pace Azaria Linden would like. You're not being patient with yourself. And actually, I've been thinking a lot about the shop. Bella will need to finish working there before she has the baby. I reckon Eliza-May would make a great manager. If she accepts the offer, then I don't need to go back at all."

"What would you do?"

"If the only thing I did for the rest of my life was enjoy your company, that would be more than enough for me. Azaria Linden, would you do me the honour?"

"Are you proposing to me?"

"I am proposing that we spend the rest of our days together."

She laughed. "You're an incredible man, Isaac, but I'm not great company these days."

"So that's a yes, then?"

She laughed. He always made her smile.

"Azaria, life is different. You're different. But the woman I fell in love with, she's still there. Jaded, bruised, yes. But gorgeous, radiant, funny, wonderful... That's all still there. It just needs time to find its way to the surface again. I'm prepared to wait, no matter how long it takes. And if I can help you to laugh again, nothing would give me greater joy."

Before she had time to respond, Kara and Starr came into the kitchen to join them for breakfast. "I'm thinking of heading back to Zululand this week, Ma. Are you okay with that?"

"Yes. No. Honey, you girls have to do what is right for you. I only want you to be happy. That's all I've ever wanted. Can you promise me that?"

"I was happy before this happened, and I'm sure, in time, that I'll smile again."

"And you, Starr?"

"Ma, I just don't know. It feels wrong to be going back. Everything's different now. Everything! I had this huge offer before I left, but frankly, I don't know if I'm the girl for the job any more."

"What's the offer?" Isaac asked.

She couldn't help herself, but Starr's face lit up as soon as she started talking. "I've been offered the chance to write a series of articles that'll be syndicated worldwide, and there's even talk of it becoming a book. I have to write about the lives of seven people, and then find a theme that links them. I've no idea what that would be, but when I first heard I jumped at the possibility. My editor said I could still work at the paper, and he'd make sure I had the time available to work on this project too. What do you think, Ma?"

"I think that when the time is right for you, in your heart, that you'll be brilliant. My only caution is to make sure you're ready. Only you can know when that is."

"I haven't booked any flights back to Kununurra yet, but I know that I can't keep sitting here crying."

"Don't rush the process," Isaac cautioned. "Grief is your sabbatical to realign yourself and your values against the shock you had. Time can heal, but how long that takes is anyone's guess."

The Legacy

James Megane had taken long-service leave from his law firm, and spent the past few weeks staying in a hotel near his family. He was still trying to persuade Eliza-May to come back to New York, and that maybe more counselling would be helpful for her, not just about her hatred of city living, but the loss of her younger sister. She refused, and said this was her home now. Isaac had offered her the job of manager, and she was taking it. She also wanted to be near Bella and be part of her grandchild's life.

Bob and Astrid had arranged a meeting with James, and asked if he'd come to see them at the barn while he was still staying in the area. During a two-hour meeting, he helped put the legal framework in place for Astrid's dream: to set up a care home for single mothers. She had spent many times over the years wondering how different it might be for young mothers who, for whatever reason, were estranged from their families, and parenting alone, if they had somewhere to stay that nurtured them while they found their feet. Over the past few months she'd witnessed a huge transformation in Bella, not just because she was loved up by her new beau, but because she was loved. She had her own space, but knew without doubt that all around her were people who cared.

Bob, to his great delight, had discovered an old derelict farm, with barns, just a few miles the other side of town, and had put in an offer. The landowner accepted, and now Cottonwood Farm was theirs.

At some point, when the time was right and Bob had adjusted to life without Astrid, he'd begin work on repairing the buildings, and then hiring staff to help manage the place. For Astrid, it gave her life meaning. For Bob, it was his way of saying thank you to the woman who brought love into his life after a bitter divorce. For both of them, it was a legacy of their love.

After their meeting, they headed over to the homestead, and the three of them joined Car, who was on the veranda enjoying some late-Winter sunshine.

"That's quite a collection of knitting, Car," Bob said, admiring the basket of baby clothes.

"Just want to make sure that Bella doesn't need anything after the little one is here. It's the least I can do."

"They're beautiful, Mom. Just beautiful." Astrid looked her mother in the eyes and said, "A beautiful legacy."

"We all want to be remembered in our own ways, don't we?" She smiled, knowing what the meeting with James was about. "Is everything sorted then?"

"Yes, Cottonwood Farm will be set up as a charitable trust for single mothers." Astrid's breathing was heavy, but she still managed to smile. It brought her joy that she was able to bring something into the world which would make a difference, even though she'd never get to meet the people whose lives she'd touch. The farm would feature a dozen self-contained apartments and a communal kitchen and lounge.

"And when do I get a tour of this place?" Car asked, winking at Bob.

"Might be best when I've tidied it up a bit, I think. I wouldn't want you stepping on rusty nails."

"I'll have to be patient then."

Two cars pulled into the driveway.

"Visitors?" James asked.

"Yes, women from my knitting group. We've decided to start meeting here instead of at the café. You're welcome to join us. There are plenty of needles to go around."

James laughed and said, "Maybe another time. I've got a few things to do in town before I head back to New York. It was good seeing you, Car. Astrid, Bob, I'll see you again soon. Take care of yourselves." He had hoped to see Azaria, but she'd gone down to the spring with Isaac. James drove down the mountain, the loss of his sister-in-law, and the imminent death of another in the family, looming heavily on his mind.

The knitting ladies opted to head inside and enjoy the comfort of the woodstove. Bob wheeled Astrid inside to keep warm, and popped the kettle on to make everyone tea. He noticed his wife smiling, happy to observe the chatter around her. Astrid's had been a hard life, filled with emptiness and heartache, and now as the door to her earthly existence was being closed, she finally had everything she'd always dreamed of: to be back home.

Healing Waters

"You smell good," Isaac whispered as he sat in the warm medicinal waters with Azaria. Stretching out, he luxuriated in the way his muscles instantly relaxed.

"It's jasmine oil. I hoped it would ease the sadness a bit."

"And?"

"It's a work in progress," she smiled. "Gosh, I can't believe how long it's been since I was in here. I've missed this place."

"I can't believe you haven't shared it with me before now. You know, I think we might have to rendezvous here more often. It's not always easy to get time alone with you Azaria Linden, what with all the women in your family always around," he said, jokingly.

"Are you saying you want to have your wicked way with me, Mr Jameson? Because, if you are, there's only one answer: actions speak louder than words! I'm sitting here naked next to you…it's not like you even have to rip my clothes off."

He pulled her closer, enjoying her sexual taunts. There she was: there was the Azaria he'd fallen in love with. She was trying, every day she was trying. And bit by bit the light shone a little brighter. And then, just when he thought she was finding her balance again in life, she'd sink back some more. There, almost there, and then back again. Just like a baby's first tooth. Seen, and unseen. There, and not there. Up and down. Discomfort, ease. Pain, triumph.

Enjoying the feel of his bare skin against hers, she leant into him until there was no space between them. They'd only ever made love once: that night on the beach in Roatan. They'd spent every night together since then, but neither of them attempted anything beyond a hug.

A slip of a crescent Moon sailed through the sunny afternoon sky, nothing more than a flirtatious wink in the heavens. These were the waters she'd birthed her twin babies in, and now she shared this sacred space with her lover. The air was cool, but the water more than warm enough. Kissing her shoulders, Isaac murmured. "You're the most beautiful woman on this Earth, Azaria. I can barely contain myself when I look at you, but it's more than that. Even if I were a blind man, I'd still see you as beautiful. You leave traces of gold dust wherever you go. Azaria, will you marry me?"

"I thought you already proposed to me?"

"I'm still waiting for your answer."

"I thought I'd said yes."

"I want to hear it again. I want to hear you say yes every day of my life."

Isaac kissed the nape of her neck, and then nibbled at her soft downy earlobe.

"Yes," she sighed, sinking into the deep honey-amber of his eyes.

As his hand cupped one of her ample breasts, the other hand wrapped around her waist and pulled her closer.

"Yes," her word barely audible.

The nape at the top of her legs began to throb. How was she going to keep standing when her legs were turning to jelly?

"Will you spend every day letting me love you?" he asked, his kisses moving down her neck and over her shoulder.

"Yes," she cried, tears of joy slipping down her cheeks.

"And Azaria, will you promise to keep doing all the things in your life that you love, and grow with me through the seasons?"

"Yes, I will."

Isaac's soft caresses eased down from her breast to her waist. "Will you let me hold you each night as you fall asleep?"

"Yes, you may."

He sighed, a dam of erupting pleasure tormenting his breath. Isaac wanted to be inside Azaria now; he wanted to be fully united. A small groan left his lips.

"Yes?" she asked, teasingly.

"Azaria…" He lifted her up, wrapping her long legs around him. "If I don't make love to you now I'm going to explode."

"Yes," she laughed.

Gently bringing her down closer, he eased inside her warmth. Slowly. Sweetly. Seductively.

"Yes," she moaned into the afternoon sunshine. "Yes."

Hidden away in the secluded spring, their modesty protected by the swoon and sway of ancient Rocky Mountain white pines, they surrendered into the bliss of loving each other until there was nothing left to do but become one.

"Yes," she whispered, kissing his brow. Her climax shocked both of them, coming from an unknown place deep inside. A place where she wasn't anyone's daughter or sister or mother. A place where she was, simply, a lover. Here, in the seclusion of the wilderness, in a place that was so familiar to her, Azaria Linden crossed to the other side in her ecstasy, and there was no part of her soul that didn't belong to Isaac Jameson.

She closed her eyes, and sent a prayer to Luna: *still reckon I'm rockin' it like a goddess?*

"It will always be yes," she laughed, sated. "Oh," she moaned, "I could get used to that. You're good, Mr Jameson. Real good."

He laughed, and brushing her damp long silver hair back from her face, said "I love you so much. I've waited, for what feels like forever, to find a woman like you. I had years of doubting it would ever happen. Who knew it would be so easy?"

207

The Call of the Ancestresses

Their relationship rose to a higher octave, and despite her ailing sister being nearby, Azaria surrendered to the thrill and pleasure of being in love. If this was her consolation prize for having lost a child, then she was damn well going to grab it with both hands. Isaac was both her anchor, and a safe port, in the storm of life. His shining, smiling eyes were the first thing she saw when she awoke each morning. He was always there, already awake, smiling lovingly at her.

"What are you looking at?" she asked him each morning.

"The most beautiful woman in the world." His reply was always the same, and every time she laughed, because she knew that when he said those words they *were* true. She felt beautiful. Wounded, but beautiful. Somehow, even though her wings were damaged and crushed, there had to be a place within her that could still fly.

After they made the bed together that morning, Azaria sprinkled drops of lavender oil onto the pillows. She hadn't done that in months, but as she did so the fragrance made her think of all the years she'd performed this simple ritual on her children's bed linen. Luna loved it, and when she moved away from home she said she couldn't sleep peacefully until she sprinkled lavender oil on her bedding.

And then, as if a long-forgotten song started playing in her heart, Azaria felt drawn outside. Without saying a word, Isaac followed her. He knew that look. It was a look that said she'd had a good idea but couldn't put it into words. Attuned to her every movement, he stayed just a few steps behind. With speed in her step, she hurried off the veranda, and then started running up towards the top meadow. The Sun was bright, though the day was still cool. Isaac had grabbed her coat from the rack, and raced up the field. He watched as she swiftly circled around the field, looking in the distance, then counting steps. Back and forward, around. Then, stopping. Desperate to put the coat around her shoulders, he walked closer. Quietly, gently, he draped it around her. Azaria smiled, and said "YES!"

Instinctively, he knew it wasn't about their relationship, but he was at a loss to know what she meant.

"I'm going to leave a legacy for Luna. A labyrinth. I'll grow it from lavender. She slept better with lavender and now I know she'll be able to rest in peace. And when I need calming, or any of the people in this family need to feel close to Luna, we can come here and walk the path."

"What do you need?" he asked, ever his practical self.

"Shovels, plenty of shovels. We can ring around and organise a working bee. We can spend the day all together, digging holes and planting lavender. I'll pop down to the nursery today and place a bulk order for good-sized lavender plants. What do you think?" she asked, as he stood there quietly, stroking her hair.

"Yes." Tenderly, he traced his finger down her cheek. "Yes."

He held her for the longest time, grateful to be alive. Grateful to have found his soulmate. Grateful that she was finding a way to literally dig herself out of the torment.

"I'll start making some calls. When do you want to do this?"

"The crescent Moon is a call to action. The next one will be in Gemini. An air sign, it rules flowers, so we can be sure that planting those lavender pots then will get them off to a good start and bring us beautiful blossoms."

Isaac smiled not only at her indepth understanding of the Moon's signs and shifting energies, but how she actively worked with them, even in her grief. Not once had she dismissed Grandmother Moon, even though she

209

had the power to move the tides and heave tectonic plates, and had caused the world to cave in beneath her.

Something shifted within Azaria that day. It wasn't huge, but enough to make her believe in something greater than herself. She'd heard the song of the ancestresses calling her, and whisper the words: *lavender bed* into her heart. It was one thing to have her family around, and to know she wasn't alone on this journey, but to have invisible family there at her every turn gave Azaria a new confidence. Maybe Luna had been right. Maybe Jake had been with her at the hour of death.

She replayed their final moments together, that god-awful day in the reckless rubble of Roatan. *Dad said you got the apples he left you.* And then, like discovering a long-lost puzzle piece, she finally understood.

Azaria fell back onto her bottom and started laughing. She hadn't laughed this hard in a long time. "Yes, I got the apples!" It all made sense now: her new-Moon wishes on the apple twigs near Car's 80th birthday, and then Isaac buying Appleseeds Health Store, and bringing her a box of apples the first day they met. Jake was giving his blessing. He was wishing her well with Isaac.

Isaac looked on in disbelief. It wasn't every day he got to see a beautiful 57-year-old woman lying in a field, laughing.

"Are you okay?" he asked, wondering just what he'd got himself involved in. He fell in love with her all over again, watching her laugh like that, her tinsel-coloured hair flicking in the wind, and tears rolling down her cheeks.

"I'm perfectly okay. I'll tell you later," she said, and kept laughing.

"Can anyone join this party?" he asked.

"Come here, you," she said, reaching her hand up to his and pulling him down beside her on the ground.

210

The Wise Crone

It was The Mystic's Moon that brought Car and Azaria together under the trees that chilly February evening. The balsamic moon, an archetype of being in the embers, guided Azaria's initiation.

She'd been delaying her Wise Crone ceremony for several weeks now. It just hadn't seemed appropriate given the circumstances. Something about it had seemed selfish. But when she woke that beautiful February morning, she knew that today was the day. She wasn't going to call her friends, but instead asked Car to join her under the limber pines where the snow buttercups were blooming.

It was early evening, and they'd brought a flask of raspberry-leaf tea, and lit some candles in old glass jars. They talked about what it meant to be a wise crone. "Our ancestresses, all those gorgeous women before us, knew her not only as the leader or elder of the community, but as a healer and teacher." Car said, knowing full well that Azaria didn't need any education about this rite of passage.

"It's different, though, isn't it Mom? There's no sudden moment when you go *oh, this is my last period.* Not much different to when a child weans themselves. It just happens softly and quietly without fuss. You barely notice the goodbye. I feel a bit lost without my Moon clock. It's been there for more than forty years of my life, and now it's gone."

"The Moon hasn't gone, though. You have always lived with her rhythms. That won't change. It's just that you won't have that red flag waving at you every month." Car smiled, her silver twisted locks shining by candlelight, like the beacon of a lighthouse protecting sailors from the shore, and said, "I'm so pleased you've decided to go ahead and celebrate your Wise Crone. I know our bodies change, and they aren't what they used to be, but we're still beautiful, Azaria. It's a different sort of beauty. We're never too old to dance, my love."

They shared stories, drank tea, sang songs, and then Car presented Azaria with a flower crown, and invited her to cross over and join the wise ones.

Car smiled, and whispered: "The women in this family always look amazing with flowers in their hair."

A silver tear, ever so silently, slipped down the side of Car's cheek.

The Father's Daughter Moon

When James Megane left the city one last time, he knew he wasn't leaving just a well-established career behind, but starting a brand-new life. He was reclaiming his family, and becoming the husband and father he always knew, in his heart, that he was meant to be.

Taking a couple of young interns with him, he set up a practice in the heart of town. Each day, he'd go into Appleseeds Health Store and buy lunch. Eliza-May's face would light up, and she'd smile shyly. She wasn't taking him back just yet, but she loved how hard he was trying. The way she figured it, she deserved at least a few months of wooing. James was prepared to wait. Eliza-May was worth it.

Isaac had bought the shop next to Appleseeds, and was expanding the business to twice its current size. He was impressed by Eliza-May's invaluable managerial skills, especially as he found himself spending more and more time at Azaria's home.

After work, James would leave the office, and his briefcase, behind. He'd take the steps at the back of the healthstore and go up to Bella's flat. Heavily pregnant, now, Bella was grateful to have her father around. James came in each evening to help with chores and check she was okay. He needn't have bothered, really, as Callum had moved in, and made sure he finished work at the pool at 5pm sharp every day. The smile on Bella's face when she saw her dad, meant that James continued the daily ritual even though he was no longer the main man in his daughter's life.

Bella revelled in all the attention, and blossomed. When James came up the stairs that afternoon, he wondered what all the banging was about.

"Oh Dad, look at this. Look at what Callum and Isaac have built me!"

There, in the centre of the lounge room, was a home-made birthing pool built from plywood and pond liner.

"The midwife reckons she's going to hire them to build a whole bunch for her so she can lend them out to her other clients. I'm so excited, Dad. I can't wait for this baby."

"Don't be in too much of a hurry, darling. Once that baby's here, time will speed up even more."

He gave her a long hug, content she was happy and safe, and then headed back to the house he'd bought. Alone.

Luna's Labyrinth

It was late one afternoon, and sullen clouds skulked across the southern sky. The overcast horizon with its pewter and ash hues was like lead against the day. Rain was nearby, Azaria could smell it in the air. Undaunted by lightning forks, she checked each of the beehives, and secured some of the skeps against the incoming storm. Settling on an old tree stump, she breathed in deeply and began to talk to the bees.

"I'm sorry I've neglected you lately. My daughter Luna has died, and I can't get used to her being in the spirit world. Life feels so different without her. I'm different. And yet, I'm still the same. That's what I find so difficult. I don't know who I am anymore now that my baby girl has left this world," she sobbed softly. "I can still smell her hair, and hear her laughter. When the phone rings, I always expect it to be Luna telling me about her day. And then I remember..."

Azaria spoke for some time, and just as she was ready to leave the field, three bees settled on her thigh. Smiling, she whispered, "You heard me."

Azaria worked diligently to put plans in place for the labyrinth working bee. Isaac had phoned everyone on her list, asking if they'd like to be part of creating this unique memorial, and Azaria marked out the path, ordered 500 four-year-old lavender plants, and bought several spades from the hardware store. She'd emailed people her reasoning for the labyrinth, and shared the significance it had had throughout history.

> Dear friends and family, Luna's labyrinth will be both a personal declaration to her life and beauty, but also open to people who feel the

215

need to surrender to the ancient and sacred spiritual path. Unlike a maze, there are no tricks, no decisions to be made. It is about surrendering to our path. I hope you'll join me. Love, Azaria.

Azaria had mown the labyrinth path through the long grasses, and marked out clearly where the lavender plants would go, and where the path would be. Her letter explained that walking the labyrinth was about learning to walk, one step at a time, just like she was trying to do since Luna died. A living metaphor for life's journey, she wrote, this one path leads us to the heart. It is the journey each of us takes to the centre — our centre — and back out again to the world. A place for reflection, she added, throughout the ages, it has been considered to be a walking prayer.

Azaria shared the astrological symbolism of the seven-circuit labyrinth, and how it correlated to the seven visible planets. As above, so below. To walk the labyrinth, was to walk the heavens. She hoped, with all her heart, that it would be like walking with Luna, wherever she was now. She omitted the other references to seven: musical tones, days of the week, colours, and chakras. But she tucked their symbolism into her heart.

Words couldn't begin to explain that the labyrinth produces an energy field that calms mind and body, and balances one's thoughts so that intuition can flow freely. It was people's willingness to be part of the creation that was important to her.

The Sun shone brightly that Spring morning, the day of the labyrinth.

Azaria thanked everyone for coming. She talked about the labyrinth model, and its three stages of the spiritual path: walking inwards represents *letting go*. Standing in the centre gives us *insight and clarity*. Walking out is about *integrating*, and then taking action out in the world.

Everyone listened attentively, even the children. Astrid sat in her wheelchair, rugged up against the cool Spring air, unable to physically help, but deeply moved by the lengths Azaria was going to in order to honour the life of her youngest daughter: her baby. Reflecting on the daughter she gave up, all those years ago, Astrid let herself, for the first time since that fateful day, cry over her lost years of motherhood.

The day was long, having started at 8am. People worked reverently, and yet there was laughter and joking, and a light atmosphere carried the day along on a breeze of birdsong, wispy clouds, and a belief in something more powerful than mundane life. Azaria could sense that people were keen to see the labyrinth completed, and to try the walk for themselves. Isaac had, with several other men, moved dozens of barrows of shredded bark between the lavender plants, so people had the option of walking the labyrinth barefoot. Azaria couldn't help notice how he kept looking at his watch. Irritation nipped at the edges of her mind. He'd been so attentive and desperate to help, but now she was wondering what was going on. Did he have somewhere else to be?

Looking at his watch once more, Isaac smiled. She couldn't understand that satisfied look on his face. Pushing the empty wheelbarrow, he brushed by Azaria and said "I'll be back in a few minutes."

She watched him walking out of the meadow, past the herb gardens, and towards the old homestead. At that moment, she saw an unfamiliar vehicle pull up. Everyone was here, so who could possibly be turning up at the back end of the day? Watching the car door open, she saw Isaac shake hands, and then he hugged the visitor. He'd made no mention that he was expecting someone. The two figures reached into the van, and then carefully placed something, which looked rather heavy, into the barrow. Slowly, they made their way towards the labyrinth. It was only when

217

they were several metres away that Azaria recognised the man: Patrick. It was Patrick!

She fell to her knees. After all their attempts to reach Patrick, she'd given up. But here, on the very day they were creating a memorial to Luna, the love of Patrick's life, he was here. Unable to speak, Patrick came and sat in front of her. "Mrs Linden," Patrick sobbed. He didn't care that there were more than thirty people in the meadow watching him. He cried like a baby, unrestrained tears adorning the sacred soil of Luna's labyrinth, the grief of the past few months escaping like a dam wall breaking. Patrick had been putting off this moment for what seemed like a lifetime, not because he was a coward, but because the torment of meeting the family of the woman he was destined to marry simply seemed impossible; cruel, even.

"I'm so sorry. I just wasn't coping. She was everything to me. I loved her more than you could possibly imagine. I still can't believe she's gone."

Feeling Isaac's safe and secure hands around her waist, Azaria spoke softly. "I understand, Patrick. I really do. It's just so hard."

They sat for some time, consoling each other, while the team of helpers put the final touches to the labyrinth.

"I've brought something. I hope you don't mind. When Isaac said what you were creating here, I wanted to contribute in some way." He gestured weakly towards the wheelbarrow that Isaac had pushed up from the car. Azaria stood up, and walked over. She gasped, her hand firmly in place over her mouth. The resemblance was astounding. So accurate, that she nearly fainted, but Isaac was there, *always there*, to keep her standing.

In exquisite detail, a life-sized bust of Luna's head and upper torso was made from clear and coloured glass. She lay there, in perfect stillness, sleeping in a bed of grass and wildflowers, all sculpted in the finest detail.

"It's extraordinary."

218

Patrick pulled a photo out of his pocket. It was what the sculptor had used to make the model. Patrick gave her the photo to keep.

"I wondered if you might want to have the model here, with the labyrinth. I understand if you don't want to, or if it's not suitable," he added, wondering if it was too much. Too much of a constant reminder of their loss.

"It's perfect. We can place it in the centre, by the wooden seat Isaac carved." She hugged Patrick for the longest time. His sweet smile and kind heart were so obvious from the second she'd met him. No wonder Luna had been so happy.

Marion arrived from the house with a barrow full of glass jars with wire handles, and dozens of beeswax tealight candles. The Sun reluctantly slid towards the horizon. Night was starting to draw in. If they wanted to walk the labyrinth, they'd need a lot of candles. There wouldn't be much light from the Moon tonight. Isaac and Patrick walked in the labyrinth, each step mindful and purposeful, and laid Luna to rest in the centre. Azaria watched as Isaac leant down and kissed her forehead. Patrick did the same. And then, together, they walked back out to the onlookers. Marion handed everyone the makeshift lanterns. She'd also brought Thermoses filled with hot chai tea.

February had brought another month of unending tears...but tonight, tonight as they walked, the tears were an offering to Mother Earth. A dedication to Luna Mahalia Linden. Each person, in turn, walked the labyrinth. Beneath the stars, Azaria felt the love of her family and her community surround her. This was the funeral they were never able to have for Luna. Tonight she was honoured in a way no one would ever forget. She watched the way Patrick looked at Starr, trying to take in every last detail as if he were watching Luna for the last time. Azaria felt his pain, and knew exactly what he was doing.

219

When everyone had completed the walk, they gathered together beneath the crescent Moon to listen to Car speak. She held her drum and spoke calmly while softly beating the skin. The gentle rhythm mesmerised everyone.

"That pulsing sound, it reminds us of something. Something deep and primordial," she said, her voice soft and clear beneath the starlight. In her heart, she knew Luna was near, listening to her every word.

"Our mother's heartbeat, pulsing blood around her body, is the first sound we ever hear. It was the first sound our Luna heard. As we listen to this rhythm, let us remember her beautiful life, and how every day she smiled and blessed this world with her vibrancy and gorgeousness. None of that was in vain. She gave us something. Something priceless. Her love will never leave us." Car continued to beat her drum into the still and silent night. "We drum because it is a sound at the core of all creation, no matter where in the world we are from. It's ancient. It's rhythmic. It is also the sound of our own heartbeat. Let us use this time to heal our pain, to find ways to move forward. To take the love from Luna we were blessed to receive, and share that love with other people." She smiled, and looking around the circle of people, said: "Our Luna has a million names now, and she flies free. She's wild like the wind. Our job is to let her be free, not to hold her back. To cherish our priceless memories, but to let her go."

Patting her drum, with symbols of red flowers adorning the skin, Car stroked out each beat, lulling everyone into a state of deep inner peace. Like a Goddess in the starlight, her gaze showed a woman who knew death was not to be feared, but embraced. Catching the eye of Astrid, she said "I know there is beauty in the Earth's fault lines, even though it has shaken us all to the core, and I know that devastating bush fires bring new flowers to life. Out of chaos, comes life. Death and birth are one and the same."

220

The Springtime

Behind Closed Doors

Starr lounged about in the colourful Honduran hammock she'd strung up on the veranda, daydreaming about Luna and watching Astrid and Car curled up together on the porch swing. She thought just how different Astrid looked with her shaved head. Reflecting on her own hair: shiny, healthy, long brown locks to the base of her spine, it struck Starr just how much of one's identity is tied up with the hairstyle we choose. She'd always shared the same style as Luna. Part of it was to make it impossible for anyone to tell them apart. She smiled at all the tricks they'd played over the years.

Admiring Car's silver locks, she wondered: how many grandmothers have dreadlocks? Car wore them like an ancient priestess, often with a wildflower and colourful glass beads threaded through them.

And then, Starr had an idea!

It was an hour after her grief-counselling session when she sat in the hairdressers' salon. Eyes, red from crying, saw the future clearly. Azaria had insisted she have weekly sessions until she felt like some real healing was taking place. Starr wasn't convinced they'd made a jot of difference.

When the hairdresser, who was reluctant to even touch such beautiful hair, finally put down her scissors, Starr said "I love it!" She knew, however, that Azaria would be devastated by the new pixie haircut, so she spent a couple of hours walking by the river. It gave her plenty of time to think. At some point, she needed to decide if she was going back to Australia, or if she'd relinquish the golden opportunity that had been offered to her and settle back in Colorado.

Sitting on some granite rocks, she watched the rapidly flowing water. Looking up high above her to the snow-capped mountains, she breathed in the alpine air. Oh how she loved this place. It would be hard to leave.

"I miss you, sis," she said out loud. "I really miss you. These have been the darkest days of my life, and I haven't even had you to talk to about it. I feel scared to move forward with my life, because I feel like I have to live two lives. My life, of course, but yours, too. You were meant to get married and have babies and live happily ever after. I can't do that for you. You know I'm not the settling down type, but I will live each day knowing that I'm living it for you, too."

Starr arrived back at the homestead, her thoughts clear, and found Azaria and Isaac tending the herb gardens. Starr walked up and waited for Azaria to turn around. When she did, Azaria cried. "Your hair! Your beautiful hair."

"It's okay, Ma. It will grow back, if I decide to do that."

"You look…so different." What she wanted to say was: you don't look like Luna. *How will I remember Luna?* She bit her tongue. Starr was not Luna's replacement, and Azaria knew that. Her thoughts were entirely selfish. But oh God, how it hurt.

"I've made a decision," Starr said, her voice soft and quiet. Her hand brushed the sage leaves near her knee. "I'm going back to Australia. I'm really sorry, but I need to do this."

"There's nothing to apologise for, honey. This is your life, not mine."

"I want to take this syndication offer. I know what I want to write about. And I know I'll be good at it."

Isaac asked "Do you fancy telling us or is it a secret?" He knew Azaria wasn't in any state to speak.

"Well, in some ways it's secret. But I can tell you! The

theme will be Behind Closed Doors. All these counselling sessions I've had have felt like being trapped behind a door. The counsellor just nods, and I want to scream at her. I want her to tell me how to walk out of this hellhole of pain that I'm trapped in. I may as well be talking to the wall for all the good she's doing. I'm sharing all these painful feelings in secret, out of the way, when what I want to do is shout to the world about how much pain I'm in. Some days I want to yell at people in the street and say 'Why are you laughing? Don't you know my sister has died?' I'm just so angry! I want to shine a light on those hidden-away places in the world."

Isaac stepped away from the rosemary bushes he'd been tidying, and came over to hug Starr. "I'm so pleased for you. That's a wonderful idea to work with. We're really proud of you, aren't we Azaria?"

She nodded her head in agreement, but the words refused to come out. Another loss. Another little death in her life. When was this going to end? When would her days be peaceful again? Whatever happened to the perfect life she used to have? Damn it!

"Is it okay if I stay another week or two? I'm hoping I might have myself a baby niece or nephew to cuddle before I go!"

Stay as long as you want, is what Azaria wanted to say, but she simply nodded.

Baby Moon

Late March came dancing along with a skip in its step saying: *Look what I've brought for you!* The days were unseasonally warm, and Azaria felt a lightness to her heart now that she was able to spend more time outside in the gardens: sunshine on her skin, and hands in the soil.

Azaria had sent Isaac to town with a basket of items for Bella. There were herbal tinctures, pots of honey, bags of raspberry-leaf tea, and baby clothes. Each time there was a delivery of birth-related items, Azaria was sure to include books. Each of them shared similar themes on instinctive parenting, like sleeping with your baby, wearing a sling, natural immunity, and full-term breastfeeding. Talking to the bees that morning, Azaria said: "We have a new baby coming into the family. Maybe she'll be a beekeeper. Or he." Then she laughed. Of course it wouldn't be a boy!

For hours she ambled around the hives, enjoying the scent of pine wafting on the breeze. The simple life of these industrious insects never failed to amaze her.

Astrid had seemed particularly bright that morning, and Azaria was somewhat thrown by how good her sister looked. Her life had been hanging on a thread for months now. Perhaps she was waiting for the baby, too, before leaving.

Sitting by a small altar near the colourful chakra hives, Azaria began tidying up the gifts she'd left for the bees. The delicate pink flowers of a calypso orchid near the base of a pine tree caught her eye. *Fairy slipper*, she whispered. *The baby must be near.*

Azaria reflected on the idea that her sister was about to leave this earthly plane, and a baby was about to be born. Life never stands still, she said to herself. She got up and started walking back to the homestead when she noticed

Isaac jogging into the meadow. Savouring every second of his gorgeousness, she melted into his smile. Handsome. Lithe. Fit. Strong. And damn sexy.

"Bella is in labour."

"How lovely. That's wonderful. Is she okay?"

"She's fine, but the midwife has got chickenpox, and Bella is refusing to have the back-up midwife. Eliza-May is there. We closed the shop. Bella wants you."

"I'm not a midwife."

"I think Bella's words were: any woman who can give birth in a hot spring is a midwife."

Isaac drove carefully down the mountainside, ensuring the midwife beside him wasn't flustered by the time she got to the little flat above the healthstore.

"I thought this baby would come at night time, not by day," Azaria said, confused by the timing.

"She's only just gone into labour, it could be a while yet," Isaac suggested.

"Yes, you're right. It's just that the women in my family tend to birth quickly."

"Should I be driving faster?" he asked.

"YES!"

"If the baby comes today, it will be born under the Weaver's Moon. Quite a shy child."

Behind closed curtains, in the peaceful ambience of the bohemian-styled lounge room, Bella laboured long into the afternoon, but her patience was wearing thin. Callum massaged her back, pouring warm water down her spine every few minutes. James and Eliza-May stayed out in the courtyard, giving them privacy. Isaac and Azaria busied themselves in the kitchen, always within earshot, but not distracting the birth process. Azaria wasn't a midwife, but she was clear about the three needs of a woman in labour. Her goal was to give Bella as much privacy, quiet and darkness as possible.

The mountains, like curtains announcing the end of a scene, declared daylight to be over as the Sun slipped away; and as day gave way to night, Azaria came and sat by her granddaughter.

"You're doing so well. The baby will come when it's ready. I don't think it's far away now. Just keep breathing, honey."

"I asked Great-Granny Car to choose a name for the baby," Bella confided between contractions.

"Oh, you didn't want to choose one yourself?"

"I had lots of names I liked, but I knew Car would find something perfect."

"And has she?"

"Chandra. It means Moon Shining. She showed me a special book she had from India. It's an old Sanskrit name. She's been knitting all these lovely clothes for the baby. I know it's a legacy she wants to leave, and they're wonderful." Bella stopped to breathe through another contraction. "I wanted her to feel like she was investing in this baby. That life will still keep going. It's so hard watching her saying goodbye to Astrid."

Azaria felt her legs quiver. "Yes, honey, it's hard saying goodbye to your child. But right now, we're going to focus on you saying hello to yours."

She gently reached down into the birthing pool and felt between Bella's legs. "Hey," she smiled. "Reach down and feel your baby's head."

Bella's face lit up as she touched the bulge between her legs. "That's my baby?"

Azaria nodded, the smile on her face warming Isaac's heart.

"What if it's a boy?" Bella asked.

"Honey, the odds of anyone in our family having a boy are pretty slim!"

As Chandra Eloise was lifted out of the water deftly

227

by Callum, who was so proud he nearly burst, and put into Bella's arms, Azaria cried. Her first great grandchild. The joy filling the room that evening was incomparable. Birthing by candlelight, Bella had pushed her baby into the world, all the while laughing at how incredible it felt.

"That was amazing! I want to do it again!"

Eliza-May and James looked at each other.

"Oh my beautiful baby, look at you. You are amazing. I love you so much." Bella cried as she looked her baby over, counting the tiny toes and fingers, and watching the little dimple on her chin. "Mom, look at my baby. Dad, come and see your granddaughter. Isn't she gorgeous?"

"She looks just like you, sweetie," he said.

"I want Rubes, Starr, Astrid and Bob, and Great-Granny Car to meet Chandra. Can we go and see them?"

Azaria stood up, wrapping a towel around mother and baby's shoulders. And then she gasped. Chandra had a wee birthmark in exactly the same place that Luna had had hers. It seemed too coincidental, and she had to stop herself from feeling dizzy.

"They can come and visit you," Azaria replied calmly. "What's important right now is that we keep you both safe and cosy for a good few weeks. You'll have plenty support from all of us, but we don't want you overwhelmed with visitors. Just enjoy your Babymoon. You'll never get these precious days back again."

So Bella and Chandra lay in bed, their breastfeeding relationship off to a fine start. Callum met their every need. For three weeks, they never ventured far from their family bed or the little courtyard downstairs, where they soaked up rays of Spring sunshine. All the women in the family brought soups and salads, and Bella and her baby thrived on having daily massages. Some days she thought about Smudge, and that horrible thing that happened in the hayshed, and then, looking at the most beautiful girl in the world, gave thanks.

228

***

The family gathered on the veranda at the old homestead one particularly vibrant Spring morning, the day Azaria dreaded, and teary eyed they prepared to say goodbye to Starr.

Five generations of women, from Car to Azaria and Astrid, to Eliza-May and Starr, and to Bella and Ruby, and to baby Chandra, all gathered on the Lafferty Homestead veranda.

"Are you sure you don't want me to take you to the airport," Azaria asked for the thirty-sixth time that day.

"No, Ma. I want to leave by cab. I want this memory, of my family, all here, on the veranda. I need this."

Everyone went back for second hugs, and thirds. The cab driver popped his head out of the car window and asked "What time did you say the airport shuttle leaves town?"

"I'm coming," she said impatiently, and turning to her mother one last time, wiped the tears off Azaria's cheeks.

Starr went and stood by the cab, wanting to leave her mother with words she could hold onto. Words that would have meaning.

"I don't know when I'll be back again, but just look for me under the silver Moon, and I'll be there. I'm always there, Ma. That's what you've taught me my whole life. That's where all us Linden girls hang out, you used to say. That hasn't changed. It never will."

"Under the Moon," Azaria whispered, nodding her head, tears flooding her dress, and squeezing Isaac's hand until it turned white.

About the Author

Veronika Robinson is an Australian writer who lives a soul-filled life in rural Cumbria, in the far north of England. Her favourite things: home, family, Monday mornings, the scent of a eucalyptus forest after a storm, kittens, lightning, ripe mango, reading by a crackling woodstove, hot sunshine, a meadow of wildflowers, cosy bookshops, friendly people, lazy Sundays, friends over for dinner, cello music, the soft light of the Moon, beeswax candles and sunrise. She is a hopeless romantic,  and although she's happy to buy and grow her own flowers, isn't averse to being swept off her feet by a good belly laugh and a box of dark ginger chocolate. Veronika is married to her soulmate, and together they have two daughters.

You can sign up to Veronika's mailing list if you wish to be kept informed of book tours and new books, and you can follow her on Facebook and Twitter.
Facebook: Veronika Sophia Robinson, author
Twitter: @VeronikaSophia
Blog: http://veronikarobinson.com/blog/
email: veronikarobinson@hotmail.com

If you enjoyed Sisters of the Silver Moon, look out for:

Book Two: *Behind Closed Doors*
Book Three: *Flowers in Her Hair*

Author photograph: David Hollins

Acknowledgements

My darling Paul. There can't be many men in this world who would encourage their wives to prioritise writing over housework. I love that you value my creativity, and boy do I love you! When I write lovely men into my stories, all I have to do is think of you: your humour, love, kindness, compassion and awareness have been the foundation of our amazing marriage. Thank you, sweetheart.

Sara Simon: how blessed am I to have you in my life, both personally and professionally? Thank you! I can't imagine my books without your artwork. You inspire me and support me in so many ways. Thank you for yet another fabulous cover!

Denise Ridgway and Mandy Bingham, my gorgeous friends, thank you with all my heart for being the first people to read my manuscript. I bit all my fingernails off waiting for your feedback! Mandy, thank you so much for gifting this story with your beautiful, soul-stirring song *Under The Same Sky*.

My daughters, Bethany and Eliza: your creativity inspires me every day. Thank you for being the catalyst to my life as an author.

My soul sisters, near and far. You know who you are. Thank you for everything you bring to my life. You're amazing. And my blood sisters, Heidi Anita and Ramona Rebecca, I love you.

My mother, Angelikah. Thank you for all those moments after school, when we'd sit in the kitchen, and you'd inspire me with my creative writing. I shall treasure those memories always.

A special thanks to Paul and Eliza for proofreading.

About the Cover Artist

Sara Simon is an artist, illustrator, writer and mother from Yorkshire. She works in a teeny studio in a creative little household on the edge of the Peak District, UK, with her husband and two sons, and can see the Sun rise over the hills from her drawing board.

She has illustrated several fiction and non-fiction books for Veronika Robinson.

She loves trees, long walks, wild swimming, the sky, gardening, the sea, canoeing, camping, chocolate, cats, and reading with a torch way after bedtime. She doesn't like cooking (except cake), driving, jazz, hospitals, or being cold.

Sara's artistic career has come full circle from pencil and paper, drawing everything that stayed put for longer than two minutes; through computer-based design for print and the Internet and the high-pressure world of advertising; and then back home to the easel, in colourful paint-stained trousers, dipping her paintbrush in her tea.

About the Songwriter

Hailing from the North Coast of Ireland, Mandy is the eldest daughter of singer-songwriter David McWilliams (Days of Pearly Spencer). Her mother, Gil McWilliams, was also involved in the folk-music scene in the 60s and 70s. This cultural and family heritage is inherent in her songwriting. Mandy writes her songs very much from the heart. With her acoustic guitar and her wealth of life experience, she creates beautifully formed lyrics and melodies. It is music that captures the light, depth, and time capsules that mould us into who we are. Her voice is pure and strong and can't help but make an emotional connection to the listener. In everything, Mandy is accompanied by her husband Graham, who sings harmonies, plays acoustic guitar and lap-steel guitar. Graham also has an integral role in the arrangement and development of new songs. Mandy's debut recording is available through her website www.mandybingham.co.uk and digitally through iTunes and Amazon.

"Mandy's voice is clear, folky, sincere, deceptively strong, and incredibly easy to listen to. "- Creative voices NI.

"Addictive country blues music"– Gigging NI

"A real talent, such mature songwriting…." – Ralph McLean, BBC Radio Ulster

Reader Questions

Q: *Which subject do you feel most passionate writing about?*
A: Anything which touches the soul, so in that sense it doesn't matter if I'm writing fiction or non-fiction. In a nutshell: it's about what it means to be human.

Q: *You write in many different forms (cookbook, fiction, non-fiction, articles). Do you have a favourite, and if so what makes it stand out for you?*
A: For me, writing is like music. It's completely mood dependent. I never imagined I'd write fiction, but now it feels like the place I'm most comfortable. I suspect, by my nature, I'll always dabble in all areas.

I have two cookbooks in the pipeline, a few non-fiction manuscripts begging for my attention, and various articles on the go. Sometimes it's like being the mother of needy children, and you end up paying attention to the one who makes the most noise. At the moment, it's fiction which is speaking loudly to me.

Q: *What motivated you to become a writer ?*
A: The exact moment was when I was around ten years old. A raging bushfire swept through our mountains, destroying hundreds of acres of beautiful eucalyptus forest and wattle trees, and killing so much wildlife: kangaroos, koalas, goannas, snakes, birds and so on. The total devastation haunted me. I remember walking through the charred remains, my bare feet black with soot, and feeling so desperate to articulate the loss of my 'home'. I spent so much time outdoors and those hills were like my garden. That is when I first felt the call to write. I wanted to express myself, and so I wrote a poem. It was around the same time that I became really aware that when I became a mother I wanted a job which would allow me to stay at home with my children. A writer ticked that box nicely.

When I was 19 years old, and living in the Adelaide Hills of South Australia, I saw a palmist. Of the many things she forecast, one was that I'd earn my living as a writer one day. I held that thought firmly in my heart. The 'writer's fork' is still etched in my palm.

Q: *Where do you gain most of your inspiration from when writing your novels?*
A: Anywhere and everywhere! *Sisters of the Silver Moon* came to me in a dream. I often get ideas while I'm in the shower or swimming. *Mosaic* came about simply because I'd turned forty. *Bluey's Café* came to me because I heard the word 'Bluey' on the radio one afternoon as I was about to make dinner. I had a great friend in childhood named Bluey, and my thought was: I wonder what it would be like to have a female character with that name? And as soon as that thought came to me, a whole series of images and storylines poured into my head. *Bluey's Café* wrote itself into my brain in the space of half an hour, while I cooked dinner. I then spent the next five days solidly typing it all down. I've never written anything that quickly.

Life inspires me. Conversations. A word. A smile. An image. A flower. A scent. Colour. Anything and anyone can inspire me to dream new ideas. Paying attention to life, and living in slow time, these are a writer's friends.

Q: *Is there a writer who has influenced you?*
A: In terms of my writing, probably every author I've ever read, for better or worse. I don't feel I imitate any style, though.

Q: *If you could spend an evening with any writer, throughout history, dead or alive, who would it be?*
Can I choose two? Kahlil Gibran and Clarissa Pinkola Estes. I grew up with Kahlil's writings on our kitchen wall. His profound wisdom has had a huge impact on me. Clarissa is the author of *Women Who Run With the Wolves*. This seminal work is something worth reading at least once a year.

Q: *When you're writing, do you work out the story/plot first?*
A: Not generally, though *Bluey's Café* came to me completely told. So did my (so far) five unpublished romance novels. Sometimes I have a rough idea where I want the story to go, but in the end the characters dictate the story, not me.

Q: *Have you ever had one of your characters change personality part way through the story in a way that you didn't expect, and had no control over?*
A: Yes! Astrid changed completely from what I'd expected, and in many ways, Bella did too.

Q: *When reading other writers' books what is it that draws you most about their writing?*
A: Although all the writing advice demands that you focus on dialogue so it can move the story along and reveal the characters, I much prefer description. I want to know what sort of world that characters live in. I want to feel what the air is like around them, and what food they're eating.

Q: *When you're writing, do you ever consciously put yourself in the place of the character?*
A: Yes, especially in love scenes! I try and inhabit their skin, the same as when I'm reading an astrology chart...it's not about me, but about the client and wearing their shoes and seeing the world through their lens. I recently had a lovely email from a reader saying she'd never read such a beautiful account of lovemaking like she had in my novel *Mosaic*. I suppose I should thank my husband for that, because all I did was close my eyes and remember what it feels like to be held in his arms in that way.

I had a similar letter about the birth scene in *Mosaic*. Although I don't agree with the writing rule about 'only writing what you know', there are times when it helps if you can draw on first-hand experience! Being a fiction writer means, while writing your book, having multiple personalities. I think it's vital that you put yourself in the place of the character. After all, if the writer can't do that then how can the reader?

Q: *Do you ever write in longhand first?*
Yes, with *Mosaic* most of it was written by hand first.
However, I'm a speed typist, and when I'm on a roll I need to be able to type, as I think too quickly for my pen to keep up with me. As a mum, I've spent a lot of time waiting outside music lessons and other such things for my daughters, so I always had a pen and paper with me. Ideas and storylines can come at any time, and you need to be prepared.

Q: *If someone were to ask you for guidance on writing novels, what would be the single most important thing you would say?*
Follow your intuition rather than rules for writers. You are the storyteller, and no one else. Trust your voice even if it goes against guidance. One of the big writing rules is: don't write a backstory. I deliberately ignore this rule because the novel, as in life, has real people. And we all have a past. We're all driven by things in our subconscious.

Q: *Which is more important to you: the writing of the novel or the reaction to it of your readers?*
A: The writing. Creating a book, for me, is like pregnancy, something growing and expanding deep within. Something that previously ceased to exist takes on new life. It's incredible! You tend to feel protective of it, too.

Although giving birth to my daughters was amazing, birthing a book feels scary: what if someone says your 'baby' is ugly or there's something 'wrong' with it? No author wants to hear that. I don't have a thick skin, I'm afraid, so yes, I want my readers to get as much from reading my books as I do from writing them, but primarily, for me, it is about the experience of creating the book. Obviously when I receive favourable comments, I hold them close and cherish every one.

Mosaic

by Veronika Sophia Robinson

Mosaic is a story of family and friendships, of love and loss. Topaz Lane is an internationally successful children's illustrator, and boy has she been bruised by love. In fact, she's sworn off men for life and is mourning the fact that she'll never have a family. A chance meeting with five women shows her that we all have wounds, and we all have gifts to share.

Bluey's Café

by Veronika Sophia Robinson
Paperback, and also on Kobo and Amazon Kindle

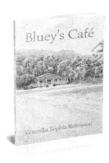

Bluey Miller lives a charmed life in Calico Bay, a small rural town on the east coast of Australia. She built her popular wholefood café from nothing, and it has garnered a well-deserved reputation for world foods. When her mother dies, Bluey discovers that there was far more to her mother's life than she'd realised. Why so many secrets? As she begins to unravel her mother's past, she's left wondering about their relationship. They had been so close over the years, yet now Bluey feels like she didn't know her at all. Her very identity hangs by a thread. Who am I? she wonders. Who was my mother?

Seemingly insurmountable challenges lie ahead, and Bluey must face them without her mother by her side. She finds strength from her local community and daily nourishment from the welcoming atmosphere of her café, but is this enough? Drawing succour from the Australian bushland around her, friendships, emerging spirituality, a life-changing romance, and the memories of good mother love, Bluey must somehow find enough courage to allow the best of the past to become the foundation for her future.

What readers have said about *Mosaic*

Our mutual friend, Mandy Bingham, lent me your first novel, *Mosaic*, which I've just this minute finished reading. This might sound weird (although maybe not to you) but it was exactly the book I needed to read today. It's a beautiful story, beautifully told. I laughed and cried. So thank you. *Edelle*

I read this in about three days, a miracle seeing as I never usually get time to read anything with having children 24/7, but you know when you find a good book, you can't put it down. I knew it would be, thanks Veronika. *Becky*

Really really enjoyed *Mosaic*; it reminds me a bit of 'Love Actually' and that's a compliment! Thank you Veronika, it arrived at the perfect time: 'Flu plus a self-imposed screen-free week. And I DID cry! Xxx *Elizabeth*

What a beautiful story it is. I so enjoyed reading it, so much so that I read it all in one go with sleeping children cuddled up around me! I think you are a really powerful healer, and your words are your medicine. They offer the potential to heal and reveal to the depths of the human heart and soul. The wise women in your story are archetypes for our time, offering grace, truth and wisdom. I love the way you include so many aspects of natural birthing and parenting, and liked to imagine younger women reading this then exploring these ideas for themselves and making them a reality when they become mothers for themselves. A beautiful, inspiring story of the many depths of love and the human heart. Loved it and looking forward to your next ones! *Clare*

It's a fantastic book. I really enjoyed it and would recommend it to everyone. It has the most beautiful description of a birth that I've ever read in a novel. I look forward to your next novel, Veronika. *Michelle*

I awoke early this morning to sunlight streaming through the house. Making a pot of cinnamon tea, I settled down in my favourite chair and read *Mosaic*. What a treat — simple, truthful, peaceful, evocative, inspiring. A time spent with friends old and new. Thank you. *Samantha*

Well I could savour no more and just sat and read it all! I can tell you it takes a lot to make me sit down in the day and read! I have cried my way through your beautiful book. I have truly loved it, and am so honoured to be in it. I really am. It is a beautiful book, and I miss all the characters hugely already! Bring on the next one! *Mandy Bingham*, Irish singer and songwriter

I just have to share that I received my copy of *Mosaic* yesterday, and managed to finish it already between naps and my son's bedtime. What a WONDERFUL read. It is poignant to all of us, and truly relevant to everyone who is human. It was an amazing catalyst for me into some of the sore places in my heart that are so deeply in need of healing; places that are affecting my mothering of my son, and are crying out for ways to heal. I literally began to remember how to cry them out as I read the book. The first page had me... the characters were immediately like my old friends, and as they shared more of themselves with Topaz, the main character, I felt like I had known them all my life... it reminded me how incredibly important it is to have a circle of women in my life... something I have been desperately missing since moving to England 2.5 years ago. Topaz is a beautiful mix of already-amazing woman and one open to expanding and learning new ways of being in

241

the world. I was inspired and reassured that there is still time to become everything I dream of. And the storyline unfolding in her life kept me turning the pages well after I should have been in bed. It was also incredibly refreshing to read a novel that fully encompasses the parenting life I find so natural and comfortable... scenes of delicious food, sweet experiences of birthing, parenting, educating — a way of being in the world that is in line with Nature. Usually, reading novels there is some place that sticks, or prickles; some place where the way "the world" assumes a way of being that just goes against what I feel, that I end up with a bad taste in my mouth. *Mosaic* left me with sweetness the whole way through, even through the bitter, painful, tearful parts. Much love, *Kirsten*

I am only just reading *Mosaic*. All I can say is WOW!!!!! It is brilliant. I will be in tears when I finish this book. Nowhere else have I read such a beautiful description of making love. It is a book that you can't put down. I am suffering from clinical depression and barely managing to read but this is gripping. Also very healing. I went through two difficult years recently which resulted in me moving back to live with my parents last November. It has left a big wound but this book is really helping. Something inside me says YES when I am reading it. Thank you so much for writing this book. I can't wait to read more of your books. Thank you for writing a book that is so helping me. Lots of hugs to you. Blessings. *Ruth*

A lovely novel with a very human theme which almost everyone will relate to. I enjoyed this book — it is an accessible read with simple but touching descriptions that capture moments in human life and nature in a very evocative way. I loved the introduction of important issues such as gentle birthing, empathetic parenting and the importance of finding a peaceful connection with the

Earth. I hope that the novel will open the eyes of readers who happen upon it and do not yet know the joys of such a way of life. I specifically liked the ending and the way the author has not shied from the sadness which so many of us, if not all, experience — bereavement, baby loss, changes that are difficult to manage and accept. I suppose life is a mosaic, as per the title, and beautiful in all its parts as well as a whole picture — a fitting title then for this snapshot of a very human protagonist and part of her uplifting, open-hearted journey. *Clare*

Thank you for sharing your heart with us. The novel was intimately moving; I would like to get one for my eldest granddaughter. I so want her to read it; beautiful seeds will be sown within. *Ruth*

What readers have said about Bluey's Café

I devoured this book. I love it. Easy to read and so enjoyable. Lovely storyline, wonderful heartful characters, amazing food, scenery. The picture painted was beautiful and the interweaving of relationships delightful. I laughed, I cried and was enlivened from yearning. Perfect to pack in your case for a holiday or to read at home cosy by the fire. *Claire*

I've just finished reading *Bluey's Café*. Sigh. It's filled me with a sense of love and hope. Just what I needed on this wet Autumnal day. Beautifully written, drawing the reader into every word of the text. Lots of mention of delicious home-cooked nutritious food and romance, I feel nourished on a deep level. *Kim*

I laughed out loud and shed the odd tear but mostly was enveloped in the beautiful world of Bluey. I have been reminded to have faith in your dreams and following your heart and to continue offering love and kindness. *Christine*

I think anyone who enjoys reading Joanne Harris will love this novel. The theme of mouth-watering wholesome cookery runs throughout alongside the entwining of others' lives — past and present, good and bad. I couldn't put it down. A feel-good read...love conquers all. *Jill*

Thoroughly enjoyed reading it :-) Fabulously written, flows and reads well. Thank you. Wonderful plot and story, a real joy. *Socpo*

Bob's Chocolate Tart

Cover 75g of dates in a bowl with boiling water.

Place 100g coconut oil, 140g ground almonds, 175g desiccated coconut, 2.5 tablespoons of honey and one tablespoon of cocoa powder into a food processor, and blitz until it is a crumbly mixture.

Place the mixture into a tart tin, and press it down to form a crust.

Drain the dates, and blend them with the juice and zest of an orange, 50g coconut oil, 175g honey and 140g cocoa powder. Whizz in the food processor until it is smooth and silky. Scrape the chocolate mix onto the crust, and place it in the fridge for an hour or two.

Printed in Great Britain
by Amazon